THE WARM WAR
by Garry Waite

Cover Design
Lynne Armitage
Jigsaw Design

Author's Photo
Jan Knight

ISBN 9781983354236

ACKNOWLEDGEMENTS

To my late mother who never got to read my first novel, My late Father for being my Father, Bob Gard for his support, encouragement and friendship, Dusty Symonds (Exec Producer BBC) for telling me it was the best story line he had read in three years, which encouraged me to continue, and my partner at the time, Jo who had to listen to each chapter as I finished it.
And to Galyna who despite many years together has never read the book.

PROLOGUE

The temperature was already reaching twenty four degrees centigrade as light broke on another Costa del Sol morning. The sky was clear, save two tiny dots of cloud vying for position in front of the, already fiery, sun. I had positioned myself in a safe corner of the sloping mountainside overlooking the beautiful lake of Istan, a few minutes from the fashionable town of Marbella and the glitzy port of Banus. This was a beautiful time of the day — not one that I saw very often — just after 7.30 am, and the sun was rising from behind me. The wildlife were still masters of all they surveyed and, waiting for the inevitable invasion of their tranquility by tourists, motor cars and locals going about their daily tasks. A short-toed eagle quartered the skyline, periodically hovering to study prey some one hundred meters below. With the deathly silence of the surroundings not being disturbed, he dropped his wings and dived ground wards into the shrubbery and wild gorse, emerging triumphantly with a snake gripped in its talons and, soaring upward to its mountain hideaway, disappeared from view.

I had set up my tripod and placed my Canon. EOS safely on the adjustable screw mounting, so I could get a complete framed picture of the newly completed villa that belonged to a wealthy English client, David Lewis, who had instructed me to photograph his pride and joy. Why he should build such a beautiful house so close to the damn wall puzzled me, given the availability and space of the surrounding countryside. The sun was now well to the left of me, affording the opportunity to take a sun-drenched shot of the Andalucian designed, six bed roomed house. The crystal clear pool was already shimmering in the first morning light and I knew these were the shots I wanted, before venturing closer than my present 300 meters, to capture the house in more close-up detail. I adjusted my 105mm lens, 60th/sec F4 and confirmed my depth of field, then, using the automatic motor wind, I took half-a- dozen shots adding a filter to enhance the pictures. As I finished the somewhat simple task, my friendly eagle re-appeared, its wings fully stretched, aiming towards its prior hunting ground, in the hope of repeating its previous success. As he hovered, awaiting his next quarry, I put on my 300mm mirror lens and gently pointed the camera toward this beautiful bird. Through the camera I could see that he was intent on his new found prey and was about to dive. I put my finger on the shutter and kept it there in the hope of following the majestic animal in its long dive, for its second helping of breakfast. But instead of hovering downwards, it seemed to move away in panic and across the blue Spanish sky, towards the safety of its cliff side hideaway. The noise that seemed to have disturbed it, was now approaching me. A rustle of bushes, a sharp snapping of sun burnt twigs, the dragging of substance against substance and, the eventual thud of dead weight on dry earth. I froze, riveted to my hillside sanctuary, feeling not unlike the eagle that had suddenly left, who appeared to be more aware of danger than I, and a cold sickening feeling ran from the centre of my stomach through my lungs, now taking painful gasps to take in much needed air; through my heart, pounding so hard that my ears hurt and, despite the hot summer's morning, the sweat on my brow, the back of my neck and on my chest, made a shiver run down my spine. There, lying not a meter away from my camera case, was a beautiful, fair-haired young woman, around twenty five, her head tilted back looking up to where the bird of prey had been, with her long hair draping behind her like a waterfall over the rugged countryside. Her blue eyes were Open, expressionless, staring coldly as the warm sun started to bathe her frozen brow. Blood was trickling from between her full incandescent red lips and her arched back making her pert young breasts force their way out from her torn maroon and dark yellow cotton shirt. Gouges from the rugged hillside caused the tanned body to leak blood droplets, as if the savage countryside had raped and imposed itself on their unsuspecting Visitor. Her knees faced each other in an undignified pose, confirming that the fall had probably broken her legs and maybe even her hips. Not that she could feel anything. I had never seen a dead person before. I had often asked myself how I would react, should the occasion arise. Would I immediately rush to offer assistance? Would I look up to see the perpetrators if indeed there were any, or, would I look to see how she had fallen? Would I cry out in fear, or for help? I felt colder, I was frightened, I felt sick — I threw up!

CHAPTER ONE

The champagne corks popped, the waiters deftly poured their chilled contents into the crystal flutes of the invited guests. Others passed through the assembled crowds, offering freshly made canapés of smoked salmon, blue cheese and strawberry, individual tartlets of curried quails eggs, Spanish *Jabugo* ham and, a further array of tasty tit-bits, especially put together for the preamble of the celebratory dinner to be held at the fashionable and popular Marbella eatery 'La Reserva'. The mixed crowd of businessmen, actors, entertainers, local politicians, senior Guardia Civil officers, local ex-pats of all nationalities and friends, were all there to celebrate the fact that I had now achieved ten years of living on the Costa del Sol. A feat in itself. I had not come here through crime, I had not lived here on crime, I did not come with millions and I certainly had not achieved millions. I had struggled to make a living as a photographer and had befriended a hotelier in my first few years in Marbella which developed into a friendship culminating in a partnership and, the opening of 'La Reserva', which through his hard work, excellent food and service and, my meagre contribution as a PR and 'people man', had turned the operation into one of the Coast's better successes.

"Well done Philip, another great success and congrats on being here for ten years. God knows how you did it, especially as you actually had to work for a living."

I smiled, "Thank you, Alan, Sandra, it's good to see you both, thanks for coming."

"Ah Phillip, you remember Marjorie my wife," said the British Consul.

"Marjorie, you remember Philip Edwards?"

"Of course, how are you Marjorie?" I said as I lifted her hand gently to my lips, "Brian has always managed to keep you hidden, you should insist that he shows you off more often." A smile passed over my lips, one that was returned by the rather petite and attractive 50 year old, "He likes to keep me out of the way so as he can join you and your cronies for your 'businessman's' lunches," she replied, referring to our, normally, monthly gatherings, where we attempt to discuss everything under the sun and consume as much food and drink as humanly possible.

"Hello Consul, I wonder if I could introduce you to my wife ..." said an overbearing character as he passed our small gathering.

I liked Brian Hurst, he had proven to be a good friend over the years. Always there to help, not just me you understand, but to all the Brits that had found themselves in a bit of a pickle with the local laws and authorities. A genial man who liked nothing better than to meet with his 'flock', down a few pints and, to be invited to say a few short words about life here, on the Coast that we all loved so much. "As long as they don't keep drawing me on the subject of Gibraltar," he would say, " 'cause it's such a hot potato, and half of them don't want to hear what I have got to say anyway!"

"You may be the guest of honour," the voice broke my thought patterns as I turned to face my partner Paul Harrison, "but I think you ought to do your bit. Announce dinner and get the buggers seated." Paul was a charming man, in his early forties — the other thing we had in common apart from a love of good food and wine — good looking and a ladies' man. Happily married to an English girl he had met out here and, the proud father of two gorgeous daughters, four and six, he always managed to keep his admirers at bay.

Many is the time that I was happy for a couple of his rejects to keep me company, as l was divorced from my Spanish wife of nine years, Maria Jose. She had taken our seven year old daughter, Carmen, back to England to be with her parents, who had an hotel in the Lake District, after an acrimonious split some two years before. We had met at the Lakes Hotel 12 years ago when I had been retained by a local PR company to put together a brochure for her parents' hotel. At the age of 31, I had been struck down by 'love-at-first-sight'. Her long dark hair, tied back, her full figure, perfect shape and deep brown eyes had made me draw breath on our first meeting. We had a whirlwind romance. Much against her Spanish father's better judgment and her English mother's wishes, I persuaded her to come to live with me in Spain, where I had always wanted to be, but where she had not lived since she was six years of age, twenty years before. It hadn't worked. Fights and unnecessary arguments had all proven too much for both of us, so she returned to the UK and we saw each other very infrequently. We got on a lot better than before, probably because we didn't see each other very often, but I still missed Carmen. I still saw her twice a year for her holidays and, there was never a problem about seeing her when I made my very infrequent trips to the UK.

"*Señores*, Distinguished guests, Ladies and Gentlemen," the roar of Paul's 'master of ceremony' voice jolted me back to reality and, the realisation that it should have been me announcing 'dinner is served!'

The assembled crowd took their places at round tables of eight, all dressed with fresh flowers and the exquisite silver that adorned our pure Irish linen cloths. Each guest had been allocated a table and at each place setting their name was written on the menu with Paul's distinctive quill script. Once again we were to be treated to a gastronomic delight prepared by our talented kitchen and watched over with love and care by Paul, himself a brilliant cook, as frequent visits to his house had shown. A *Parfait of Chicken Livers with a Redcurrant and Ginger Sauce and Toasted Brioche,* preceded a *Chilled Tomato and Red Pepper Soup garnished with Spring Onions and Sour Cream.* A short break before one of the house specialties of Home-made *Pasta Parcels filled with Langostines and Crayfish Mousse on a Crayfish Sauce,* a champagne sorbet to cleanse the palate before being presented with a *Fillet of Veal in a Light Madeira Sauce with Fresh Basil and Pink Grapefruit* and a side salad of mixed lettuces tossed sparingly in one of our herb dressings. A dessert of *Tropical Fruits in a Tulip Biscuit on Three Fruit Puree's* completed a superb dinner. Pinord Chardonnay and Mindiarte Reserva from the Rioja accompanied the starters and main courses and a local Malaga Moscatel, Cartojal, was served with the sweet. Coffee, petit fours and liqueurs rounded off the evening.

My partner was Sandy Tate a stunning Australian lady who had made some money in her home country as a TV producer and was over here looking at the possibility of 'doing something' in the same line. We had met at the launch of a new magazine some six weeks earlier. She was tall, leggy, well tanned with a slim figure and looks that belied mid thirties. Also on my table was Marjorie and Brian Hurst, and Doctor Peter Livingstone and his wife Sue. Looking around I saw so many faces, most of whom I had known since my early days in Marbella. Sitting with Carlos Jimenez, deputy head of the Guardia Civil, was my pal Gerald Peters. Gerry had been down here about the same length of time as I had and had earned a reasonable living as a journalist, both locally and, as a stringer, for such respected publications as The News of the World and the Sun, back in the UK. "You may not like what I write, or who I write for," he always says, "matter of fact neither do I sometimes, but it pays the rent."

His real desire was to write an exposé of the corruption that was reputedly rife in the days of the Gonzalez government. He was a rugged looking fellow in his late thirties with a great sense of humour and an insatiable alcoholic thirst which had caused many a quiet evening to turn into a debauched night on the town, culminating in chocolate and *churros* at the local fruit and vegetable market at sunrise. At the table next to them was Marbella's deputy mayor, Arturo Sanchez, an astute businessman, brilliant at PR and a lover of his beautiful town, beautiful women and the *corrida*. To his right was Juanita (Jane) Mendez, the stunning looking 30 year old who was the Editor of "Marbella Marbella", the newly launched glossy magazine for whom I took the occasional picture. On the table next to the, temporarily redundant, fireplace, sat Chris Yeo and Julio Martinez, partners in Marbella's top real estate agency based at the nearby five star hotel, Puente Romano. With them was Ricardo Cuevas, director of the local English language radio station, part of the country's largest broadcasting and charity company, Onda Cero.

Associates, business acquaintances and close friends all enjoying the evening splendour in this, one of the most beautiful towns, in one of the most beautiful countries, one could wish to be in.

"And now ladies and gentlemen, our guest of honour Philip Edwards."

Paul's rousing voice once again tore me away from my thoughts and brought me back to the task in hand to say a few words and thank everyone for coming. I rose to my feet accompanied by warm applause. "It is hard to imagine that ten years has passed so quickly, but it is heart warming to see so many friends here to celebrate the anniversary of my stay in Spain, which, like many of us, I have always considered to be my home and I would like to thank especially, our Spanish hosts," I acknowledged the gathered representatives of the country, "for making me and all of us, so welcome."

There was a ripple of applause accompanied by a typically British, "Here, here."

"And even though all of you are aware that this party was only designed by Paul so as you could part with more of your money," — every guest had paid 15.000 pesetas for the privilege of dining with us this evening. Paul was always coming up with different ideas to create party nights that usually had a waiting list, as guests, old and new, tried to book tables, — they all laughed, "I do seriously thank all of you for coming and making this evening so very special.

Here's to the next ten years of growth, integration and friendship in our multi-national community," I said as I lifted my glass to toast. Everyone stood and returned the salutation. As I sat down again I put my hand on Sandy's, who was smiling warmly and I gently kissed her lips.

I awoke as the sun crept through the thin gaps of the curtains causing the dust in the air to glisten and swirl like a child's kaleidoscope. 'Ten years on' I thought, and such a far cry from the formative years of toil in the UK. The flat lands of Lincolnshire had been replaced by the hills and mountains surrounding the palm tree lined streets of Marbella. The narrow lanes of period terraced houses of Stamford were a contrast to the modern developments and luxurious villas of the Golden Mile. The oak-beamed ceilings and rustic charm of the George Hotel, replaced by young aspiring drinking spots and, traditional old Spanish bars and, *ventas*.

They had been good days. Boarding school, public school, not a great achiever, I had always wanted to be a jockey, but it was obvious by the time I was fourteen that I would never be the right weight and height, so I developed my hobby of photography until I became proficient. Rather than riding horses, I started taking pictures of them and created quite a reputation amongst owners and trainers. It was because of this, that my meeting with the legendary Josh Gifford resulted in me working with a colleague of his, who had a PR company in London. After some time travelling between London and Stamford I moved to the big city and started my career in earnest. But Spain was calling and my frequent trips to the coastline made me determined to live here. The meeting with Maria Jose was the final push I needed and within one year from then I had found a rented apartment and was off. And I hadn't looked back.

I rolled over and sat on the edge of the bed, stretched, and ran my fingers through my sadly thinning hair. My mouth was feeling the wear and tear of last evening's excess of *Carlos Primero*, I cursed myself for agreeing to photograph David Lewis' house today. The alarm clock said 6.30 am and I looked at Sandy's tanned body stretching half out of the bed with her long hair draping over the pillow toward the floor, and swore I could have gained an extra hour if only mutual passion had not overcome the need for sleep and recovery, on our return to my apartment on the Puente Romano Marina in the early hours of this morning. I showered, shaved and managed a quick *expresso* which dissolved the inevitable fur on my tongue, before brushing my teeth, mouth washing and putting on some Calvin Klein Eternity

Feeling like a completely new human being — it's strange how the older you get, the less stamina you appear to have to cope with the late nights, early mornings and excess of alcohol, food and sex —- I slid into my pride and joy, a BMW 325i convertible, and headed toward the Istan road, for the ten minute journey, thinking how fortunate I was to be alive.

CHAPTER TWO

The stench of my own vomit was worsened by the excesses of the night before and, had the effect of making me even more nauseous. I turned toward the prostrate body in the hope that the whole event may have been an illusion caused by a mild hangover, but no, she was still there, and the smell of' death was now apparent. The noise of her fall, and my retching, had caused the previously quiet countryside to come alive with the chatter of birds, as they fled from their overnight resting places. Recovering my senses and, feeling more akin to a frightened schoolboy than a mature, scared, man, I stepped carefully toward her. Why? Did I think she was suddenly going to turn and accost me, draw a knife or a gun? I placed my hand on her neck in the slim hope of feeling a faint throbbing that would indicate some life. But nothing. She was cold. I looked up the side of the hill trying to ascertain from which direction she had fallen and, probably foolishly, to see if I could see why. There was no shouting or panicking, indicating to me that she had been alone when she fell. Or maybe, she was pushed? I faintly heard a car engine, but it was no more ominous than any of the other vehicle sounds that were audible as the local villagers set off down the winding hillside road, to Marbella and beyond, to earn their daily bread. A hush had now once again fallen over the parched terrain and I sat there hopelessly at a loss. It was just after 8.30 am. I had been here for an hour. My mind went back to the warm sweet smelling body of Sandy lying next to me in the king size double bed, the fan oscillating gently above us, her urgent mouth finding every part of my body, draining me of my physical love, as we eventually drifted into a satisfied sleep. Remembering that same body stretched over the bed this morning and recalling my reluctance to attempt today's task, made me even more aware of how I had wished this appointment had never been made.

As if suddenly coming to some definitive decision and overcoming my fear and nausea, the fact that I was a photographer became first and foremost in my mind. I picked up my camera, changed the lens and started to photograph the young woman from all angles, without disturbing the body. I couldn't believe my own motives, yet I knew that if I didn't take those shots now, there would be a time in the future when I would regret it. I put my camera back into the case and withdrew my mobile phone, not as yet turned on to meet the demands of the day. Now it seemed that the pest that only appeared to disturb meetings with clients, or relaxed lunches with friends, was my only salvation from the unholy state that I found myself in this summer morning. I dialled the offices of the Guardia Civil.

A number I knew well, but normally only used to confirm a dinner date, the venue for the forthcoming businessman's lunch, or just to ask my friend if he was free for an after work drink. The phone responded quickly, "*Diga!*" said the efficient, if not friendly voice, at the other end.

"Puedo hablar con el Señor Carlos Jimenez?" I asked somewhat nervously, *"Quien es?"* came the quick reply. *"Soy Philip Edwards"* I said, only to be answered with,

"Lo siento señor, pero el señor Jimenez no está in su oficina en estos momentos. No ha llegado todavía. Quiere dejarle alguna mensaje?" 'Why wasn't he there damn him?'. He always says he's in work every morning by 8.00 am. Did I want to leave a message? How long would he be? Did he have a hangover?

"Si", I was thinking as quickly as possible, *"Digale que me llame, por favor. Mi numero es, 908 959155."* She repeated my mobile number and I thanked her. I took out my electronic note book and looked for Carlos' home number and quickly punched it in. The phone rang and rang and eventually cut off. I placed the phone on stand-by, thankful that the blasted thing even worked in this dense shrubbery and hillside. What should I do now? Call the ambulance? Pointless. Call the police? Better if I waited to speak to Carlos. Call Sandy? And say what? "Hi darling, I'm going to be a bit late for our lunch date, as I am at the bottom of a ravine with a blonde whose beautiful body is open for all to see, with two broken legs, perhaps a hip or two, and more than likely a broken back and neck." I couldn't carry her up the side of the

hill, even if I'd wanted to.

'Why did you choose my bit of mountain to land? I'm only here to take some bloody photographs.' The phone warbled and took me away from my selfish misery. *"Hola! Philip, soy Carlos, que pasa amigo?"* I suddenly felt a stirring of comfort, a friend on the end of the line who would surely be able to help me out of all this.

"You won't believe this my friend," I said and started to explain the morning's events.

Eventually his worried voice said, "Don't move, I will be with you in fifteen minutes." Just after 9.00 am, I heard a voice shouting my name urgently. The usually smiling face of the genial deputy of the Guardia Civil was above me, his thick set figure bearing down.

"Donde estas Philip?" he shouted.

"Aqui, Carlos" I replied waving my hands.

"Uno momento," his voice reassuring me, as he and an assistant officer made their way down the somewhat precarious track.

Treading carefully down the same path that I had negotiated nearly two hours earlier, the two uniformed men clasped at protruding branches and solid rocks. "What made you come down here in the first place?" grimaced the giant of a man as he put his huge hand on my shoulder.

"To take a photo would you believe?" I said trying to smile.

"What exactly happened Philip? Tell me every detail you can remember."

There was nothing much to tell him, but I went through everything, from me taking the pictures of the hovering eagle, to the phone call to his house, although omitting to tell him I took the pictures of the dead girl, thinking he would feel I was somewhat morbid and unfeeling. He barked an order to his colleague, who immediately got on the walkie—talkie and relayed some instructions. Carlos went over to the girl's body and, without disturbing anything, studied the area and the crumpled form, with the eye of an experienced civil guard who had seen far worse in his earlier years in Madrid, a time he did not talk about much, unless you had managed to get him to consume the best part of a bottle of Chivas Regal.

"I have called for a pathologist and scene of crime officers," he said, mopping his brow, as the heat of the morning sun was now upon us. Sheltered from the little breeze there was, the temperature in our mountain hideaway was rising rapidly.

"What are your movements for the rest of the day?" he continued.

"Not a lot," I replied. "I have to take some shots of Igor Metchnikov at about two, they are doing a profile on him, and then, I thought I might go to the restaurant for a snack with Sandy and to see Paul. Why?"

"I will need to talk with you again and, so probably, will the crime officers. This girl did not fall, it is likely that she was thrown."

"How do you know?" I asked, my own fears now being realised.

"Because the blood on the left hand side of her mouth is older and dryer than the blood on the right hand side of her mouth and her body, indicating that she was bleeding from her mouth before she fell."

I looked at him with some admiration.

"Don't worry my friend," he continued, "I am no, how do you say, Sherlock Holmes, we will leave the correct conclusions to the experts. You may go now. I will contact you at the restaurant later today."

I picked up my case and started to walk back up the path.

"Oh Philip," his deep voice made me turn around, "I will need the film that is in your camera."

"What?" I said with genuine surprise in my voice. "I uh .. I only have photos of the house for my client," I fumbled, obviously lying.

"And the photos of the eagle?" he said questioningly, "as one of the Coast's leading photographers, you would not have left an opportunity like this..." He pointed to the prostrate body of the dead girl, "to pass you by."

Being defeated by a friend was a less painful experience than being discovered by an enemy. "Let me develop them" I pleaded, "and I will give you the original negatives and the photos over lunch later - promise."

"*Seguro?...*" I nodded,

"*O.K. Hasta luego.*"

I continued my climb upwards, my legs feeling like lead and my hangover becoming worse rather than better. I stood at the top of the hill next to the familiar green livery on one of the Guardia Civil Nissan Patrols, surveying the scene and wondering why this should happen to me. I had been here for ten years and nothing like this had happened before, even when I was looking for an exciting picture. And I certainly would never have expected to be as close to the event as this.

Two more Guardia Civil vehicles pulled up alongside me in silence, but with their lights flashing. Two plain clothes officers got out of the first car and a uniformed officer and a man in plain clothes with a black doctors bag, from the other. I greeted them, and pointed downwards. They all walked to where I had just emerged. I got into my car and drove in the direction of Marbella not sure whether I needed another coffee, a brandy or both. I decided on both and called into Kings, a local tapas bar and drinking hole frequented by "the media" as it was under the offices of both 'Marbella Marbella' and the Onda Cero Radio station.

"Un cafe solo y un Magno por favor," hoping the thick black coffee and the syrupy brandy would help me to recover.

"Good morning Philip," I looked up to see Jane Mendez in the doorway. With her short cropped blonde hair, tight 501's and a light cotton blouse she certainly was a more pleasing sight than my morning had so far produced.

"Great party last night. You look as if you're either still celebrating or recovering." I beckoned her to sit down and she ordered a decaffeinated coffee with milk. I could never see the point in drinking that stuff from a sachet when one needed the buzz that a good strong cup of real coffee gives.

"When are you going to take the pictures for this month's centre spread?" she asked.

"I have an appointment with Metchnikov at two today, it should take me a couple of hours and you should have the prints tomorrow morning."

"Great," she said beaming her full smile that lit up her eyes and crinkled her nose. She paused, "Philip, are you alright?" For what reason I am not sure, but I started to tell her all about my morning. Apart from Carlos, who I felt was slightly different, I was able to tell her all. When I finished I looked up at her and she said, "Christ, what a story!"

"Trust you," I said, a nervous laugh starting, "you can't have the pictures though, Carlos needs them."

"When he's finished with them, I'm sure we can have them back. Listen Philip, we have to keep an eye on this story. I'll give Carlos a ring later."

"No Jane. Don't let Carlos know I've told you anything. I'm seeing him later, I'll sound him out then."

"O.K.," she said getting up, "but keep me informed. Your coffee and brandy is on me."

I nodded some sort of thank you and decided I had to get back to the apartment to develop the film. I acknowledged the boys from the radio station as I left the busy bar and got into my car for the five minute drive home.

As I arrived at the Marina, boat owners were

starting to make ready their crafts for coast hopping or perhaps a longer journey to Gibraltar or Morocco'. Sleek millionaire's cruisers, elegant tall ships, standing with their naked masts erect, waiting to get out to sea, where the wind will take their mainsail, and blow it into a full white harness of energy, that will push the craft majestically across the Mediterranean, controlled only by the adept handling of the man at the tiller.

Sandy opened the door, a towel wrapped around her and her wet auburn hair glistening in the shaft of sunlight falling in from the open terrace that looked over the port. I put my arms around her and kissed her long and hard trying to get back some of the warmth and love that my body had lost during the short morning. "What was that for?" she asked as we pulled apart, and I once again I related the story. Leaving her somewhat aghast I went towards my darkroom to prepare the pictures. I hadn't even finished my job for David Lewis, I would have to ring him later and arrange another time.

"Philip," I turned to see Sandy standing with her elbow resting on the door frame and her hand in her wet hair, "Jane's right you know, this could make a bloody good story."

CHAPTER THREE

The alarm sounded, dead on 7.00 am and, the gentle giant stretched his right arm outwards to deftly stop the grating ringing, his face still buried in the pillow of his huge, empty, bed. What little black hair he had left was matted to his head from a hot, close night. That, and something to do with two *Pacharans* too many from the night before. He pulled himself up from his bed, rubbed his baggy eyes and ran his tongue over his for covered teeth. He opened the curtains and looked out over the countryside that surrounded his *finca*. The dry parched land craving water from the cloudless sky, a familiar feature of the past year. He went into the bathroom and stood under the powerful spray of his shower. Carlos Jimenez was 48 years of age and a high ranking officer in the Guardia Civil. In fact he was the deputy commander for Marbella and district. You couldn't get much higher than that. He had lived in this house for ten years now. He bought it fifteen years ago when he was a sergeant in the civil guard in Madrid and he and his young wife, Marie Lollie, used to come to Marbella on their annual holiday. It was their intention to live here permanently when Carlos retired. Something he had intended to do when he was fifty. They had planted trees and shrubs knowing that when they were in full bloom, so would be Carlos and his wife.

He had been trained with the special forces

to tackle terrorist activities in the troubled north of Spain. ETA had long been a problem in that part, as the Basque country fought for independence from the rest of the mainland. He had always likened the problem to the pointless struggle in Ireland only not quite as bloody and evil. His promotion to captain had been greeted ecstatically by his family. He had never been a brilliant academic and, his parents were fairly simple folk, so, him achieving the dizzy heights of captain of an elite force that was treated with great respect among loyal Spaniards, was a, matter of great pride to his father, who had lost a leg at the age of eighteen fighting for his King and country during Spain's wretched civil war. His father had died soon after Carlos' promotion and he could remember crying as they slid his flower covered coffin in to the wall, next to where his grandfather had been placed some 20 years earlier. The young captain saluted his father as the tears flowed down his cheeks. He swore he would never cry like that again. But how wrong he was to be.

There had been a spate of terrorists attacks in Madrid especially aimed at Judges and politicians who were determined to stamp out ETA and its fanatical content. Carlos had already had to supply officers from his squad as bodyguards to leading members of the government.

Their job was to check vehicles for hidden explosives and generally keep an eye on their charges.

Every morning he would rise at 6.00 am and drive the short distance to his offices and barracks in the capital city. His wife worked in Corte Ingles, the massive department store group, who had huge stores in most Spanish major cities. She would drive her little Renault 5 — an ideal car for manoeuvring around the packed, traffic jammed streets — and park in the staff car park before going to her perfume department, where she looked after a staff of six, on the designer section. She always used to come home wafting of the scent from half a dozen different perfumes as prospective purchasers would continually ask her to act as the 'tester'. Carlos wondered why she ever bothered to put perfume on before leaving the house in the morning as she was sure to come home smelling completely different.

She enjoyed her job, she was well respected by the staff and clients and popular with the management and everyone who came in contact with her. Her beaming smile, petite body and five foot something frame was in complete contrast to her husband's bear like six foot two height and, girth that appeared to match.

The April weekend had passed like most. They had gone out to dinner on Saturday night to their favourite restaurant the recently opened El Amparo in the Callejon de Puigcerda. A delightful, comfortably furnished room with a beamed ceiling, pink tablecloths and overhead lights and lots of plants. The maitre, Eduardo, greeted them warmly and brought two dry sherries to the table with the menus. Marie Lollie had chosen a *Lobster Salad* followed by *Sea Bass with a Thyme and Tomato Compote* and Carlos, *Red Peppers Stuffed with Cod* followed by *Roast Lamb with Baby Garlics.* They had a bottle of Viña Sol with the starters and a bottle of Faustino 5 with the main course. In truth Carlos had most of the red as he invariably did. Sunday was spent with friends at a local country *venta* after a horseback ride through the surrounding countryside. It took them a good hour to get there but the scenery was worth it, as was the food. Simple grilled shellfish and salads washed down with house wine from Navarra.

That Monday was different as Marie Lollie had an extra day off owed to her, and Carlos' mother and sister were coming over, as was Marie Lollie's sister. They were going shopping and having a 'girls' lunch out. Carlos' mother Maria Teresa loved these days out.

She was frail now and didn't get out very much, but when she was with her family she would do as much as she could to keep up with the other girls, especially at lunch time.

Carlos was letting his wife borrow his car, a Citroen Pallas, so that the ladies could travel in comfort. No, he wouldn't take the Renault, the sight of his bulk in the front seat was too much to bear and on the odd occasion he had used it, friends and colleagues had found it most amusing. He phoned the duty officer on Sunday night and arranged for a

car to pick him up from home at 7.30 am to
ferry him the half hour journey across town
to his offices.

The next morning he leaned over and kissed
his wife gently on the forehead, broke a
carnation from the bunch in the bedside vase
and placed it on her pillow and left. It was
the last time he would see her like that. She
didn't feel a thing. No sooner had the women
settled themselves into the black Citroén and
she had placed the key in the ignition, than
there was a thunderous roar and
simultaneous bang that shattered the peace
of the suburban street. The bonnet of the car
somersaulted backward and the passenger
and driver's doors were blown outwards by a
huge ball of orange flame as black smoke
billowed upwards. The boot was blown
skyward as the fuel tank exploded at the
same time. The heat caused the roof to bulge
outward and the paint peeled, like burning
skin. Any screams from the occupants were
instantaneous and muffled by the holocaust
of flames and twisting metal. Then, there was
a strange silence. The cacophony of early
morning bird song ceased as shocked
starlings fled their havens, leaving the
crackling of fire in the tree lined street, where
the shrubbery stood scorched and shrivelled
and windows of nearby houses lay shattered.
That hush of death was broken by
neighbours who, after the initial shock, were
leaving their homes to see what had
happened. Children were screaming, women
were crying and the men, who were not

working that morning, ran toward the burning vehicle. But there was nothing that could be done. The heat was intense and the four women were incarcerated in their burning pyre.

The phone on Carlos Jimenez' desk rung for the umpteenth time in a morning that had already brought a bomb scare at Corte Ingles — thank God Marie Lollie isn't working today he had remarked — an attempt on a circuit judge and a demonstration outside of the Parliament building where Felipe Gonzalez was holding a press conference. He picked up the receiver with the customary. *"Diga me!"* The voice of his duty officer made his stomach tighten and his heart pound.

A feeling of nausea waved over him from his hot brow to his leather- boot clad feet. He sat rigid as a lump stuck in his throat.

"Reports are coming in from our Lagasca station of a car bomb. A black Citroen, number of occupants unconfirmed, so far no reason for the attack ..." the officer's voice continued, but Carlos heard nothing. His mind was like a silent movie, pictures and images rushing past his eyes, people talking and laughing but no sound: He and Marie Lollie, dinner, walking, riding, laughing and crying. His mother, his father, his nephews, his family, his life, his loss, Their loss. Why God, why?

By the time he had got to the scene the ambulances and Guardia Civil vehicles were already there. The fire department had extinguished the fire and all that remained was the blackened burnt out shell of twisted metal and the stench of burnt skin. His worst fears were confirmed and he could not move from the car. He leaned against the bonnet to support himself as he felt his knees quiver and his body weight double. Tears welled up in his dark eyes and he wanted to scream and wail and break his heart, but his pride and position made him hold in everything until he was on his own later that night when he cried like a baby. More than he ever thought possible. More than he hoped he would ever do again.

He had been given compassionate leave. He had buried his wife, mother, sister and sister in law, all in three consecutive days. He had put the house on the market and was prepared to take his vacation in the *finca* in Marbella. He would put that on the market too and soon he would be rid of all the painful memories.

The drive to Marbella was long. The A and C roads had not yet been replaced by Motorways. When he opened the door and the shutters to the rustic house, the sun drenched the table and chairs and, the house came alive with thoughts, smells and memories. He was reminded as to the reason for the purchase of their dream home and, there and then, decided to keep the house as Marie Lollie, he was sure, would have wished. It was over a solo dinner that night in Santiago's on the *Paseo Maritimo* that he thought about the moves that could change his life and make him leave his sadness behind. One year later he opened the same door to the *finca*, but this time, for good.

He brushed his greying black hair back and decided not to make his customary coffee, but to go to the local market bar on his way to work. He often popped in here as the coffee was good and he could get a croissant. He could never understand his fellow countryman's obsession for bread with scraped tomato or garlic oil for breakfast; not when you could have a hot croissant with some butter and peach jam. Alfonso was there behind the bar, *Ducados* smouldering in his mouth, smiling through his wrinkled, weather-beaten skin, as he dispensed coffee, anis, coñacs, chocolate, *churros* and banter with farmers, market men, street vendors, policemen and housewives.

The stories this room held. The life and passion of a friendly race that went back three generations all in one room. First world war, civil war, second world war, Franco, ETA, Bosnia, the socialists and now the spring cleaning mayor of Marbella Jesus Gil y Gil, all in one lifetime! He dipped the corner of his croissant into his thick dark coffee cut with a splash of milk and, browsed through a *Diario Sur* that someone had left behind. He was going to be late for work this morning, he had a small hangover, a self-inflicted illness he acquired by eating and drinking with his '*guiri*' English friend Philip Edwards. He didn't have much time for the Brits in general. Come to think of it he didn't have much time for most foreigners. They came to his country and imposed their way of life without trying to integrate, with their British bars, British food, English language radio and newspapers and a lack of effort in learning his language. They weren't all the same though. Philip was a good sort, as was Paul and most of the people that were at the party last night. At least they spoke some Spanish. Some of them very well, and enjoyed the good things of life, as well as the local colour and traditions. He was due for a barbecue at his house soon. He would start on the list this weekend. He paid for his breakfast and decided to walk to the office. It would clear his head.

"Buenos días jefe," said the officer on duty as he walked through the door. "There has been a telephone call from a Philip Edwards, would you call him on this number," he said passing Carlos a slip of paper.

The scene of crime officers looked at the body as the pathologist confirmed that death appeared to be caused by suffocation and that the girl had sustained a blow to the left hand side of her face, prior to being thrown from the cliff top. There were no abrasions other than those caused by the roll down the hillside, implying that the girl was not thrown from a moving vehicle but rather dumped from the top. There was no identification on her. No jewellery, no bag, no obvious scars or marks and only an obscure label on the back of her cotton knickers. He would not place a time of death until after the autopsy, but confirmed that he didn't feel she had been dead long as she was still relatively warm and her body muscles had only just started to relax and rigor mortis had not started to set in.

He also stated that there was bruising to the inner thighs and vaginal area implying that forced sexual intercourse had taken place. She had probably been raped, but further examination would be necessary, before confirmation could be given.

The scene of crime officers went to the top of the cliff to see if they could find any clues. There were mixed tyre tracks, that of the Nissan Patrol, the BMW that had just left and other indistinguishable marks.

'And I chose this day to have a hangover,' thought the Guardia Civil officer

CHAPTER FOUR

I eased the BMW off the *careterra* into the Puerto Banus exit, past the new Corte Inglés development and headed under the tunnel towards the port entrance. The barriers were down as I approached and pressed the security button. *"Si?"*

"Tengo una cita con el Señor Metchnikov en el barco Wave Dancer." I replied realising I was ten minutes late for my appointment. The barrier lifted as I drove into what had once been a millionaire's paradise. The luxury vessels of some years ago had been replaced by smaller craft with matching budgets. But since Jesus Gil y Gil had become Mayor of Marbella, Banus and San Pedro, and his son Mayor of Estepona, the towns, and especially, Puerto Banus, were looking to return to the old image of quality with quantity. Metchnikov had plenty of the latter if he was short in the former. He had a lot of money. Nobody knew quite how much, but the ship alone had been estimated at some $8 million. He had space for a small helicopter on the back and a Ferrari on the dock side. He was good news, at the moment, for the town. I parked in front of the floating hotel and climbed the gangway to see a bevy of women who always seemed to be at his beck 'n' call. A large man with hair tied back in a pony-tail met me at the top and took me into the salon. An opulent room filled with fresh flowers, crystal glasses and 'beautiful people'.

Metchnikov was sitting with a glass of champagne, surrounded by women, and the odd minder "Philip Edwards, I presume?" he said getting up from his sumptuous surroundings, "please come in," his voice rasped, "have a drink — champagne?" I wasn't sure that it was that good an idea, but I accepted. "You have brought your camera and you are ready, hmm?" his thick Russian accent rang with both enthusiasm and authority. I took the offered glass of champagne, Perrier Jouet no less; he clapped his hands and motioned everyone onto the upper deck. It took me some time to get my equipment out and set up. But the man was in no hurry.

Igor Metchnikov had arrived in Marbella four months ago. His ship — you couldn't really call it a boat - had sailed into the port of Banus quietly and without fuss. Some said it would exit in the same way. But he had made his mark. No one was sure of who he was or what he did. He had ingratiated himself to a waiting public. He had made friends quickly and had spent a lot of money in a lot of places. Full restaurants found tables for him, garages picked up his cars and ferried them backwards and forwards as he wished and, women did anything and, everything, to get an invite to join him, and his friends, on his yacht.

The photographs I was taking, were to accompany an article Jane had written about the new pioneers of Marbella. Because of his impact on the town, she felt that he certainly ranked among the top of that category. We took some good shots of him in the lounge with the girls draped over him and a couple of him on his own. Jane's article concentrated on the man's rise to financial stardom, how he made his money and what made him come to Marbella.

After another glass of champagne I said my goodbyes and went down the gangway to my car and exited. I had hope to get to the gym before going to the boat, but time was against me. I would try and go later in the afternoon. I tried to work out every other day to keep fit and to keep my weight down. I also did martial arts which I thought seemed a good way to discipline mind and body. I knew I could use it effectively if I had to, but rather hoped I wouldn't need it. Likewise with the gun club. Handgun shooting was a passion of mine from a young boy. Watching too many war films I guess. But it was fun and I had met some interesting people. Most of whom now dine with us at the restaurant.

The sun was getting toward its full strength now as I drove towards La Reserva, the breeze cooled me. Not as effectively as the air conditioning, but more fun. I had asked Sandy to bring the pictures with her that I had left drying in my dark room. I pressed my remote control as I approached the underground car park of the restaurant and the garage door lifted, at first hesitantly and, then smoothly, upward. It was half past three. I was late. Not an unusual thing for Spain, but people knew I liked to be on time.

But, today, I thought, I will probably be forgiven.

The restaurant had already started to get busy. The usual cross section of characters, business people, shoppers, young trendies and the retired not so trendy, relishing light lunches of Terrines, Warm Salads, Grilled Fish and for those with more time, the excellent menu of the day. Sandy was at the bar talking with Paul and got up as she saw me come in. She kissed me lightly, but warmly.

"Sandy has just told me all about it mate," said Paul. "Good start to the next ten years eh? If you are going to have that sort of luck, keep away from here!" he laughed.

"It's no laughing matter," I said, pour me a large gin and tonic —— on second thoughts give me a glass of cava."

"Spanish Champagne?" enquired Paul, sarcastically "Are we celebrating that you have already found out who dunnit?"

I explained about the photo session with Igor and his 'girls' and how I had already had a couple of glasses. "For God's sake don't tell anyone else about this or Carlos will throw a wobbly," I continued. "He's coming down later, for these photos, perhaps he will have some news." Paul opened the envelope and took out the photos and his face drained somewhat of colour.

"What's wrong?" I asked, "never seen a dead body before?"

"No. She is very attractive isn't she?"

"Was," I replied.

Arturo Sanchez came in with a few official looking chaps, presumably from the town hall. He acknowledged us from the doorway and, in English, thanked us for a great night. Julian Gomez our restaurant manager greeted them and took them to his favourite table. Sandy and I ordered the menu of the day although I was unsure how hungry I was, but I know that there are not many things that put me off a good meal. I had *Gazpacho* and *Grilled Lamb Cutlets with a Redcurrant and Port Wine Sauce* and she had *Melon and Avocado Salad* followed by *Tagliatelli with Salmon, Caviar and Wild Mushrooms.*

We had just started our main courses when the imposing figure of Carlos appeared. I stood up and shook his hand, he reached down and kissed Sandy on both checks as I pulled up a chair for his bulk. Paul brought over another bottle of Chardonnay and two more glasses pouring one for Carlos and the other for himself. Without asking Carlos, Paul ordered some *Serrano Ham* and *Manchego Cheese* for the friendly policeman to pick at with his wine.

"Well?" I asked after what seemed an age of silence, "what has happened?" Taking an olive from the table and chewing purposefully, as if trying to work out what to say, he deftly removed the stone from between his teeth, took another mouthful of wine and related what had happened since I had left the scene. "So basically," he summed up, "we can confirm that she was murdered between about four to six am, thrown over the top of the hill at about a quarter to eight and whoever did it obviously thought that no one would be waiting halfway down a cliff side to see it all happen. They probably think that she went all the way down and is now lying at the bottom of a ravine where she will decompose and never be found. If it hadn't have been for Philip, we could all have allowed our hangovers to take their natural course," he smiled and took a piece of thinly sliced cured ham and a cube of crusty bread and chewed methodically. "We don't know who she is, or was," he continued, the only thing we have to go on was the label on the back of her *bragas*."

"And?" I interjected impatiently.

"Well, her underwear appeared to be fairly new and there was some indecipherable hieroglyphics on the label. We have confirmed that the writing is Russian, therefore, naturally assume, so was the young lady."

"Russian?" we all said at once.

A year or so before, I was lying on the beach, and listening to the general chatter of people and picking out the usual languages of Spanish, English and German, the odd French and of course a mild influx of Bosnians but then I heard a completely alien tongue and realised it must have been Russian. I remember thinking there would have been a time when I would only have expected to hear that tongue if we were all invaded! Now they appeared to be coming

41

over in their droves, and, sailing large yachts! "What are you going to do?" I asked. He picked at a piece of mature cheese and ruminated.

"Nothing at the moment."

Paul looked at him curiously, "Nothing?"

"No, we must wait and see if anyone reports her missing. I do not want to tell all the TV stations and newspapers that we have an unidentified Russian girl lying in our morgue. Someone, somewhere, will know she is missing. And the person or persons that think she is dead and buried may well make a mistake. At the moment, it is all we have got."

"Jane wanted a story," I said.

"Not at the moment, and Philip, do you have the pictures?" I handed him the envelope. "Thank you, you can have them back when this is sorted out, or when we can issue a statement. Now my friends, I must go back to the station. By the way, I will be having a barbecue at the *finca* the weekend after next, you will of course come?" We all nodded and grunted our agreements to what seemed an incongruous request given the events of the day.

"A call for you *Señor* Philip," said Julian as he approached with the portable phone.

"Thank you Julian. Hello, Philip Edwards."

"Hello pal, its Gerry," said the worn voice at the other end of the line, "how's your hangover? Not as bad as mine I hope!"

"No it's fine. How you doing?"

"Better than this morning," he joked, "in fact

so much so I now feel I could manage a game of golf. I know you're a busy chap but I wondered if you could manage 18 holes before the pressure of work becomes too much for you to bear."

"Sarcy bugger, where and when?" thinking that a mindless session of watching the eight handicapper annihilate me at his favourite sport would give me time to think.

"Five o'clock at the Marbella Golf Club and I'll book the tee time. It should be very quiet. I'll see you there."

"I'm going to play golf with Gerry this afternoon," I looked at Sandy, "are you doing anything?"

"I'm going up to see someone at Coin Studios about an idea." The studios in the inland market town had remained dormant since the BBC's abortive attempt at a soap opera called Eldorado ground to a halt. God knows what she could achieve up there, but it was not my position to interfere with her plans. We left the restaurant together and I kissed her goodbye arranging to meet later on that evening at home. It was just before five when I took the car out of the garage and drove through the main street out of Marbella in the Malaga direction.

It was normally much quieter at this time of day even in the summer and saved the run out to the *autovia* that by passed the town. Five minutes later I was passing the Costa del Sol hospital on my left and Los Monteros Hotel on my right. The Robert Trent Jones designed course was on the other side of the road necessitating a manoeuvre off the *careterra* over the bridge and back on myself. The drive up toward the clubhouse confirmed everyone's worse fears about the shortage of water. The greens were holding out, but the fairways were in a sorry state. 'I can always blame my game on the poor conditions' I mused. I pulled up in front of the pro shop to find Gerry had already arrived and was putting on his shoes. He waved as I got out of the car. "There's only two other parties on the whole course, so there won't be anyone holding you up," he grinned.

We loaded our bags on the buggy and drove up to the first tee.

He always made me tee off first. I think it helped to boost his confidence. I placed the ball on the tee and, remembering everything I had been taught, lifted the wood as far behind my head as possible and followed through smoothly and effectively connecting with a perfect crack that sent the little white bullet a pleasing 100 meters or so. I smiled smugly at my partner, who politely doffed his cap.

It was a beautiful day and although the sun was hot, the countryside around the course was blessed with a constant cooling breeze. We chatted about nothing in particular, until we got to the third green where he succeeded in taking that hole from me as well, when I could bear it no more. He was a journalist. He knew everyone and knew just about everything that went on down here.

"What do you know about the Russians?" I blurted.

"What?" he looked at me quizzically. "Well, they live in a very cold country, they have a peculiar alphabet, a funny language that only they seem to speak, they used to be the enemy, but since we all became friends, there is a lot of unemployed spies and they all seem to be leaving their homeland"

"I'm trying to be serious." I said.

"So am I, why do you want to know?" Even though he was a very good friend, he was a journalist first and foremost, and as much as I wanted to tell him, I felt it was unfair to put him in an awkward position.

"It's just that I have seen and heard so many of them about lately," I lied, "that I just wondered what they were all doing here."

"They're on holiday. Wouldn't you went to get away from there? You said it was bad enough in the UK."

He hit a perfect drive down the fourth fairway.

"Yes, I know that, but I was just wondering."

"Well," he continued, "to be honest I don't know too much. But seriously, they are coming over in their hordes, buying up villas and apartments and more interestingly time-share."

"Time-share? What on earth for." I grimaced as my ball went half the distance of his and, well to the left, into the rough.

"Search me, but apparently they appear to be arriving with suitcases of German Marks and American Dollars and, paying cash for whatever they are buying. If you went to know more about that, talk to Baz Brown at Costalite Resorts near the Melia Don Pepe. He's the resort director there and they have been doing fantastic business with the Ruskies. Also, Chris Yeo told me the other day that he had someone buy an eighty million peseta villa on the Puente Romano estate, not a drop shot from your pad."

"Whew, that's the best part of four hundred and fifty thousand quid."

'Yup",

"What do you know about Igor Metchnikov?"

"Why do you ask?" he said sharply.

"Just curious."

"Well, that's a different story" he said as he lobbed his ball onto the green. "A very different story!"

Over the next two hours or so, Gerry painted a startling picture of the man that everyone had taken to in our town. He basically told how Metchnikov had been reputedly involved with arms deals, black market, especially during the troubles in Bosnia, illegal passage, drugs, prostitution and more. In other words he said, "one of your general all round kind of nice guys!" Money was easy to come by in that sort of business. "One tanker of fuel delivered to an embargoed country at war, nets more than a million dollars. Think of all the redundant weaponry that a man like that can get from Russia and sell on illegally at between a twenty and fifty percent commission."

"So, why has he been allowed to settle here

and why hasn't someone like you written about him?" I asked as we walked up the final stretch to the eighteenth green, right behind the club house.

"Secondly, I like living here and want to continue to do so and I would prefer not to disappear overnight. And firstly, there is no real proof. Certainly none that I could get hold of. And, let's face it, he's good for business at the moment.

His yacht is one of the biggest Banus has seen in a long time, he spends money and he appears to be doing a lot for the town, It certainly fits into Jesus Gil's idea of a wealthy and prosperous new Marbella. And, until he does something here, there would be no reason to doubt that he is a philanthropic businessman". He got the last hole on his sixth shot and I was close behind on a bad nine, my mind full of all sorts of confused thoughts, making my concentration somewhat lacking. He had gone around in an acceptable 88 while I had trailed with a miserable 98 — still at least it was in double figures — but, even with the handicaps adjusted, I was still buying the beers as usual.

We went to Los Canos, a popular beach bar which was only minutes from the club, despite having to go around the *careterra* yet again. We would have stopped at the club for a drink, but since the company had been involved in a legal wrangle the place had virtually come to a standstill and had all but shut. A great advantage when trying to get on the course but certainly not good for a business that at one stage was one of the finest golf and country clubs on the Coast. Still, it's an ill wind....... we recruited some of their kitchen staff to increase our professional brigade. Over a beer and some *calamaritos* I decided to tell Gerry all about it, on the promise that he would not break the confidence that Carlos had placed in me. It didn't take long to recount, what to me appeared to be, a very long day. We ordered two more beers. "Crumbs," he eventually said, "what a day."

"So you won't say or do anything?" I asked for his co- operation, "Carlos has promised that as soon as there is a story we can have it," a similar conversation that I had had with Jane.

"No, mum's the word. But listen maybe we could make some sort of unofficial enquiries. Do a bit of poking around on our own."

"You must be bloody joking," I said, "I am not going to open a can of worms. Let's leave it to the police." I took another swig of beer and studied him carefully. He was thinking about it, damn him. Once a journalist...................

CHAPTER FIVE

Gerald Peters didn't need an alarm clock. He just got up when he woke up, unless he had a particularly important assignment, which was getting less frequent these days. He never could understand the habit of rising to an alarm. He had had an argument some many years ago with a girlfriend's father who was a very successful fruit and vegetable merchant in Devon. One day the father was bemoaning the fact that the struggling journalist, who would be out until the very early hours in search of a story, spent most of his morning in bed, whereas, Gordon had done a day's work by the time Gerry's heavy eyes had opened.

"Tell me Gordon, when you go to bed at nine thirty at night, are you tired?" asked the cheeky young cub.

"No " came the immediate reply.

"And when you get up at five in the morning," continued the brave young man, "are you tired?"

"Well, yes," hesitated the older man. Obviously waiting for the punch-line.

"Well," said Gerry with bravado, "when I go to bed at night, I'm tired and, I get up when I'm awake. I think that's a far better way of living, don't you?"

Needless to say the prospective father-in-law didn't agree and decided that his daughter should not keep the company of such a sloth and was dispatched to finishing school in Paris, almost immediately. He never saw her again. Her loss, he would say, but on reflection? She was the daughter of a millionaire and had since married some chinless lawyer and probably "went to the country' each weekend. You wouldn't catch them down the 'Hare and Hounds' on a Friday night, or in Torremolinos for their holiday. Which, of course, is where he found himself nine years ago this July. He wasn't impressed. Some pals had suggested he go there as he was assured there was 'a lot of crumpet' about. As most of them were sorry, unhappily married hacks, he should have realised that their tastes in women were different. So, he ventured down the Coast bit by bit each day. He wasn't keen on Benalmadena although Fuengirola was better. As he went further West, he thought he was going back to Torremolinos, as he passed Calahonda, where the whole of the U.K. and some of Germany, seemed to have settled. But, things did get better, he saw the attractive port of Cabopino and fifteen kilometres more, he found himself in Orange Square, in the old town of Marbella.

The old plaza filled with the sweet smelling orange trees, small exclusive boutiques, pavement cafes and, restaurants, made him aware of the style that existed in Marbella. This he liked, but continuing his search further West, it took him to Puerto Banus — 'there's hundreds of stories there' he thought — and onto the old town of San Pedro, which he fell in love with. He scoured the local Sur in English and found a house, beach-side, to rent and, went along to see the old lady who owned it.

"I have to go back to the U.K. for some treatment," she had said, "and I could be gone for at least a year."

'A year would be fine' he thought 'long enough to know whether I like it here and can make a living'. They agreed a rent. The lady confirmed she was leaving at the end of the following month. Sufficient time for him to go back to London and tie up some loose ends. No sooner had his plane touched down in Gatwick, he hi-tailed it to Fleet Street and went to see his editor at the news desk of the Sun, billed as Britain's biggest selling newspaper.

"You're wanting to do what?" shouted the seasoned newspaper man. "What the fuck do you think you're going to do in that God forsaken dump?"

For a journalist, Gerry had often thought that his editor lacked somewhat in the vocabulary department.

"It's full of fucking, pimps, whores and fucking losers."

"Yes," retorted the hapless scribe, "and a lot of fucking good stories waiting to be written."

Sun newspapers wouldn't keep him on full salary, but the editor was willing to pay him as a stringer and also encouraged their sister newspaper, The Times, to do the same. So, with a promise of sweet FA, Gerry arrived in San Pedro where, for the next few years, he was going to make a living as a freelance journalist, writing for whoever would pay him and, thankfully, they did. The Sun, The News of the World, the Times and, occasionally, the rag mags that published the 'tits and bums' and the 'my mother was raped by an alien' type stories.

He pulled himself to the edge of the bed, scratched his head, rubbed his stubble face and sat for a few minutes with his head in his hands. What it was that made him drink three or four more iced Cointreaus, he didn't know. If it hadn't have been Cointreau, it would have been something else.

It wasn't that he was an alcoholic, he knew that, it was just that he liked to drink. It wasn't boredom either, he had plenty to do and, it wasn't loneliness. There were lots of people that he knew and, lots of women to keep him company, as and when he wanted. No, it was just that he liked a drink, although this morning he wished he had had at least one less. He didn't feel as bad as he had done on other occasions though.

He went into the bathroom and put on the shower and just stood there for five minutes letting the tepid water batter his head and shoulders, somehow purging his body of its outer toxins. It had been a good night though. The food was excellent as always, the wine was plentiful and he had sat with Carlos Jimenez. He liked Jimenez, he was an honest copper, hard working, who valued his friends and acquaintances. Not many police he knew from the old days in the UK had his principles. Carlos had often been helpful to Gerry. When he had a story to do for the

British papers, he could rely on the Deputy Commander to confirm or deny certain information or allegations, which often lead to Gerry's stories being the most accurately written in the British press.

In the kitchen, he squeezed himself a few oranges and, made a cup of instant coffee, he couldn't be bothered to dirty the filter machine and, put in three big sugars. He needed the energy he thought. He put some ice into the glass and, with only a slight hesitance, picked up the Smirnoff bottle and added a shot. Well, a little drop might help him feel human again. And it did. On the way to the terrace he remembered that he had not listened to his answer-phone when he had got home last night. He rewound the messages and pressed play.

"Gerry, Jane Mendez, shit I must have missed you. If you come back before you leave to go to Philip's party tonight, can you please bring your article for this month's edition. Deadline was yesterday you sod! love you." He didn't normally miss deadlines and, anyway, he had already had it with him to give to her, when he left home.

"Listen you toe-rag, you owe me one hundred thousand pesetas and I want it before the weekend, or I'll let your tyres down and poison your chickens. Seriously old son, you're over two weeks late ..." It was the voice of Honest Horace, purveyors of fine second hand carriages for the discerning, or a bunch of crap for the less fortunate. Enter one less fortunate, who had bought a four year old

Ford Sierra that had had one genuine owner. Obviously, the other members of the demolition derby team were not that genuine. But he would give him the balance this week "Peters, McNee, Sunday Times," Gerry's ears pricked up, "there's a chap who seems to be in your area that we have been looking at on and off for the last year or so. His name is Metchnikov. He's a Russian, with a load of dosh, likes fast cars and fast women, shags for his country and steals from his grandmother. Find out what you can and come back to me. We might have a story ..."

He took a large mouthful of spiked orange juice and went out on to the terrace. Metchnikov, he knew him, he had been there when the yacht had sailed into the Port and then asked himself how someone like that, had got all that money. His contact at the Port had told him that he had paid his mooring fees for six months. Why didn't he buy one? There must be plenty for sale. If he was going to stay for as long as he implied, he could obviously afford it. The man had certainly made his mark. He had a Ferrari, a Rolls and an entourage of women and minders. He could be seen most nights at 'Oh! Marbella' at the Don Carlos Hotel or Olivia Valere's at the Puente Romano. He had never caused any problems though. He had been known to tip Maitré D's with watches, reminiscent of 'the good old days' when the Arabs would flash their untold wealth. He would entertain friends at La Meridiana and watch them dance the night away at La

Notte. He had never seen him in Paul and Philip's place and neither of them had ever mentioned that he had been in. Perhaps, La Reserva was not exclusive enough for the big man. Obviously there wasn't enough razzmatazz and publicity for him. The *Ayuntamiento* were keeping quiet about their new visitor. Jesus Gil had not met him and there were no apparent plans for the popular mayor to do so. Arturo Sanchez had met him. He received the cheque for the roads at a specially convened press conference on board Metchnikov's yacht. In private, Arturo had said that personally, he wasn't keen on the man and, hoped that the general opinion that he would leave as quickly as he had arrived, would be true. Rumour had it that he was going to buy a restaurant on the Port, but preliminary enquiries made by Gerry showed that it was a rental only deal. Why would someone only rent things if he had the money to buy. Unless of course he didn't intend to hang around for very long. He thought there might have been a story, but he hadn't been sure that he wanted to put his nose in, just in the hope that someone may buy it, but he would keep an eye on him. However, this phone call now meant that he could be a little more earnest in his investigations.

He looked out over his garden and pool. He had lived here in the same house for nearly nine years. He had bought it very cheaply. The poor lady, Gladys, from whom he had rented the three bedroom villa in the first place, had died a year after her treatment for bone cancer.

He liked her, she was kind and he remembered being sad when her son had phoned from Bournemouth to tell him. He had been sending her 'story letters' about what was going on in her beloved adopted country. It was good 'short story' practice for him and he enjoyed keeping her informed. She didn't want to go back, but her family insisted, so as they could take care of her. She had more friends here than there. Her church, her theatre group - she still acted until her illness slowed her down and the lines were not so easily remembered — and her whist drives, all helped her to enjoy life. The weather eased her arthritis, her pension went a lot further and gin was a lot cheaper. She had bought the house when there was hardly anyone in the village. Even Sean Connery hadn't arrived by then. When she died, she left a thousand pounds for Gerry to thank him for the letters which she had kept in a binder which was returned to him. "You must get them published and call the book, 'Letters to a Dying Old Lady' she had told him one day. "You're not dying you silly old moo," he would say. But she was. And she did. Arthur her son had said that his mum had asked him to send off the binder with the cheque and, a letter explaining that her son was not allowed to sell the house for six months, giving Gerry time to find another place, or, that he had the same length of time to find the money to buy it at the price that she had put on it, which Chris Yeo had later told him, was considerably undervalued. Something that the old girl was very well aware of. He had had a few bob saved and at the beginning of that year his mother had died — they weren't very close — and, as he was the only son, the estate passed to him. It wasn't much, but it was certainly enough to buy the house and, he did like it. He bought it well before the six months were up. Perhaps he would get the letters published and he would dedicate it to Gladys Biggs and to the memory of a kind old lady that so loved life and her adopted Spain. He took a mouthful of his coffee and decided it was too sweet. He left it.

It was nearly lunchtime. Actually it was only just passed breakfast, but in his case the two were in tandem this morning. He squeezed another half a dozen oranges and added them to a long glass of ice and vodka and felt decidedly pleased with himself. The memories of dear old Gladys had cheered him and, the phone call from the Features Editor in London had revitalised his sagging journalistic prowess and, he was quite raring to go. But first a game of golf. Which one of his cronies would be free to play this afternoon. He could take the opportunity to thank Philip for last night and, the fact that he would surely beat him, would make a fine ending to, what he considered was going to be, a nice day.

He liked Philip. He respected him as a photographer, liked his honesty and genuine concern for people and their plight and, thought that he and Paul ran a fine restaurant, where he, and many others, had had some great times. He was aware that the guy had worked hard to survive down here all these years and was, at last, reaping some reward. He enjoyed his golf with him as well. Not just because he invariably won, but that he was good to talk to, always gave him a break on a story if he thought one was coming up and, nearly always bought the beer at the end. .

He had just sunk a pleasing five meter putt, when Philip asked him about the Russians. But when he asked about Metchnikov he was taken aback. Why on earth would a photographer ~ it was accepted that Philip never called himself a photographic journalist — and a partner in a restaurant, want to know about a sleaze ball like Metchnikov? So it came as a bit of a shock when he told him about the dead body and the Russian connection. 'Was this all too much of a coincidence?' he thought.

He wanted to tell Philip about the editor's phone message concerning the Russian, but he daren't. Now, a dead Russian girl, the name of Metchnikov being mentioned and, who was it who bought that property in Puente Romano? Maybe he would go and see Baz Brown, maybe they are all connected? Maybe he had a story. He had given his word that he would say or do nothing. But that was only in regard to the dead girl. He didn't say anything about the other things. Yes, first things first. He must get on with the story about Metchnikov, maybe it will all piece together. On the other hand of course, there could be absolutely no connection at all......................Unlikely.

CHAPTER SIX

I had had a restless night's sleep. The events of the previous day were running through my mind as I attempted to put them into perspective. I tried to be logical and methodical. Was I making more of this than there actually was, or was there some connection between it all. I decided to take Gerry's advice and go and see Baz Brown at Costalite resorts in Marbella. l rose from the bed to find Sandy was already up and in the shower. I went into the kitchen and squeezed some oranges and put the coffee on. She came out of the bathroom and came over and kissed me. "You're up bright and early," I said.

"Yes, I'm going up to Coin again this morning. I didn't have much time to talk to you last night. Anyway, with . everything else going on, I didn't think you would be very interested. The studio is involved with a London production company and they are talking about filming a series down here on the lines of Dallas and Dynasty, you know, fast cars, fast women, fast yachts and fast bucks."

"Sounds better than the last attempt," I said pouring the coffee." What will they want you to do?"

"I don't know yet, we're just talking. What are you up to today?"

"I'm going to see this guy Baz Brown."

"Why are you getting yourself involved?" she interrupted, "you don't know what you are doing, or what you may be getting yourself into."

"Listen, you are one of the people that said there could be a good story in this. Maybe there is." I said pointedly.

"Well, for God's sake be careful," she said as she moved towards me and put her arms around my waist. "I've only just met you and I wouldn't want to find you at the bottom of some ravine."

Her jesting remarks ran a shiver down my spine and made me aware that, maybe, I could be getting myself into something a little out of my depth. But, variety is the spice of life.

"I'm going back to my place tonight," said Sandy. "I've got a girlfriend coming around. Girls' stuff you know. I'll ring you later."

"OK," I kissed her on the cheek, she stood back and looked me in the eyes, before kissing me fully on the lips.

"I do care you know," she said as she turned to go into the bedroom. I went into the bathroom to shower and shave.

The sun was well and truly up as I got into the car and headed towards Marbella with the roof down. I turned right at Gil y Gil's obelisk, between the King Edward building and the Palacio de Congressos, Marbella's exhibition centre and conference hall. The Melia Don Pepe was virtually in front of me and the beach-side holiday resort was nearby. I parked the car near the reception area and went into the comfortable office to ask for the resort director.

"Who may I ask is calling?" said the beautiful young blonde at the counter. Long flowing hair, blue eyes, as tall as me, with legs up to her armpits. I guessed she was Scandinavian or Dutch, although her English was virtually without trace of an accent.

"Philip Edwards," I replied, "I'm a colleague of Gerry Peters. He doesn't know me."

I looked around the office walls which showed pictures of the resort and stock shots of other resorts in different countries. They explained their affiliation with RCI, the exchange network and, how owners were able to travel to more than 1500 resorts worldwide. Time-share was a popular holiday concept that the Americans developed and the rest of the world, as usual, jumped on.

"Would you come this way," said the Legs. "Mister Brown will see you now." She escorted me into less palatial quarters into a small, but adequately furnished, office. A short, smartly dressed, man got up from his desk, came over to me and shook me warmly by the hand.

"Hello," he beamed, "Baz Brown, how can I help you?" A strong but pleasing Southern Irish accent broke through the educated man's voice. He was in his late thirties, I guessed, well tanned and perhaps a little overweight. He gestured toward the sitting area and we both took a seat.

"It may seem a strange request," my mind thinking rapidly, as I now realised I didn't know exactly what it was I wanted to know, or how I was going to ask for it.

"I'm a writer and photographer," I said knowing the second part was true, "and I am doing a piece about the exodus of Russians to this country on holiday and buying time-share and property. Gerry said that you were probably the best person to talk to, as your resort has a big Russian influence.'

"He's right about that," said the genial Irishman, "would you like a coffee?"

"Thank you."

"Legs," he shouted, and the blonde reappeared. I found both the nickname and the lack of intercom or telephone contact amusing and he registered my smile. As 'Legs' floated off to make the coffee, he smiled.

"It's a pretty bloody obvious nickname for her, isn't it really? Her name is Legiyah, her mother was Spanish and her father English. Apparently it means a 'bright woman' which is true. She's a good girl, she's been here since I came here last year. My wife isn't too keen on her though," he laughed and I joined in. "Now then," he continued, "we have the largest and, I would say, most successful Russian line on the Coast. We are selling about two a day on average and they are nearly all red weeks, that being the most popular and hence the most expensive times of the year. The buyers seem to range from professional people, to young trendies and their families, to the downright strange. But their money is all the same.

"How exactly do they get their money?" I asked.

"Search me, but they pay in cash. And, it's not Rubles. We don't accept them," he quipped, "it's either dollars or Deutsch Marks; and, they have plenty of them."

'Legs' brought in the coffee and I could now see why the Irishman had this sitting area and a low coffee table in front of it. "You ought to speak to my line manager, Uri Karpov," he continued taking a mouthful of the insipid coffee. She might look good, I thought, but coffee making was not one of her forte's. He was obviously used to it. "He's American, but from Russian family. He's been here since we started the Russian line this year. He's not here today, but I can make arrangements for you to see him tomorrow if you like"

"Thanks," I replied "that would be most helpful. About the same time?" I asked as I got up to go.

"That would be fine. Legs, show the gentleman out please," and again he shook me warmly by the hand. *"Hasta mañana."*

The air-conditioned building was more noticeable as I stepped back out into the midday sun. As I got into the car, the leather burned through my back and the steering wheel was hot to the touch. I decided to call in and see Chris Yeo at his agency in the Puente Romano. Juan the doorman touched his peaked cap as he opened the door of the car for me, "Good morning *Señor* Edwards, leave your car with me." he said in good English, probably one of the half dozen or so languages that he knew well enough to communicate with the multinational clientele. 'I wonder if he speaks Russian,' I thought, as I opened the door to Chris' office and was greeted with a belt of cool air. The Eton educated, aristocratic, chartered surveyor, got up from his leather bound executive chair and beckoned me towards him, past his bevy of secretaries and negotiators. "Philip dear boy," his effeminate gestures not bothering me, or any of his close friends, at all, "to what do we owe this honour? Are you wanting to invest some of the hoarded millions of pesetas you have, into a beautiful hillside property or did you want us to sell your idyllic '*pied a terre*' — or have you just come in because you know I have a job for you?"

I took most of their brochure pictures for them. The types of property they dealt with, meant that they could always pay the photographer to take decent shots, as opposed to sending one of the staff out with their little Canon.

"Good morning Chris. None of that actually, although the job would be welcome. I wanted some information about the Russians."

He was a tall slim, 50 year old, with a shock of bleach blonde hair, combed back deftly covering his balding pate.

"Ooh," he gasped mockingly, "going in to the spying game are we?"

"Sort of," I laughed, I just wanted to know if you had had much dealing with them and if they had bought any property from you."

"Well," he said running his fingers through

his mane, "the only one that comes to mind, which is probably the one you are referring to," he implied knowingly, "is a beautiful villa, beach side, set in its own grounds which we recently sold for eighty million pesetas. If I remember, it was put into a Gibraltar company and, the gentleman who bought it, was acting on behalf of that company. He was a diminutive little chap, with round glasses and, he just opened a suitcase and paid me in dollars. Seven hundred and twenty thousand of them in one hundred dollar bills. Absolutely incredible."

"What was the name of the company?" I asked. "I couldn't tell you dear boy. If you want to know that you would have to speak to our lawyer, Ricardo Nuñez."

I knew that would be a client confidentiality and that he could not help. Anyway, at this stage, it was of no real interest. I had just wondered whether the Russians were buying property. As an afterthought, I asked whether Metchnikov had approached him for anything.

"Funny you should say that, we have been acting on his behalf to find a restaurant for him in Banus. We found him one on the front line. They wanted seventy million pesetas for it —I know, silly isn't it — but Metchnikov said he just wanted to rent. So we found one on the second line back. He hasn't made a decision yet 'though."

"Thanks Chris, you've been most helpful," I got up to go.

"May I ask why you want to know all this my friend?"

"Just curiosity and something someone said the other day. It's nothing important, don't worry." I started to leave. Chris followed me to the door.

"I thought you wanted the job," he said placing a brown envelope in my hand. "I would like the pictures by the day after tomorrow if you can."

I thanked him and walked to my car. It was one thirty, I decided to go to the restaurant and see Paul. There was a space outside, so I parked there rather than go into the garage. My partner was in the office doing the books.

"Hello mate," he greeted me the same most days, "are you OK?"

"Yes, fine thanks. How are things?"

Scribbling rapidly, he said, "We've had a good month. How August will be I don't know. If it's as bad as last year, I suggest we close so as we can give all the staff their holidays at the same time." It was a known fact that some of the better restaurants found August to be one of their less successful months and some did indeed close.

"*Señor* Philip," Julian had come in, "*Señor* Hurst is at the bar and wants to know if you are both free to join him."

Paul told me to go through and he would finish what he was doing and then come out. I walked through the bustling kitchens into the restaurant and up to the bar. I

"Hello Brian," I held my hand out in greeting, he took it warmly.

"Hello Philip, sorry to disturb you, but I had a meeting in Marbella and I thought I'd pop in for some lunch and, as I hate eating alone, I thought I'd like to invite you and Paul to join me, if you were free."

"It would be a pleasure," he knew I enjoyed my lunchtimes, especially with friends. Julian poured us a glass of cava and gave us the menus. Paul joined us and the three of us took the last remaining table outside. We ordered two *Vichyssoise* and a *Filo Pastry Parcel with Spinach and Chicken* and three *Fresh Salmon with Hollandaise Sauce* and a bottle of white wine from the Rioja. While we were sipping our wine and nibbling at crudities and olives, it occurred to me that Brian may well know more about are Eastern friends than anyone.

"There appears to be a lot of Russians coming over here Brian. Apart from the obvious weather, why has Spain become such a sort after spot?" I enquired, chomping, nonchalantly on a piece of raw carrot.

"I'm not too sure," he replied, "because we don't get too involved obviously, but I have heard certain things. For instance, it is very difficult for the Russians to get visas to come here. There is only one Spanish Embassy and that's in Moscow and, they have to queue a devilish long time. And corruption is rife. It's the old story, if you can afford it, you can get anything you want. They have to pay up to a thousand dollars for a visa and the associated bribes as well. Timeshare has a lot to answer for too, as it is being sold off site in Russia and buyers are being promised *residencias* on the back of their 'property' purchase. Which of course is totally untrue. So they come over here and find that they can only stay the length of their holiday time. Estate agencies sell houses on the same basis, although there is more chance then for the purchaser. It's an expensive business for the tourist. As it is, the return air flight is some five hundred and fifty dollars."

"Where do they get their money?" I asked, giving Brian a moment to take a mouthful of wine as the starters arrived.

"Well, from what I understand, there would appear to be three types of money. The old communist money, the young aspiring professionals and the black market and Russian Mafia money.

When glasnost started, those people who had been good communists were rewarded by the establishment. You must remember, people who were directors of factories, companies and the like were not put there for their abilities, but because they were good and loyal party members. When westernisation began, these people were rewarded with involvement in the businesses they were running. In Poland for instance they were offered shares in their companies, but in Russia they got more. So, all these people found themselves with a great deal of cash coming in. And of course they were dealing with American Dollars and German Marks as Rubles are worthless outside of their own country."

The staff cleared the starter plates and brought the main courses. Brian ordered another bottle of wine. The second lot of money has come about by the young professionals getting involved in business and of course travelling outside of their country to make money. And then of course, there is the perennial black market, which while things are in short supply, there will always be people willing to obtain them as long as people are prepared to pay for them — at a price of course!"

"So, how many of them are there here, do you know?" I asked, picking around the centre bone of the salmon steak.

"Only the Spanish immigration authorities would know exactly, and even then they will only have the official figures." explained Brian, "but guesstimates put it at some ten thousand since charter flights into Malaga commenced some eighteen months ago."

"Jesus," I was shocked, "that's quite a lot. Where are they staying?"

Brian shrugged his shoulders, "Mainly in Marbella, so I believe, but there isn't exactly a sort of community. Some Russian journalists started a newspaper in their own language, some weeks ago, so they must feel that there is a market." He finished his last piece of broccoli and placed his knife and fork down and with a contented look on his roundish face, he took another mouthful of wine and topped his glass up, before draining the remainder of the bottle in our glasses. One of the boys cleared the tables, both Paul and I declined sweets, but Brian chose a *Chocolate Marquise* to satisfy his sweet tooth. Paul and I sat there amazed, neither of us were aware that the Russians were arriving here in such numbers. We finished our lunch and Brian paid the bill.

"Thanks for the company chaps, it was most enjoyable."

"Thank you, I replied, "both for the lunch and the information."

As he got up to leave, he turned towards me. "By the way, why did you want to know all that?"

"Just curiosity," I smiled. But curiosity was getting the better of me.

CHAPTER SEVEN

Igor Metchnikov put down his mobile phone and picked up his glass of champagne. He finished the last round of toast with Beluga Caviar smothered over it. He was not a handsome man and he didn't try to be so. His pot belly, the result of the recent years of success, folded over the top of his black baggy trunks. He was happy with his lot. If the women didn't come to him for his good looks and personality he would buy them with gifts and friends and if all that failed he would have a whore when and where it pleased him, he didn't give a shit. Come to think of it he didn't give a shit about anything anyway. He had had it rough as a kid and had spent most of his early life working hard, so now he was making up for it. The Spanish girl was lying on the after deck, her long dark hair flowing backward across the teak with her breasts pointing proudly upwards and the mound of her trimmed black pubic hair the only contrast of her perfectly tanned body. He would have her again, later. Before dinner. This was the life. A far cry from his childhood days in the Ukraine some forty years ago, long before that fool Gorbachov had dreamed about a new and free Russia His mother and father had worked on a state farm just outside of the medieval city of Lvov. They often had only just sufficient money to enable them to feed little Igor. It didn't take long for the young Russian boy to learn how to survive. He would steal other peoples chickens and sell them. He daren't take them home, his father would flog him. They may have been poor, but they were honest. Too honest for their own good as far as Igor was concerned. Poor Papa, he was a fool. Working like crazy and dying when he was forty five. Feeding the state and not himself. Letting his mother scrub and clean and milk the cows and shovel pig shit.

'Not for me', thought the street wise kid. 'There's more to life than this.'

It wasn't long before he progressed from chickens to western goods that were unavailable in the USSR. There were always people prepared to buy American cigarettes, food and the like. He had contacts now. He had moved up the ladder. He had left what little schooling he had been getting and had learned the ways of the world.

"Best education you can get" said the older boys and young men that he had fallen in with. "Money is the only commodity in the world worth having. Every communist dream — to be a capitalist."

And so started Igor's climb to wealth and infamy.

Then there was glasnost when all the do-gooders decided that the USSR was going to be a 'free' state. Democracy was going to change everyone's lives. The Berlin wall came down and the politicians tried to change what had been in existence for 75 years. Communism may not have worked, but what were to be the alternatives? There wasn't enough money around to pay decent wages and the shops were not suddenly going to be full of goods. The queues still existed and of course inflation raged. But it gave Igor and his friends the opportunity to increase their revenue. The more there wasn't, the more demand was created and the harder people like Igor had to work to keep up with that demand. In fact business was so good, that Igor had a team of people working for him now and, like in all similar circumstances, he had created enemies.

Sergei Barenkov was much the same as Igor except that he had no parents that he could remember. He came up via the streets and too had built a strong business in the black market. The problem was, that although Igor was expanding into all areas of the Ukraine, Sergei was still in their hometown of Lvov and he wanted it to himself.

Things came to a head when two of Igor's boys were found in the back of their car, gagged and tied back to back with a cheese wire twisted, Spanish gar-rote style, around their neck. It had cut through the veins. It had been done in such a way that each time they moved it cut more and more through the already severed skin, until eventually the jugular just exploded, causing them to die helplessly, their bodies soaked in blood. When news reached the gang leader, his face grew red with anger, his body trembled with rage. He picked up his desk chair and hurled it through his apartment window out into the snow covered streets. He looked at the town where he had struggled to make a living. He didn't know whether his parents would be proud of him, as he had more money than they had ever dreamed of, or whether they would be so disgusted with him, and what he had done to survive, that they would despise him forever. No matter, they were dead. And he had been told that there was no God, even though his parents believed, so he would never see them again in heaven or, be answerable to them, for his actions. He turned to the assembled men who had brought him the news, now shivering as the winter evening penetrated the previously warm room.

"I want a meet with Sergei Barenkov tomorrow night, in public, in the square, at eight o'clock. Let him know and tell him to be alone."

Igor wanted rid of this man and he wanted out of this town. He wanted to go to America. California, the beaches, the sun, the women, drugs and prostitution. He could make a lot of money. They paid more for their whores there than here. The overheads couldn't be that much more expensive, he smiled.

Sergei Barenkov was no idiot. He knew that Igor wanted him out of the way. The feeling was mutual. Metchnikov had got too big for his fur lined boots and he was going to do something about it. The message to meet came as no surprise to Sergei, why else had he had the two boys strung up like poultry to the market, if not to push Metchnikov's hand. But if Igor thought he was going to be alone then all his money and power must have made him feel Godlike. He summoned his men and selected three to go with him. He would position them in the adjacent doorways with silencers fitted to their hand guns. He gave instructions that when the two rivals met they would walk toward them and as Igor would not recognise any of them they would be free to walk down the street. As they got alongside him they should fire at close range. It was simple, he, Sergei, would not carry a gun and should there be a problem, he would be in the clear. He sent one of his other men to the meeting point some two hours earlier to make sure that there was no ambush.

At 7.30 pm Barenkov was in place. His men positioned strategically in the nearby doorways. He stood wrapped up against the cold. Nothing untoward was visible and although Igor had not yet appeared, he felt uneasy. People were going about their early evening business. Cars were traversing the square. A bus pulled up and the passengers disembarked. Others got on and it slowly pulled away. A taxi dropped off a client, the passenger paid and was engaged in some conversation. Sergei lifted his collar up over his neck and adjusted his ear muffs. He hadn't really heard the shouts and if he had he wouldn't have thought that they were for his benefit. People were running out of the way as the taxi mounted the kerb and sped along toward the unaware figure of Barenkov. He turned at the last moment to see the lights of a car upon him. Like a frightened rabbit he was transfixed. The thudding sound was a combination of the immediate breaking of two legs followed by the impact of the upper torso on the bonnet. The force of which pushed the body upward and onto the windscreen cracking it as the bloody face of the victim seemed to adhere itself to the ice cold glass. The driver braked and the body flew forward and landed in a crumpled heap in the gutter.

As if it was a street rat, the driver drove purposefully along the pavements edge and guided his nearside tyre over the head of the lifeless body, ensuring his task was complete. The screams and shouts of the spectators filled the night air as the taxi drove away as if it had just picked up another passenger. The cab was found burned out, at the bottom of an embankment on the outside of the town. The real driver of the vehicle strapped into the driver's seat, his lips sealed forever.

The cork flew out of the bottle as champagne spewed out after it. "A toast gentlemen to all the taxi drivers in the Ukraine they do such a great job."

They laughed and raised their glasses.

"Gentlemen," Igor continued, "we are expanding our operations considerably. I will brief you as to who runs what and where. But I am going into the war business. The war in Bosnia and Croatia is hotting up and they are in need of arms and fuel. We have a surplus of arms and we can get the fuel. To the future!"

They all raised their glasses again but this time a little confused. Metchnikov was going out of their depths. A little black marketing was alright and they didn't mind bumping off the odd bit of competition, but arms and fuel sounded complicated and dangerous. But they would be happy to watch the shop in the Ukraine.

Success continued to come Metchnikov's way. He had built sound business interests to front his illegal and immoral activities. He had visited 'his' America and had bought a home there. He had taken back to Russia the American hype and had used that to turn basketball into a spectacle which had become exceptionally popular with the Russians. His team were doing well. The spin-offs were good too, in as much as clothing and the merchandising, while not as profitable as it would be in the States, was returning him a reasonable profit. But more than this he was gaining respectability and credibility. His circle of friends and acquaintances had grown and he had managed to become somewhat of a personality among the professional elements and had even started to be a benefactor to cover his nefarious activities.

It was at a reception for the inauguration of a new children's wing at the local hospital, to which he had contributed, that Metchnikov's career was to take a turn toward the most filthy and cruellest form of crime imaginable.

Doctor Olga Petrova was in her late thirties and worked as a paediatrician at the hospital.

She was an unattractive short woman with swept back, short black, hair and moustache to match. An obvious lesbian, she reminded Igor of the typical Russian spy villain in the Western 'Bond' films that he enjoyed watching so much when he was able. She quizzed him about his known association with America and explained that she had a scheme which she knew would make money. She didn't want to talk there and then but arranged to meet at Igor's office the following day at one o'clock. Metchnikov was always keen to hear of new ways to increase his already mounting fortune and readily agreed to the meeting.

The next morning he opened the door to his office and greeted Olga Petrova. She wore a heavy fur coat over trousers and a jacket. A far cry from the regulation white coat and uniform of the hospital, but still undoubtedly a dyke. He offered her a seat and poured some tea.

"I am aware of some of your dealings," she said to Metchnikov taking out a cigarette and lighting it. "Do you mind?" she had asked too late. Metchnikov gave a sideways shake of his head. "So I therefore ask that this meeting be kept in the strictest confidence," she continued, "and should you not wish to become involved, that our conversation goes no further."

"I agree," said the intrigued Russian.

"During the course of a year there are hundreds of children born in the Ukraine to poor peasant girls, some whose families do not know, some who have no family, nearly all of them are of a limited intelligence and lack education. They get pregnant at fourteen and fifteen years of age. The children are unnecessary and largely unwanted. In the West there are thousands of childless couples who would give anything, especially money, for a healthy new born baby. You will recall that there was an exceptional black market trade in babies in Rumania which has since stopped, leaving, as you would say, 'a gap in the market.'" Igor unconsciously rubbed his hands together while watching the scheming, ugly witch. "I have not offended you?" she asked.

"No, I am very interested" he said, "please continue."

"Obviously, with my position and contacts," she stubbed her cigarette out in the glass ashtray, "I am able to get as many of these babies as we could handle. But I, and my colleagues, need the help and muscle, not to mention capital, to mount such an operation that would need forged documents and visas, which only someone in your position would be able to arrange."

It was as simple as that. The woman sat back in her chair and crossed her stubby legs. Igor didn't like her. But then again he did business with thousands of people and he couldn't think of more than half a dozen that he would even drink with.

"How much will these people pay for one of your babies?" he asked.

"It depends" she replied lighting another slim cigarette, confident now that she had got the gangster's attention. She didn't like the man, but she didn't need to. She just needed his co-operation and influence. "If the family are wealthy Americans, up to 35,000 dollars. But our preliminary enquiries have shown that there are many that will happily pay between 25 and 30,000 dollars."

"You say 'my colleagues'. There are obviously more of you. Who and where are they?" enquired Metchnikov finishing his tea.

"I have two doctor friends in two other hospitals in the Ukraine. We met at a seminar several months ago. My friend here is a gynaecologist at our hospital. We all have discussed the possibilities and agree that there is a lot of money to be made."

"How will you 'acquire' the children from their mothers?" he poured himself another tea, not offering Olga one, as she had not touched the one in front of her.

"Some will be born prematurely, others will have natural illnesses at birth. They will all have to be kept behind and the mother will be sent home to await the outcome of their child's treatment. They will of course live for a short while and then be pronounced dead. We will issue a death certificate and that will be that. We will also issue a new birth certificate which we will use to obtain the necessary paperwork to allow the child to travel to which ever country the parents come from. During this period, they will be kept in a safe house." She smiled, for the first time, with a hint of satisfaction.

"There is more to this than a simple visa or passport you know?" Igor said getting up and walking around the room. Olga Petrova followed him with her eyes. "The Americans, or anyone else, will not accept a child unless they believe it to be above board and totally legitimate. We would have to have some form of release forms from the mother. A lawyer would have to arrange the 'adoption' and all necessary paperwork. It would have to be seen to be totally legal."

He returned to his desk. "Give me some time to think about this and I will make a decision. Come to my office the day after tomorrow at the same time." They shook hands and he opened the door for her to leave. He sat down once more.

'There is not a lot of money in this' he thought, 'it would be far more profitable to sell a tanker load of fuel. But wars won't go on forever, well not always ones that I can get involved in. However children are born every minute and there will always be childless couples waiting to pay for the one thing missing to their totally blissful westernised existence.' He would have to speak to his lawyer Dimitri Yakov, he handled all Igor's affairs, legitimate and illegal. Maybe there was something in this project that could be worthwhile. He lifted the tea pot and drained it. It was cold.

Dimitri Yakov's office was in a small but select area of the old town of Lvov. Hidden from prying eyes and secluded enough for his mixed clientele. Igor had no appointment, he didn't need one. But he felt it was best to be there first thing in the morning and better to call in rather than have the lawyer come around to his flat. He walked in unannounced, The short, bald, bespectacled man was sitting behind his cluttered desk, a cigarette hung from his lips and an electric fire in the corner blasted heat into the stuffy room.

"Igor my friend," said the little man as he got up from the chair and came around the desk, "how are you?" '

"I am well," replied Igor, removing his scarf and using it to dust the grime from the two ragged brown plastic client's chairs on the opposite side of the desk.

The little man scurried back to his seat. "What can I do for you," he enquired.

"I have a new proposition," said Igor undoing the huge buttons on his heavy coat and placing it on the furthest chair before sitting in the one nearest him.

"What do you know about adopting children?"

"You wish to adopt a child?" asked the startled lawyer.

"No you fool, I simply need to know the laws regulating the adoption of Russian children by foreigners," Metchnikov was impatient. He found Yakov irritating, but he was thorough and a terrier. Give him a problem and he wouldn't let go until he had a result. He was also trustworthy. He had to be.

Many of his clients had too much on the diminutive man and the world wouldn't miss one more legal parasite. Dimitri went over to his large metal filing cabinet and collected a file and a large book from above it.

He returned to his seat and blew the dust off the book — "I don't get many enquiries about adoptions" ~he said making excuses. He lit another cigarette, the other was still burning in the over-flowing ashtray. He opened the book and shuffled through the papers in the accompanying file. Igor loosened his tie and undid his collar. He was warm. "Well, as you may know," started the lawyer, "there is to be a moratorium on the adoption of healthy children from Russia." He cleared his throat, "however this does not apply to children with handicaps and infirmities." .

"You mean it's OK to adopt a cripple or an ill kid, but not a healthy one?"

"Well, yes, it would appear so. Although some sources say that illegal adoptions ran into several thousand between then and now. Our government is attempting to control foreign adoptions by centralising the process and forming non-profit making government accredited agencies. The government have imposed penalties for persons involved in 'baby selling'. The organisation, Pravo Rebenka, the right of the child, currently oversees inter-country adoption and has jurisdiction over the entire country, with the exception of Moscow and St. Petersburg.

They have also established working agreements with several foreign adoption agencies. Adoptions in Russia by private individuals are becoming increasingly more difficult."

"Encouraging more illegal adoptions?" interrupted Metchnikov.

"Yes, I suppose so," commented Dimitri. He wiped his brow with a soiled handkerchief. "Shall I continue?" he asked. Igor nodded affirmatively. "All applications must be made to Pravo Rebenka. Parents must be at least twenty five years of age. There must be no more than forty years age difference between parents and children. Couples should have been married for at least two years. One past divorce each is allowed. Practicing Christian families are given preference and they should preferably have no children of their own.

"Christ," interjected Metchnikov, "it sounds more like Hitler's prescription for the perfect bloody family."

"Ahem, yes," huffed Dimitri as he lit another cigarette. "Shall I?" he indicated the papers in front of him. "Yes, carry on" said Igor; "Approximately nine to twelve months after they have submitted their dossier and formal application and have a child assigned to them, they must travel to Russia and stay for two to three weeks. The whole process takes about a year and costs about twelve thousand five hundred dollars, not including their travel expenses."

"Where do the kids come from?" asked Metchnikov.

The lawyer studied his papers. "Mainly from orphanages. All are more than a year old and most suffer some form of mental or physical handicap."

"Who the fuck would spend that sort of money on damaged fucking goods, when they could get better?"

"Well, it would appear that 'good goods', as you imply, are harder to get."

"Yes, but not impossible, hey Dimitri?"

"Uh, no Igor, I suppose not." said the lawyer sweating more profusely. He got up and turned down the fire.

"If I asked you to arrange the necessary legal documents to take a child out of this country, would you be able to do it?"

The lawyer thought for a moment. "I suppose so. It would take a bit of work and a fair amount of money, why?"

"Because I may want you to do it for me. Find out how much it will cost and how long it will take." Igor got up and picked up his coat and scarf.

"When did you want to know this?" asked Yakov as he got up from his chair and followed him to the door.

"I will 'phone you tomorrow," stated the Mafia man as he pulled up his collar and made his way down the stairs. "First thing in the morning," he said as he turned back to look at the dishevelled character at the top of the landing.

The following morning, around midday, giving him sufficient time to compile the information, Igor phoned the lawyer.

"What have you got?," he asked.

"Well, it is possible," replied the man, "it would be necessary to have birth certificates and release forms from the mother, to obtain visa and travel documents. Also we would need the name of the new parents.".

"How much would all this cost?"

"Around two thousand dollars," he replied hesitantly.

"Good, thank you, I will be in touch." He put the phone back in its cradle and laid back in his chair. That seemed a reasonable amount of money. There would surely be some hidden costs that had not yet been covered. Some bribes here and there, the cost of a safe house to keep the children. It would have to look a bit like an orphanage and it would have to be moved periodically to avoid government interference, but that shouldn't be a problem. If the cost of legal adoption was twelve thousand dollars and parents had to wait and, they were going to end up with a year old semi—reject then they would surely pay twice as much for a healthy infant child and have it within weeks as opposed to a year or so. He would devise a plan and an agreement with the dyke. He would set up an agency, by name, to front it all in America, or any other country they move into, and use Yakov's practice as the registered offices. He had just under an hour before Petrova arrived. He started writing furiously.

The bell rang. He got up from his chair went to the door and saw her stout figure through the spy hole.

"Good morning," he said as he opened the door, "you are very punctual." He let her take her own coat off and he sat back in his chair immediately, proffering his hand to the chair in front of his desk. "I have given the matter a great deal of thought and I am prepared to give the operation a try." The woman beamed with a sense of achievement. Her colleagues had been dubious about involving someone of Igor Metchnikov' s standing in the underworld, but she had persuaded them that the stronger the man the more likely it was to succeed. They thought he would dismiss the idea out of hand, but Igor had the reputation of always trying out new ventures. "On the following conditions," continued the man almost sounding like a professional consultant. Well, he was a businessman, a very successful one. "I will arrange all the necessary paperwork to register the child, supply visa and travel documents and to arrange the marketing in America. In return you will supply the child, the forged birth certificates and death certificates where necessary, the signed release form from the mother. I suggest you do that before she goes into the theatre. There must be a way that you can get her to sign a form along with the others that she has to sign regarding hospital responsibilities etcetera."

"That would not be a problem" interjected Petrova.

"Good," Igor continued, "The cost of paper work and documents will be around two thousand dollars. Other costs and upkeep of the child and care etcetera will be in the region of fifteen hundred dollars per child. Lawyer's fees and the like, around another thousand. The children will be sold for twenty five thousand dollars giving us around twenty thousand dollars. You and your colleagues will receive ten thousand.

"That is only half," she blurted, "and we are taking all the risks."

"No," replied Metchnikov becoming impatient, "I am taking the risks and this offer is not open to discussion. I'm sure that if you don't want to do it I can soon find someone else."

"But," she started defensively, it was her and her friends idea, how could he take over. Then she looked into the evil eyes of the man across the desk. 'If you are going to play in the big league' she thought, 'you have to abide by their rules.'

"That's fine, I will relay this information to my friends. When do we start?"

"You will start when I tell you. That will be when we have everything in place and have a suitable set of parents. I will call you"

"Very well," she got up to go, "and remember Olga, we have not signed anything. This handshake," he extended his hand, "is as tight as any contract to which you will ever have to put your signature." She held his hand. It was warm. 'Cold heart' she thought.

Three weeks later, via the contacts that he had arranged in America, they had their first opportunity. The parents were comfortable, mature and desperate for a child. They had the money. Yakov had spoken to them and asked how quickly they could travel to Russia. They had said within days. Igor phoned Olga. "We have an order," he said, and replaced the phone. Olga Petrova was on duty when the seventeen year old came in. She said she had no family. She told the child that she needed a Caesarean She was ideal.

The doctor gave her the papers to sign. An hour later she was in the theatre. Two hours later she was informed that her baby had died during the operation. The child was distraught. She was sore, she hurt, her heart was breaking. She cried. She knew it would be difficult to bring up her baby but she was going to try. Her sister would have helped her. She would have made it. Why her? The birth certificate was arranged. There was no record of the girl's baby. Dimitri Yakov prepared the visa and travel documents for young Catherine Burnet, the new daughter of Adam and Delyse Burnet from San Francisco. The proud parents paid their 25,000 dollars in cash, shook hands with Dimitri and left their hotel, to return to their beloved America. Metchnikov met Yakov in the bar, ordered two vodkas and toasted their success. Within one month they had supplied three and with the other hospitals being involved this number was to grow. 'Not a bad business,' thought Igor as he counted his share, 'and it will rim itself with just a little supervision.'

CHAPTER EIGHT

The envelope that Chris Yeo had given me contained instructions on how to get to a villa in Los Nagueles, a very exclusive part of town, just off the main *careterra*, by-passing Marbella's city centre. The name of the client was enclosed and I had to telephone him well in advance to make an appointment to go to the house to take the pictures. I had phoned him yesterday evening when I returned to the restaurant to have a light dinner with Ricardo Cuevas, director of OCI. The client, David Hill, had readily agreed to meet me at his house this morning at midday. It was nine thirty, that gave me time to go and meet with Uri whatever-his-name-was at Costalite resorts, at ten as agreed. I packed my camera case and two new rolls of film. I quickly swilled my glass and coffee cup and saucer under the tap and was just on my way out when the telephone rang. It was Sandy.

"Hi Babe, how are you?"

"Fine," I replied, "what's happening?"

"I'll tell you later. Are you free at lunchtime?"

I replied in the affirmative, sure that I had nothing else to do after the villa shoot. .

"Then we will meet at Ogilvy and Mailer at two thirty; My treat. Bye."

I got into my car and pulled out on to the road that would take me toward Marbella for the five minute trip to the time- share resort. I parked the car in some sort of shade and left the roof down. I went into reception to find 'Legs' behind the desk.

"Good morning," she said her broad smile lighting up the room.

"Hello," I said giving my sexiest smile back, obviously to no avail, "I have a meeting with Uri, uh, I'm sorry, I don't know his other name."

"Karpov," she replied. "Please take a seat, I will tell him you are here. Mister Edwards isn't it?"

"Philip, yes." I sat down and watched her for a few minutes before a tall, good looking, man entered the room. His short brown hair topped an angular face with a strong chin, broad shoulders and a slim body. His open smile revealed a perfect set of teeth that were obviously all his own!

He was wearing dark blue trousers and a short—sleeved light blue cotton shirt with a patterned blue tie. "I'm Uri Karpov," he extended his hand in greeting, "please come this way. Perhaps you would like a coffee." I accepted. He had an accent that was more American than Russian, I thought. He walked us to the small coffee shop that appeared to be primarily used by the sales staff and ordered an iced coffee for both of us. "Now," he said showing me to a table in the comer, "Baz tells me you wanted to talk to me about the Russians and them buying time—share. How can I help?"

I took a sip of the cold black coffee. "I really just wanted to know a little more about how they come to buy time share, how they get here and where they get their money?"

"You work for the government?"

"No," I replied quickly, "I'm a writer photographer, I am doing a story that's all."

"Very well," he emptied the pack of sugar into his glass and stirred it slowly. This company is probably the most serious and successful when it comes to marketing time-share to the Russians. We have offices in Leningrad, St. Petersburg, Moscow. Russian people cannot legally come here unless they have a visa. They can still only come here if they own a property or if they intend to buy one. This means that we have to pre-qualify them. In other words our offices in Russia show them videos of the resort in our language. If they like what they see then they must arrange to come out on a fly-by. That is where they pay for a flight over and we supply them with accommodation. As long as they bring sufficient funds to make a purchase, they will get their visa."

"Does that mean that they have to buy?"

"No, but they nearly always do. They are dying to buy something with their surplus of dollars."

"Where are they getting the money from?" anticipating his answer.

"I don't know. Old money, new money, Mafia, who cares. As long as they buy."

"Once they have bought, does that mean they can travel freely backwards and forwards?"

"No. Firstly they are only given a Schengen visa. That is the freedom to travel within the European countries in the EEC that are linked by borders. Britain and Ireland would not be accessible to them. Also they only have a one entry one exit visa. If they state before coming that they wish to visit Morocco for instance, they must obtain a double entry and exit visa."

"Are they led to believe that their timeshare entitles them to live in Spain permanently?"

"Some companies do this. We do not. Some Russians arrive and overstay their visas and wait to get caught. It is becoming a problem. You must remember that it is the Spanish government that insists on the visas, it is nothing to do with Russia. They don't care how many people leave the country at the moment."

"So how do people like you get here and stay?"

"Most of the people I know here are educated people. Young professionals, students and the like. Obviously, nearly all of them speak good English and most of us speak Spanish. Some, like me have work permits and *residencias* and live here all year long. It's different for me as I am Russian/American. My father and I emigrated to America when l was young. It's still difficult for me as an American to get a work permit, but as I am a director of the company that has invested money, that tends to qualify me. It is very hard for us to get these permits. Others try and fail. Some stay and chance working, or meeting and marrying a Spaniard in the hope that they can remain."

There was a silence as I felt I had no more questions.

"Now, if there is nothing else, I am afraid I

must get into my morning meeting and get my team into selling mode. It was nice to meet you, if I can be of any further help in your research, or sell you a timeshare," he smiled, " then, please 'phone me."

"Yes," I said getting up, "thank you very much for your time, I do appreciate it."

"You are welcome," he said and showed me out of the bar, through the reception and to the main entrance. I felt I was getting quite an expert on this Russian business and if things ever got bad, perhaps I could sell timeshare to them. It didn't seem too difficult. They come over from Russia with money in their pockets to a resort they have already seen on video and, what appeared to be the promise of a better life - and buy!

I drove out of the car park, around the roundabout and turned left between Kings and McDonalds, 'a total contrast' I thought, and back onto the Golden Mile before turning toward Señorio de Marbella, past Restaurant La Meridiana and over the back hills to Los Nagueles.

The house wasn't difficult to find, it was certainly big enough and on seeing it, I felt that I would probably need more than the two and a half hours I had given myself to do the job.

The price of the property was around the 85 million pesetas mark, about half a million pounds, and therefore warranted one of Chris' amazing brochures, for which he charged the client handsomely, hence the reason he could afford to pay me. I rang the door bell by the heavy wooden doors that led to the open courtyard. A voice came over the intercom. "Philip Edwards," I confirmed and the Buzzer sounded as I pushed the huge door inwards. A fit, well groomed man in a sports jacket, despite the heat, greeted me with a slight American accent. He was in his late fifties, or early sixties, but had obviously looked after himself. He was well tanned as most retired residents appeared to be. He opened the front door and beamed a welcome smile. He showed me around the property, taking me around the rooms and, sharing with me, his obvious love for his house. It prompted the obvious question as to why he was selling.

"My wife died only a few months ago and the house is too big for one person. I have no children, so I feel that I should move into something a little simpler. Somewhere where I don't need staff and can be happy in my own company."

"I'm sorry," I replied.

"Oh, there's no need to be, we were very happy, but she had been ill for some time. She would want me to enjoy the rest of my life. I'll leave you to it then. Anything you want, just holler and I'll see you for a drink when you have finished." He left the lounge and I wandered around getting the feel of the place and then started to take some shots. There was a lot of house and a lot of superb pieces that needed including in the brochure. It was fast approaching two o'clock and it was obvious I was going to have to come back to finish the shoot. Anyway, I had to admit, I wanted to take some night shots, as the gardens and pool were spectacular and Mr Hill had assured me that when the lights were on, it was a veritable Garden of Eden. I explained my intentions and he said I could return any evening as he was in most of the time. I promised to phone in advance however. He poured me a glass of cava. "I always drink this in the mornings," he said raising his glass, better than Alka Seltzer and more fun."

We chinked glasses and I took a mouthful of the ice cold nectar and smiled contentedly as the bubbles danced on my tongue.

"What do you think of the house?" he asked. "I think it's wonderful Mister Hill and I don't think you will have a lot of problem selling it. There are a lot of people coming to Marbella at the moment, with money, looking for quality places. How long have you lived here?" I asked.

"Well, it belonged to an old friend of mine who died of cancer. He was older than me and single, we had a business relationship rather than friendship although we did become friends. My wife and I were on holiday and fell in love with the place and bought it. It was only about two years ago."

"Well, it's very lovely and I hope whoever buys it appreciates it for what it is."

"Thank you Philip, that's nice of you to say," he said genuinely.

I glanced at my watch. "I'm sorry, I must go" I said. I only had ten minutes to make the restaurant, no problem. I said my goodbyes and told him I would be in touch tonight or tomorrow, He waved a jocular goodbye as I slipped into my car and he shut the great wooden doors behind me.

I dropped down on to the Golden Mile again and headed toward Puerto Banus to take the Nueva Andalucia turning that would take me through the golfing centre of Marbella, past Los Naranjos and to the small, intimate eatery, known as Ogilvy and Mailer. Whilst sounding a little like an advertising agency, this was actually, one of the better places to eat in the area. Sandy was there already, sitting on the shaded patio to the back of the restaurant. Carol, one of the partners, greeted me warmly. "What's Sandy drinking?" I asked. "Cava," came the reply, "The same for me," I said as I went to join Sandy at the table under the shade of a tree. She got up to greet me. Arms around my neck and, a warm kiss on the lips.

"I'd forgotten how it felt," she smiled.

"It hasn't been that long," I returned the kiss. "So, what's been happening?"

"Well," she nibbled at a piece of raw celery, "it looks as if they are going ahead at the studios with this action series and they need a line producer.

"A what?"

"A line producer. That's the person who runs the show on a day to day basis. In charge of budgets, welfare, actors, crew, that sort of thing. As they had seen on my CV that I was involved on a couple of Aussie soaps, they offered me the job."

"Lots of money?" I enquired

"Well, a reasonable salary to start with and points on the programme — that's like shares — if and when it is sold and is successful."

"Great," I said genuinely pleased for her, "when do you start?"

"Pre—production starts next month."

"I'm very pleased for you. You do realise that being from Australia, you could have trouble with a work permit and resident's permit."

"I have discussed that already and they are going to make me a non-share holding director of the production company, employed for my relevant and necessary skills. There's not exactly a plethora of TV personnel on the Costa del Sol. So, — that's why lunch is on me!"

"That's great, 'cause I'm starving."

"Tell me about your last twenty four hours or so," she said putting her outstretched hand onto mine.

"Let's order first, I'm famished." Carol came over and we plumped for *Salmon Carpaccio* and *Thai Fish Cakes* followed by *Italian Summer Chicken* and *Calve's Liver* with *Bubble and Squeak*. "And a bottle of Raimat Clos Casal, thank you Carol."

We spent a lovely lunchtime, the food was superb, the weather was perfect, a light breeze took the edge off the hot sun, and the company was great. I told Sandy all about my visit to Costalite, Baz and the conversation with Uri, my meeting with Chris and the lunch with Brian. I also told her about dear Mister Hill and his beautiful house and that she should come with me when we do the night shoot.

"You've been quite busy yourself then," she said, and smiled. I was enjoying the company of this lady. We had ordered our coffee and, brandy for me, when my mobile phone rang.

"At least we are not in the middle of eating," I said apologetically, "Hello, Philip Edwards."

"Philip, this is Carlos. I would like you to come to my office as soon as you can."

"Is their some development on the girl?"

"Not yet my friend, but there has been a triple murder in Marbella and we think that they are Russians."

"Good God Carlos, I'll be there in half an hour"

"What is it Philip? asked Sandy as she held my hand.

"It was Carlos, they have discovered a triple murder in Marbella, it must have been what was on the radio this morning." I finished my coffee and brandy and Sandy paid the bill. "I'll see you later tonight at the apartment, yes?" She kissed me goodbye, I said my adieus and got into the car.

I arrived at the Guardia Civil's station on time and walked in to be greeted by the imposing man. If you didn't know him, I had always thought, and, he stopped you for some misdemeanour, he could certainly make you tremble.

"Buenos dias Carlos."

"Hola Philip, pasa?" I went into his

comfortable office and took a seat as he closed the door behind us. His after lunch coffee cup was on top of a pile of papers and, had not yet been cleared away, and his desk was in some form of organised chaos.

"This morning the bodies of a man, a woman and, a child were discovered in an empty house on Urbanisation Las Cancelas. They had all been strangled with what looks like piano or cheese wire. The man and woman were in their late twenties and the child, a girl, was three or four. Once again, there was no identification, but the label on the woman's underwear was the same as the girl on your hill."

"So you naturally think that they are all Russian?"

"It's all we have to go on at the moment. Except this was no jealous lover, no whore being beaten up or someone falling out of a car. This was first degree murder. Cold and premeditated and I don't like it in my town."

"What are you going to do?

"I am going to have to put out descriptions in all the newspapers. I need to find out who they are, where they came from and why they are lying dead in a derelict house in Marbella; And —— who your young woman was at the bottom of the ravine. It's all too much of a coincidence."

CHAPTER NINE

Katrina Omst woke early, she was crying as she had done for the last eight months. She held her swollen stomach yet again, half hoping that it wouldn't be there this cold spring morning. She knew it would be though. Nothing was going to change. If only she hadn't have gone on a summer camping weekend with her friends. It seemed like a good idea at the time. Fresh air, fishing, songs around the camp fire, bird watching and climbing. All the pursuits of a normal healthy sixteen year old.

He wasn't really her boyfriend — she didn't have one as such -— she was too busy at school trying to make something of herself. Her parents were good to her, but they didn't have much and she was determined to make a better life for herself. It had been a lovely day, they had kissed for fun before, but it seemed, that night, as if everyone was doing it. The sounds coming from the other tents of laughter, moaning and general sexual banter, made her feel that she should be joining in. It was her first boy. He was good looking, with black hair that fell over his forehead as he looked down on her, he had deep dark brown eyes and was a few years older than Katrina. His firm young body was warm to the touch and smelled good as, she could feel him gently guide himself into her waiting body. It didn't hurt, she had always thought it was meant to. She drew breath as his mouth covered hers and he pushed gently but firmly further up into her young body. Slowly raising himself up and down, she could see his arm muscles swell and feel his groin tighten as beads of sweat, appeared on his brow and, ran down his spine into the small of his back. She felt him tense and moan as he released his young passion. She could feel his orgasm although she did not have one of her own. She would one day though, even with this short encounter she could see why her older friends enjoyed it so much. An evening of childlike, harmless fun, had left her with an everlasting memory of the boy she had never seen again.

Her sister was six years older than her, had found a job as a typist and had met an ambitious young man, whom she had married a few years ago. They had had a delightful baby girl. 'I wish it was her who was pregnant again' she had thought.

This episode had meant she had left her home on the pretences of getting a job with her sister in Lvov. She was staying with them and was trying to continue her studies. Her parents were upset when she left school and even more upset when she left home. But her sister Natasha had told them that everything would be alright.

She had presented herself to the local maternity hospital and had told them that she had no family and was on her own. She had met a nice doctor, Olga Petrova, who had assured her she would be looked after. Her sister and her husband were good to her and she did what she could around the house to help out and continued her reading and writing. She was studying English and French as one day she wanted to live in Europe where all the glamorous people lived. She had decided to keep the child despite her sister telling her of the problems of raising a child without a proper father. But she was determined.

She got out of bed to go to the bathroom when a cramping pain caught her in the lower stomach. It was as if someone had punched her. She buckled and winced. There was another one. 'It can't be now' she thought and grabbed her dressing gown. There was another sharp pain and she cried out. Natasha came into the room. "I think it's coming she said," with tears welling up into her eyes. She put on a track suit while her sister threw something into a suitcase. They got a taxi and arrived at the hospital. Olga Petrova was on duty and came straight to the observation cubicle. "You will be alright, she said as her skilled hands moved deftly across the swollen stomach, "your baby has turned, it has decided to come out the hard way. We will have to operate to save the child, and you a lot of unnecessary pain." A feeling of horror came over Katrina. No one had prepared her for this, she just thought that she would go into hospital and, with a push and a shove, it would pop out like a pea from a pod. In a daze, she signed the forms that the doctor placed in front of her and she was prepared for surgery.

She woke for the second time that day, this

time the lump was gone, but the pain was severe. She saw the blood dripping slowly down the tube into her arm, from its hanging bag just above and to the left of her. She could not see her baby. Was it a boy or a girl. Maybe all this would be worth it. She would be a good mother. As time went on she was sure she would meet someone who would love and care for her and her child. It would be alright. She would go back to her parents one day. They may be able to accept the 'fait accompli' as opposed to watching her every day for nine months. She tried to attract a nurse, but every move caused the pain to increase. Eventually a young woman came over. She asked to see her baby, but the nurse said she would have to wait until Doctor Petrova arrived.

She drifted back into a disturbed sleep until she felt someone's hand on hers. She looked up to see the re-assuring face of the kind doctor.

"Can I see my baby doctor?," asked the frightened child. The smile turned to sadness as the doctor held her hand very tightly,

"I'm sorry my dear, you lost a great deal of blood. We had to make a decision. We tried our best, but we could not save the baby. I am so very sorry."

Katrina's heart ached. It pumped harder, she felt sick in her fragile stomach, the pain came to her eyes as her throat tightened. She started to cry with a pathetic whimper, which developed into uncontrollable sobbing. She started to wriggle and pull at her bed clothes.

A nurse brought a tray with a prepared syringe.

Katrina started yelling "No, no, please God no, please no, please, please." She screamed as the nurse gently held her so as the doctor could inject the tortured child. The screams died down to a gentle cry, the struggling stopped and, the heart— broken Katrina drifted into a tranquillised sleep.

In the warmth of a luxury hotel suite, Dimitri Yakov, offered his guests a glass of iced vodka. The woman refused. She was a very elegant creature in her early thirties. Her shoulder length blonde hair suited her tail slim body. She was a woman of class. The man, who accepted the small glass with pleasure, was equally as elegant. Dark blue, all wool, double breasted suit, with matching silk tie and handkerchief in a paisley pattern. His hair was black with just a hint of grey, and swept back off his high forehead. "Your health and that of your new baby," said Dimitri as he threw the contents swiftly down his throat. Adam Burnet followed suit, as his wife Delyse, cringed, as she could feel the neat vodka hitting the back of her husband's throat. There was a knock at the door and in came a young woman holding a small neat bundle. She handed it to Delyse Burnet who gently took it in her arms. Looking down at the crumpled face of a child barely three weeks old, tears came to her eyes. "She's beautiful Adam, look." The husband came up and put his arm around his wife, "Yes darling, she is," he replied, placing his curled finger under the sleeping baby's chin. "You didn't mind us calling her Catherine after my mother, did you Adam?"

"Of course not honey, as long as she doesn't take after her too much," he quipped,

"Thank you Mister Yakov," said the tall American as he handed over the balance of the money in dollars. Dimitri handed him an envelope with all the necessary papers enclosed, confirming that the young baby was definitely, Catherine Burnet. "It was pleasure to be of service," replied the creepy little man as he shook their hands, "A pleasure."

A month had passed and Katrina was still not over the shock. She still cried every morning and most of the night. The hospital had kept her in for two more weeks due to her operation and, because she was heavily sedated most of the time. The hospital psychiatrist had attended her every day before pronouncing her fit to leave. She had not seen her baby. She had never held it. It was as if it had never existed. All she knew, was that it was a girl. The pain in her stomach had gone, but the one in her heart, would never go away. She had gone back to her sister's to recover, but now she felt the time was right to go back to her mother and father. Should she tell them or not. She would make up her mind nearer the time.

Her parents were pleased to see her home. They held her tight and she cried. They asked her what was wrong and she just said she was happy to be home again. They were also happy when she said she wanted to continue her studies. Life went on for young Katrina, but the hurt was never far away. There were celebrations when she reached her eighteenth birthday, and, passed her exams and went to University. Her parents were proud of her. They still didn't know her secret. 'Why should I tell them?' she had said to herself. Graduated and now twenty one, she had a boyfriend. She had told him everything, and they were quite happy. They both had jobs in the evening and were comfortable. They might get married, but at the moment they were happy as things were.

He had gone out to work. She was relaxing in the armchair with a tea and a magazine with the TV in the background. The newsreader had just finished the world news and was now going onto the national news. She glanced through the magazine on her lap, until the words, baby, illegal adoptions, deaths and young girls found their way through the maze of journalistic words. She sat up in horror and listened "So far nothing has been proven, but police and government agencies are looking into the possibility that it could be part of an organised international crime syndicate that has been operating for some three years. Up until now, three young women have come forward with information that police say is helping them with their enquiries She got up and turned off the television. 'Could it be?' she asked herself.

'After all, she had had no problem with the pregnancy up until the birth. No, it couldn't be. Things like that don't happen. Anyway, it was four years ago. But the thought plagued her.

The next day she phoned her sister at work and told her what she had seen. She was going to go to Lvov and speak to the hospital. "Don't," said her sister, "it will only bring back bad memories and you have been doing so well." She told Gregorio and he said he would come with her. "No, I want to go alone." On the long bus journey to the medieval town, those past days, all that time ago, were recollected. What was that woman doctor's name? Petrova? that was it, Petrova.

"She isn't here anymore," said the clerk at the entrance. "Well, where is she?" demanded Katrina. "I have no idea," replied the hospital clerk. She followed the signs to administration where there was a senior woman behind the counter. She asked to see the registration of birth of her child.

There was no record of the birth, neither was there a death certificate. In fact, there was no record of the baby at all. Shell shocked Katrina went out into the cold wind. Everything was a haze. What would she do. What could she do? Should she go to the police? Natasha and Boris listened to Katrina's story.

"We must go to the police," said Boris. "If this has happened to others, then we must report it."

The police inspector allotted to the case was

sympathetic. He took down all the details. This so far was the most explicit information that they had received and an immediate search for Olga Petrova started.

It was soon in the news, both on TV and in the papers that it was a well organised group of doctors, but no mention was made of any ring leader. The police had summoned Katrina to their offices to get her to identify Petrova. This she did. But where was her baby. During interrogation, Petrova confirmed that Katrina's was the first child that was sold, but she couldn't remember all the details. She thought that the couple were from California and that their name was Burnet Alan? Andrew? She wasn't sure. She showed no remorse

On the news that night, it was confirmed that Petrova had been placed in custody along with another doctor from a nearby hospital, both awaiting trial. Two days later, it was reported that Olga Petrova had been found hanged in her cell.

Katrina was scared. She decided that she was going to do something. She was going to make an effort. She packed her bags and left her sister and brother-in-law, thanking them for everything and promising to keep them in touch, but she was going home to Gregorio and, to tell her parents everything.

The shame she may have felt at the outset was now outweighed by the anger and sadness inside her and she wanted her parents to understand and to help.

After the initial shock and tears her parents

listened to Katrina's story and were dumbfounded and deeply angry. Not so much with their daughter but with a society that could allow this to happen. She wanted to go to America and find her child. "Impossible," said her father. "You don't know where to start, you have never been abroad before, they speak a different language, it's dangerous, and, you have no money."

"I do know where to start, California. I have their names, travel doesn't worry me, I want to travel, my English is good, I'm not afraid and, I want to borrow some money from you to put with what I have saved Papa." Her father looked at her and her mother looked over to her husband. "Please papa, this means so much to me," said Katrina with tears in her eyes. "I have to find my baby." Gregorio was coming too. He said she needed support. They would make the journey together.

The journey to Los Angeles was long and tiring for them both. Poor Mama and Papa, they were terrified to let her go, but she was a determined young girl and they were happier that Gregorio was going with her. Her parents admired her strength, even though they wished she had come to them sooner, before the baby was born. If she had, perhaps none of this would have happened. But Papa was right, she was frightened, she really had nothing to go on. Her parents had scraped together and borrowed some money, together with what she and Gregorio had, it was sufficient to get them to America and live for a couple of weeks or so. Their visas were valid for a holiday and she knew their time was limited. They would have to get a job doing whatever. She would start going through all the telephone directories for the State. The task was daunting. And even if she found the child what was she going to do? Did she think the mother would just let her have her back. Hardly, as far as they were concerned, they had a legally adopted child.

The young couple found themselves a clean and tidy motel room in downtown Los Angeles. The next day they started their task straight away, by going to the local library and, beginning the search for Burnet. The librarian pointed them in the direction of the telephone books and her heart fell as she saw shelves of thick directories all for the State of California.

With heavy hearts they started with Los Angeles, found the 'B's and then they glanced at each other as they looked down the pages at all the 'A. Burnets'. Gregorio picked up the directories for San Remo and did the same.

This will take forever. They made photocopies of all the A. Burnets in the State of California and went back to their motel room to formulate a plan.

"We are going to have to phone every single one of these people" said Katrina.

"I know" replied Gregorio, "apart from the time it is going to take, I daren't think of the cost!"

"I hardly think that is relevant at this moment, do you?" said Katrina.

There were over two hundred A. Burnets. If Petrova was wrong and his first name began with a B or a C, then they would have a totally impossible task. Maybe God will be on their side. They would start tomorrow by going to the AT&T offices and settling themselves into a booth. They had split the areas between them. Gregorio had Los Angeles, San Diego and Long Beach. Katrina had, San Francisco, San José and Monterey. They would pretend that they were from the Russian Embassy and were checking on visas issued to an 'A. Burnet' four years or so ago. It was like looking for a needle in a haystack. They would never find them.

"Good morning, is that Mrs Burnet. This is the Russian Embassy, we are checking visas issued to you and your husband. Could you confirm that you visited the USSR? I'm sorry? You have never visited Russia. We must have the wrong Burnet, I'm sorry to have troubled you."

"Hello, is that Mister Burnet? I'm sorry to trouble you, this is the Russian Embassy. Could you confirm that you had visas to visit Russia four years ago?... Oh, I see. I'm sorry. We must be confused."

Exhausted and cramped from all their phoning, they made their way back to their room. Tired, hungry and feeling down. They had achieved nothing and seemed only to have uncovered the tip of their task. They laid in bed.

Gregorio put his arms around the beautiful young woman and his hand crept upwards, to cup her firm breast. Gently kissing her neck, he pressed into her back. She turned around and let his mouth find hers. A long passionate kiss that would have led to more if Katrina had not put her finger on his mouth and said, "Not now darling, I'm sorry, but I really don't feel like it. I have too much on my mind."

"I know my love, it will be alright", and he gently kissed her forehead and ran his hand through her hair, as she drifted into a troubled sleep.

The next morning they awoke with a renewed resolve. Today was to be the day. They got to their booths at the AT&T offices and set about their task. By lunchtime, they had still got nowhere. Katrina was flagging. She was becoming despondent, she was tired and upset. They went across the road and had a McDonalds. They had tried one in the Moscow restaurant when they collected their visas. It was sufficient to sustain them. Katrina started to cry, "We will never find them. Papa was right, this was a stupid idea. I should have left things as they were. Let's go back to the motel and make arrangements to go home. I have had enough."

Katrina laid on the bed and slowly cried herself to sleep. Gregorio, slipped on his coat and went back down to the telephone offices and picked up where Katrina had left off. San Francisco. Some eighty Burnets of which she had managed twenty odd.

"This is the Russian Embassy," said Gregorio for what must have been the hundredth time "we are trying to check on the visas issued to you in nineteen You have never been to Russia, I'm sorry to have troubled you."

"Good morning, Mrs Burnet?"

No," came the reply, I am the housekeeper."

"I am from the Russian Embassy," continued Gregorio, "I am just checking on visas issued to Mr and Mrs Burnet some four years ago."

"What about them?" said the housekeeper abruptly.

A shiver went through the young Russian, 'had he found them?' he thought.

His mind raced, he now didn't know what to say. "Can you confirm that they did indeed travel to Russia." he spluttered.

"Of course they did," came the response.

With his fingers crossed he continued, "It's just that we do not seem to have a record of the entry into Russia of their daughter." He held his breath. There was a silence.

After a short time the housekeeper said, "I know nothing about that," Gregorio's heart sank, "As far as I know, the baby was adopted over there, but if you have any questions, you will have to speak to Mr Adam Burnet and he and his wife are in Spain at the moment ."

"What?" came the shocked response. 'Spain,' thought the untraveled young man.

"Yes, they have a house in Marbella. Now if there is nothing else, I really feel I have answered enough of your questions. If you wish to write to them, I will forward the letter. Goodbye." And she hung up.

Gregorio's heart was racing. He paid the bill and started to run. On his way to the motel, he grabbed a bunch of flowers from the street vendor and opening the door to the room slowly, he laid the flowers next to the still sleeping girl and gently kissed her on the lips. She stirred.

"We've done it!" exclaimed Gregorio, "I've found them!"

"What?" cried Katrina, "where, who are they, where do they live?" she flung her arms around his neck. "Tell me, tell me please," she blurted, not knowing whether to laugh or cry. Gregorio related everything to her. Her excitement turned to passion.

They made love.

That evening they went out to celebrate the success of the first part of their mission.

"So now you see, we send them a letter explaining everything, which the housekeeper will forward", said Gregorio naively.

"Come on Gregorio," Katrina took a mouthful of the warm red wine, "what do we write. 'Dear Mr and Mrs Burnet, you are not going to believe this, but la-de-la-de-la and please can I have my baby back'." He looked at her as the realisation that they were really not that far ahead suddenly hit him.

"I'm going to Spain," said Katrina decisively. "I can't", said Gregorio, "I have to get back. Anyway we can't afford it." "I didn't say 'we'," replied Katrina, "I said 'I'."

116

"No!" said Gregorio emphatically, "it's too dangerous for you to travel all that way on your own."
They looked at each other across the table. Her stern gaze piercing his eyes. He knew he had lost.

CHAPTER TEN

As she sat in the 747 to Madrid, she was pensive. Sub- consciously rubbing her finger where her grandmother's wedding band had been. She told the pawn broker that she would send him a money-mail to include postage, in a month or so. Her grandmother wouldn't have minded. She was sure that she would understand that it was for a good cause. Poor Gregorio, he was so sad when she left. It had taken them a while to get her a visa to enter Spain. The Spanish Embassy eventually granted her a single entry and exit visa for a fortnight's holiday. She didn't know whether that would be sufficient. She fingered the piece of paper with the only information that this whole exercise had produced. "Adam Burnet, Marbella, Spain." She couldn't speak Spanish.

The internal journey from Madrid to Malaga had taken just under an hour. The difference in temperature of the Andalucian climate, to Madrid, in the more Northern part of Spain, was obvious as she stepped off the plane. She made the long walk from disembarkation to the arrival hall. There was a bank where she changed some dollars into local currency, realising that she did not have much to live on. She saw a sign that said *Tren*, and correctly assumed that she was heading in the direction of the train station. She soon found that she could only travel to the unpronounceable town of Fuengirola, where she would have to get a taxi.

By the time she got to Fuengirola, it was getting late, so she found a small, comfortable hostel off the main church square, grabbed something to eat nearby and had an early night.

The next morning the sun shone through her bedroom window and she could hear the sound of the locals going about their daily routines. After showering she went into the square where the old men sat and chatted on their park benches under the shade of a huge tree. The sound of crates and bottles echoed around the square as the delivery lorries unloaded their orders for the numerous bars and restaurants nearby. She walked into one and was about to order a tea, but the smell of freshly ground coffee made her change her mind. As she sipped the hot thick milky drink, she noticed a telephone directory on the bar by the 'phone. And next to it, she couldn't believe her eyes, a Russian newspaper. Not from Russia, but from Spain. She smiled as she saw the familiar writing that she had not seen for some time. She glanced at it quickly, but then opened the telephone directory. It was a bit confusing as it seemed to be broken into towns as well as names. She found Marbella and looked for Burnet. Nothing. 'It would have been too simple', she thought.

She continued to drink her coffee and glanced through the thin paper. Under employment she saw a large advertisement looking for Russian/English speaking staff for a time share operation in Marbella. It was worth a shot, she didn't know what it entailed, but she felt there would be no harm in ringing. The secretary told her to be there at two o'clock in the afternoon and gave her directions to Costalite resort, near an hotel called the Melia Don Pepe.

Uri Karpov was a striking young man. He had an open smile and dark blue eyes. His light brown hair was immaculate as was his shirt and the crease in his trousers. She didn't think she had ever seen such a good looking Russian. He was tanned and obviously fit. His smile made her immediately smile back. They talked, first in Russian then in English. He explained what she would be doing and how she would be trained for the job. Anything she needed she only had to ask.

"What about my visa?" she enquired.

"Don't worry about that at the moment, when the time comes we will sort it out."

"I need somewhere to stay nearby."

"I will ask some of the other girls. Perhaps you could share until you find your own place."

She left the offices and caught a bus back to Fuengirola. She felt good. She felt that this may be just what she needed so as she could take her time to find the Burnets. Opening the door to her room, she wondered whether she should find a similar hostel in Marbella. She started to pack her bags again. He was nice wasn't he? Mmm. She picked up the photo of Gregorio, planted a delicate kiss on the picture, placed it at the bottom of her suitcase and closed the lid.

Katrina blinked as the early morning sun penetrated the stillness of her small room. She had managed to share a small apartment with Diana. She was a fun girl. They had hit it off straight away and her English was improving all the time, even though some people had commented that she had developed a slight Liverpudlian accent. Diana had a shock of ginger hair and a personality that was just as wild. She was on the sales-line too, but obviously dealt with the English clients. Katrina had undergone a short training programme under the guidance of the ever-charming Uri Karpov. This week she was due to go 'on the line' and start selling the product. She could see how her fellow countrymen had fallen in love with the beautiful apartments. The crisp white buildings, modern furniture and manicured gardens were a far cry from her parents small house in the Ukraine and, the greyness of it all.

Here everyone seemed to be happy and contented. They laughed a lot and were always out with friends and eating and drinking. It was a happy way of life and she was enjoying it. But she could not forget her main task and, now that she had the stability of some income and somewhere to stay, she could get on with finding her baby. She had written a letter to Gregorio and also to her parents telling them that she was well and had got herself a job so as she could afford to stay a bit longer in Spain. She had exhausted most lines of enquiry. She had even asked the local foreign residents association if they had a Burnet registered. They didn't. If the worst came to the worst she would have to write to the Burnets in America and hope that they would respond. But there were other avenues to explore yet. She had been told about an American Club that meets regularly. She was going to get in touch with the organisers and see if she could find them that way. She was not giving up hope.

Her first day on the sales-line she sold a week's timeshare to a young Russian family. Uri was keeping an eye on her and he closed the deal for her. He then took her to the bar and bought some champagne for her and her 'line', to celebrate her first sale.

That night curled up on the settee eating a sandwich she was glancing through Marbella Marbella when an article caught her eye. An attractive woman in her late thirties looked out at her from the glossy pages. 'A fashion designer of some note from America' said the article. She had joined forces with a local designer and boutique owner in Puerto Banus to sell 'designer wear' using materials from all over the world. Indian silks, Irish cotton, Scottish wool and more. This talented designer was a semi resident on the Coast, her husband was in 'import and export', hence the availability of all the materials that she and, her Spanish partner, sold from their shop Cocos on the front line of the exclusive port. Delyse Burnet, said she was married with a little girl of four years of age.

Katrina went into a cold sweat. It was too much of a coincidence not to be the woman she was looking for. Her day off was Friday, she would go down to Banus and find her. This had to be her. Her eyes filled with tears as memories came flooding back: that, and the realisation that her trip may now have been worth it. But she still had to get her child back and how was she going to do it. Perhaps she should confide in someone who knew the area, the law and the customs. Someone who had been here a while. Uri Karpov, she knew he would help her. She would speak to him tomorrow at work. Although, maybe she had better make sure that this was the person she was looking for before she made any approaches to anyone. She would leave it until after her trip on Friday.

She had borrowed Diana's car before on her days off and, this time, after she dropped her off at the club, she once again took the little Golf GTi for her own use. She drove the short distance to Puerto Banus and parked in the car park and walked into the marina from the back of the buildings. She wandered along the front line until she came across the bright yellow frontage with the name Cocos emblazoned in blue and windows displaying their colourful, chic, overpriced outfits. She nonchalantly looked into the shop to see if she could see the object of her trip. There was a young woman behind the counter, but it wasn't Delyse Burnet. It was early. It was only just 10.15 and nothing much was happening yet. She would go and have a coffee in the bar next door so as she could wait. What happened if she didn't come into the shop? How long would she wait? Was this going to be a waste of time? She had just finished her second cup of coffee when a black BMW pulled up outside the shop. Out of the Californian registered vehicle climbed a woman, whom Katrina recognised immediately from her picture in the magazine. She opened the rear door and helped the young occupant out. Katrina's stomach flipped. Her heart pounded in her throat, there, in front of her, was a beautiful young girl with fair hair about four years of age. She was numb. It was her daughter. She knew it. The woman closed the door and walked around to the driver's door. "I'll only be a few minutes darling and then we will get back home for your phone call," said Delyse as she walked with her daughter into the shop. Katrina couldn't move she didn't know what to do. She couldn't just get up and ask her outright. She thought quickly. The woman said she was going to go back home. Perhaps Katrina could follow her. At least she would know where she lived. The Americans' car was facing East, so the chances were they would exit at the Cristamar end of the Port. With shaking hands and wobbly knees she tried to catch the attention of the disinterested waiter, to no avail. She couldn't speak, she took a 500 peseta coin from her purse, left it on the table and walked as quickly as she could to her car. She fumbled for her keys, opened the door, fired up the engine and drove to the exit. She handed the ticket to the attendant along with another 500 peseta coin. As she pulled out, she realised that she had to go in the opposite direction in order to turn around and get to the Cristamar end. Around the roundabout and back on herself, she saw the black BMW pull out of the port and turn left heading down towards her on the opposite side of the road. Damn! She went on faster until she could turn around and catch up with the westward moving vehicle. They went under the underpass and headed toward San Pedro. Katrina had the car in her sights but kept two or three cars behind. At the traffic lights before the town of San Pedro, the BMW indicated that it was turning right. Katrina followed.

The car drove at speed up the Ronda road, the nippy GTi having no problem keeping up. The two vehicles started the climb up the hill. Katrina had no idea where she was but they were both keeping to the main road and despite the hills and bends she knew she would find her way back again. Past the Madroñal tennis club, the BMW turned right down a narrow road and pulled into a drive way some 200 hundred meters along. The occupants got out and amid chatter and laughter made their way in to the house. Katrina sat rigid, not knowing what to do. She had kept her distance. They hadn't seen her. She slowly got out of the car and wandered down to the house. A large villa with a beautiful garden and pool. In the garden there was a swing and a slide. A Labrador bounced around with a beach ball and the little girl laughed as she tried to take it away from the dog. The mother looked on. Katrina was crying. How could she even think of taking the child from a loving family who could obviously give her daughter everything she could not? But, she was her mother. She had to do something. At least she now knew where she lived.

Saturday morning was normally quiet as it was 'change-over' day, the time when one lot of holidaymakers were replaced by another. That meant there were fewer people being persuaded to go and 'have a look' at the Coast's time-share resorts. Katrina had arrived earlier than normal as she had been unable to sleep. Her mind was racing as she had been trying to decide what to do. She could talk to Uri. They had had drinks together with other members of the team after work and he always seemed so nice. She would ask him for some advice, maybe he would know the Russian representative from the Consul who could help. She saw the figure of the good looking man at the bar having coffee and talking to the Sales Director, Baz Brown. She approached and could hear they were talking about sport, so she interrupted and asked if she could speak to Uri. Baz excused himself, finished his coffee and returned to his office.

"What is it?" Inquired Uri.

"I need some advice," said Katrina hesitatingly.

"About sales? If so you will have to speak to one of the senior salesmen as I have to go into town — and I'm late."

"It doesn't matter" replied Katrina, taken aback, "it was personal."

Uri, reached out for her hand. "You are troubled Katrina." Her eyes were watering. "Look, I am out all day to day, why not join me for dinner tonight and you can tell me all about it, eh? I will pick you up at eight thirty, OK?"

Katrina smiled, "That would be nice, thank you." He squeezed her hand gently and left. Her eyes followed him as he went through the glass door. A feeling of warmth came over her. She did like Uri. All the girls fancied him but they had never seen him with anyone important. Tonight could be more interesting than she had thought.

CHAPTER ELEVEN

It was Friday morning, nearly the end of a full working week since my event of the falling blonde. I was reticent about going back to the hillside, but I had to finish taking the shots of David Lewis' house, if I ever wanted him to pay me. I had been lying on my back for the last hour or so, staring at the dimly lit ceiling, illuminated only by the morning sunshine that was creeping through the closed curtains. Sandy was lying peacefully next to me, her soft breath rhythmically caressing my neck. I had been cataloguing the event of the last few days, trying to put things into perspective. How were the murdered people associated, if indeed they were, and, more importantly, why were they killed? If they were Russians, — why Russians? and did someone like Metchnikov have anything to do with it? He was not a particularly nice chap, not top of my dinner list, but I couldn't see him involved in anything like this, —- and why?

The gentle bleeping of the alarm stopped my thoughts. I got up and opened the curtains. A beam of morning sunlight cut its way through the room, shining, like a theatre spotlight, on to Sandy's sleeping face. She stirred and turned over to avoid the brightness. I slipped on my bathrobe and went into the kitchen to squeeze some oranges and make some coffee. I turned on the TV to catch the eight o' clock news. I stopped the juicer to listen to the article.

Carlos had indeed issued descriptions of the four people who had been found dead. Height, complexion, hair colour, approximate ages, distinguishing marks, everything, except actual photos, as they, of course, would have been impossible to use because of the severity of the fatal wounds.

'The people, two of whom are believed to be of Russian origin, were found dead under mysterious circumstances in two different areas of Marbella. Police have set up a special incident room and are anxious to hear from anyone who may have information regarding the people described. Contact this twenty four hour number. 2828282.'

Sandy came in and put her arms around my waist and kissed the back of my neck. "Morning," she sighed. I gave her a glass of juice.

"Good morning," I replied, "sleep well?"

"Mmm, what's on the news?"

"Well, Carlos has released the descriptions of the dead girl and the others. It will probably be in the Sur this morning. Let's hope that something comes of it."

"What are you up to today?" she asked, pouring two more coffees.

"I have to go and finish taking the shots of Lewis' house and then I'm going to the restaurant to see Paul. We could meet for lunch if you like. Oh! and then we could run up and see David Hill and finish the work on his house. You'll love it. I'll ring him later to confirm."

It was another glorious morning as I put the

roof down on the car and made my way out on to the familiar Istan road. Ten minutes later I had parked in front of the house. I looked up into the still blue sky and watched for the birds and other wild life and, inwardly, probably waiting to see my eagle. I had a couple of hours to complete my assignment and I trusted it would pass without incident. It did.

The restaurant was already busy as I parked my car in the underground car park and walked back up the ramp, acknowledging Rafael the caretaker on my way. As I passed through the occupied terrace tables to the main entrance, Carlos' green Nissan Patrol pulled up a little further along the street. The big man got out of the car and waved. I returned the greeting and waited for him to walk the 50 meters or so, to join me. We shook hands and went inside to the bar. Paul was there to greet us and poured two *finos*.

"Any luck with the report on TV?" I asked, being the first to mention the subject.

"Not yet," he replied sipping the cold sherry and popping an olive in his mouth, "but it has only been a short time. We have placed an announcement in the Sur this morning and one in the Sur in English for next Friday, and, I have put it into that Russian newspaper as well. I'm hopeful."

Sandy came in and Carlos greeted her with a gentle kiss on both cheeks. She came over and planted a kiss on my lips and ordered a glass of white wine and soda. '

"We start pre-production this week," a

130

contented smile lighting up her face.

"Ah, yes," said Carlos knowingly, "this is for the new TV production is it not? I have already had someone on the phone to my office regarding permissions for locations in the town."

Carlos' pager bleeped intrusively, he excused himself, promising to be in touch should anything come up, and made his way back to his vehicle.

"I phoned David Hill, we can go up there later tonight, so as we can do interiors and then the gardens, as the light fades. It should look quite dramatic. Shall we have some lunch?"

"Mmm... yes please, I'm famished, then I can tell you about my work for a change."

We left the apartment at 7.30 and drove the short distance to Los Nagueles. David Hill greeted us both warmly and took us through to the patio in the centre of the house. "It's absolutely beautiful," said Sandy as her wide eyes took in the elegant house and beautiful flowered patio and gardens beyond. I left them talking as I set about taking the photographs I needed to complete the selection.

When I finished all but the night shoots, I went back to the lounge where the two of them were drinking. "Dry Martini Philip?" asked the friendly American as he raised the jug into view. "Old habits die hard," he said as the clinking of fresh ice against the glass could prompt no other reply than, "Yes, thank you." I walked towards him to take my glass, "I've all but finished, but as dusk is settling in, I would like to take some shots of the garden. Perhaps you could turn on all the pool and garden lights."

"Sure," he replied, "I'll do it now." and left the room.

"What an interesting guy," said Sandy. "Did you know he worked for the CIA for virtually all of his life?"

"Really?" I said with genuine astonishment. "I never knew the CIA paid this well," I passed my arm around the room, indicating the opulence.

"His wife had money, she came from a wealthy New England family. Father was a governor and all that sort of stuff."

The lights in the trees and shrubs came on and the haze of light, deep in the water of the pool, shimmered to the surface. Garden wrought iron lamps, dotted around the terrace and pool areas, made a wonderful sight. We all went outside and they watched as I set up. Using a wide angled lens and, a fish eye for fun, I got some good shots that I knew Chris would be pleased with.

If only I had the money to buy a house like this, I mused.

"By the way," I said as he topped up my Martini glass, "did you see in the papers and on TV about the murdered people in Las Cancelas?"

"Spanish TV and papers?" he enquired. I nodded. "I'm very sorry to admit it," he continued," but I never watch Spanish TV or read the newspapers. In fact my Spanish is dreadful. The older you get you know, the more difficult it is to pick up a new language." I knew he was right, I had had enough problems myself.

"Well, the police are asking for information about them and another woman that were found dead last week," I purposely avoided going into my unfortunate role in the whole thing, "they believe that two of them appear to be Russian."

"It's like old times," he quipped. "All these Russians everywhere, searching for the sun. It was in the Sur in English the other week about how many of them are visiting the coast. Now the Cold War is over, this could be the Warm War." He smiled and raised his glass, "Cheers," he said and we raised our glasses.

"Let's go straight home," said Sandy as we got into the car and waved to our host, "we'll have some cheese and wine and then I'm going to take you to bed and make mad passionate love to you." We did.

I was awoken by the shrill of the telephone. I stretched out my left arm to grab the receiver. "Hello."

"Philip? Soy Carlos, buenos días"

"What time is it?", I asked thinking it was still the middle of the night.

"7.30 my friend. I'm sorry to wake you, but I think you will want to know what has happened. Could you come to my office straight away?" The voice was calm but commanding. For this man to 'phone on business at this time on a Saturday morning

133

it had to be important.

"I'll be there in twenty minutes," I said as I swung myself out of bed and replaced the receiver.

"What is it babe?" asked Sandy sleepily.

"It's Carlos," I replied as I went into the bathroom to turn on the shower. "He wants me to go down to his office, says he has something. Probably a development on the girl."

After a quick orange juice and an *expresso* coffee, hurriedly made by Sandy, I kissed her and told her I would be back later, or I would phone. It was a lovely morning, the same as it was that fateful Monday last. I drove into Marbella and parked just outside the station on the opposite side of the road. Carlos was in his office "Coffee?," he enquired pointing to his early morning tray.

"No thanks, I've just had one," I said stifling a yawn.

"In that case come with me," he said replacing his cup on the saucer. He opened the door and we went down the corridor. The air in the building was heavy with early morning cigarette smoke from the black tobacco that the hardened Guardia Civil officers always seemed to smoke. Something that they all appeared to do continuously, apart, that is, from Carlos.

He opened the door to an interview room where a woman in her forties and a female police officer were sitting at a table. The woman looked as if she hadn't slept for a week and had been crying. She glanced up as we came into the room. "This is Dolores," said Carlos. "She came to us this morning. She is the nanny of the child that was found murdered. The child went missing yesterday."

A wave of sadness passed over me. Not just for the brutal murder of one so young, but the torment that this poor woman was going through and the blame she must be feeling for letting the child out of her sight.

"What happened?" I asked as we made our way back to Carlos' office. Settling himself down in his leather chair, he explained.

"Dolores works as a nanny/housekeeper for an American couple named Burnet who live in Madroñal. They spend about equal time here and in America. She says that he is some sort of business man and she designs clothes. They arrived back in Spain some time ago as she was doing business with someone down here — she doesn't know who — and they have both gone to Madrid on business now. They left on Monday and are due back next Friday. They phone every evening to check on their child. On Wednesday, Dolores' niece was going to pick up the young girl from playschool and take her to the zoo in Fuengirola and, give her supper, before bringing her back to San Pedro.

Dolores had an appointment at the hospital and was unable to pick her up. When she got back to the house at eight in the evening, there were two messages on the answerphone.

One was from the owners, the Burnets, asking if everything was alright, and saying that they would not be phoning the following day as they had an important business meeting and dinner. The other was from her niece, saying that she went to the school to pick up Catherine, but she had already been picked up and, the playschool naturally assumed, that someone had collected her as normal. Dolores panicked, phoned her niece and, they went to see the lady at the school. The realisation that someone had gone away with her was now obvious and she went down to the local police station in San Pedro. They put it through the system, but could not put two and two together as I had not released the information on the dead bodies by then. They instigated the normal missing person search. The following day they interviewed Dolores more thoroughly and took photographs of the child away for identification purposes, and went to the play school to talk to the staff. Nothing connected until late last night when the information I sent out earlier, was distributed to the Local and National Police as well as other Guardia Civil offices. The duty sergeant in San Pedro saw it and called this office, who in turn woke me at six a.m. Dolores was brought here first thing this morning and has not been able to stop crying. She hasn't spoken to the Burnets yet, as she was too scared to answer the phone last night. She hasn't got their phone number so we will have to wait until they call tonight. Meanwhile, I have to take her down to the morgue for her to identify the child and see if she recognises the other two. Then I will send a policewoman with her until she gets a call from the Burnets when I will have the task of telling these people that their only daughter, a beautiful four year old, has been kidnapped, brutally murdered — and I have no reason why."

"But why were the kidnappers — if they were the kidnappers — murdered as well?" I asked, giving him time to take a breath.

"If I knew that," he paused, "I could probably clear the whole mess up. Do you want to come down to the hospital with us?"

"No I don't think so, thanks" The idea of going to the morgue at the best of times, let alone before breakfast, would do nothing for my stomach, but I would be interested to know if Dolores recognises the man and the woman."

"I'll keep you in touch," he replied, "and now you can return to bed and your beautiful lady."

My mind was full of all sorts of explanations as to what had happened, as I drove back home, none of which made any sense. I stopped on the way to pick up some *churros* for our breakfast. I phoned from the car to tell Sandy I was on my way home and to get the coffee on.

The smell of fresh ground coffee greeted me as I opened the apartment door, Sandy was dressed and had laid the table on the terrace. I sat down, overlooking the marina, in the warmth of the morning sun and dipped my *churros* into a pile of caster sugar, deep in thought. "Well, aren't you going to tell me?" asked Sandy as she brought the coffee and cream to the table.

"Sorry, yes, it's just all a bit too confusing and I don't know how any of it fits together, if indeed it does." I began to tell her virtually word for word what Carlos had told me. When I finished she was as dumbfounded as I was. "What did you say the family's name was?" she said getting up and going into the lounge. I turned my head to follow her, "Barnet or something, I'm not sure."

"How about Burnet?" she asked putting an open copy of Marbella Marbella on the table, revealing a picture of a very attractive blonde taken in a shop in Puerto Banus.

"Is that her? I didn't take that, I don't even remember reading this."

"It's last month's. You remember you were in Barcelona for a week or so and Gary took the pictures. You probably didn't read it because you're not that interested in ladies fashions!"

The phone rang, it was Carlos.

"She has never seen these people before, she has no idea who they are. So I'm not as far forward as I had hoped."

"Listen," I interrupted, " l have an article here in the last edition of the magazine about Mrs. Burnet, I'll fax it to you. I don't know whether it will be of any use."

"Anything can be of help at the moment Philip, anything." He replaced the receiver and I could feel his frustration and anger. He hated violence, especially murder, as anyone who knew him, understood why.

CHAPTER TWELVE

The crowd roared as the tall good looking young man picked up the ball and ran for all he was worth. Opponents came at him from all angles, but he deftly swerved and crisscrossed, pushing his hand out to stave off his attackers and then finally dived over the line to the cheers of the university audience. Uri Karpov got up from the ground and was lifted into the air by his team mates. While he still didn't really understand or appreciate this game, his ability to run had made him a valuable team member. And there was something special about scoring the winning touchdown. The chatter and laughter in the locker rooms was at a crescendo as Uri let the hot water cleanse his pummelled body. The post mortem of the game had taken place and the coach was pleased that his team had kept their place as university champions.

Uri waved goodbye to his colleagues as he made his way to the gates. An older man with greying hair held open his arms as Uri, some six inches taller, embraced his father. "You played well my son," said the proud man, "it was a good game."

'No matter how long we live in America I don't think my father will ever lose his Russian accent,' thought the graduate. 'Ten years on and he still talks like someone from a spy movie.' The two men walked towards the car to make their way to downtown Los Angeles. During the drive Uri's mind went back to when they first arrived at LA International Airport some ten years before. Uri's father was a respected physicist and his mother a gynaecologist. They had lived near Chernobyl where his father was involved in research and his mother had a small practice. They were not wealthy, just respected. Professionals did not earn much more than manual workers because of the Communist ideals. Uri had been a bright pupil and had obviously inherited his parents' academic qualities. He was also already bright enough to realise that he did not want to stay in Russia all of his life. He had his father's gift with Maths and Sciences and his mothers gentle, artistic manner, giving him a love of music and the languages. He had studied French and English in his own time and had excelled with his sciences. Before his thirteenth birthday, tragedy befell the family. His mother, who he loved so very much, was killed in a car accident. His father was devastated and Uri grieved for the woman, whose gentleness and protective hand, had guided him into his thirteenth year. He could not imagine life without her. At the time, he didn't know why, but one day his father made him pack a small suitcase to take only necessary items. He said they were going away.

He knew not where, but, he packed his language books, presents from his dear mother, and obeyed his father. They drove for what seemed forever, stopping only for the toilet, as his father had brought bread,

141

sausage and water.

The young boy found himself in East Berlin. He had never been to Berlin before and was only aware of its place in history caused by the outcome of the second world war. Now he had no idea what he was doing there. His father told him that they were visiting friends and that Uri was to stay in the car and not say a word until he was told otherwise. It was very late and dark, as the rain danced on the roof of the car which his father had parked in a back street. He could hear his father speaking to a man. The man was not Russian although his knowledge of the language was excellent. He sounded as if he could be English or American and Uri had thought he hoped that he would one day be able to speak a foreign language as well as his father's friend. He remembered his father coming to the car and telling him to drink the cup of hot chocolate he had with him. 'What a treat' he had thought as the thick milky liquid warmed him and kept the damp out of his bones. His eyes grew heavy and he drifted into a deep sleep. The next thing the young boy remembered was groggily waking up and getting on a plane from West Berlin, leaving behind the repression of the East, for the new world of opportunity. He had never heard the whole story from his father, but now it didn't matter. Here he was in the land of the free and, at University. His father was working for some government department but never discussed his work and Uri had never met any of his associates.

Life was good for the young University graduate. He had no idea what he was going to do with the remainder of it, but at this time, he knew he wanted to travel and see more of the world. He had his group of friends and they would go out with the girls and go to bars and clubs. They would drink moderately, pop the odd upper and fuck regularly. His father did not always approve of the young man's pastimes but never caused a confrontation over it. The car pulled gently into the driveway and the two men got out.

"Are you having dinner with me tonight Uri?" asked the older man.

"No Pops, I'm going out with the guys for a burger or something, and then a club ."

"In that case," replied the Russian, "I will have dinner with Mrs Metcalfe."

"Good on you Pops," Uri smiled, "do everything I would."

"I haven't got your stamina," he laughed, and went into the front room while Uri bounded up the stairs into his room which was the biggest in the house and doubled as his study and romper room. Pop and travel posters adorned the walls of the tiny room. On his dressing table was a picture of his mother and him as a young baby. It was the only memento he had of her. It had been in the back of his French book. He had put it there the night she died. He remembered putting it under his pillow as he sobbed himself to sleep. The other photos and bits and pieces he had, had been left behind when he and his father had defected to the West.

The phone rang. He picked it up. It was his pal Ricky to arrange where to meet that evening. It was decided that Ricky would pick up Uri from his house and they would meet the gang at Toni Roma's and have some ribs and a few beers.

They ordered. A pile of ribs with that special sauce, pitchers of beer and some Chardonnay for the girls. The atmosphere was conducive to a good Saturday night out and the room was full of laughter and, the unmistakable aroma of barbecued foods. Sally was sitting next to Uri, playing up to him as she always did. She was a nice kid. They had had a few good evenings together, but Uri didn't want to get serious with anyone. He could only see that that would cause problems. He liked being a free agent. The conversation revolved around the same things that most American teenagers and, those in their early twenties, talked about. Sport, music and sex. But Uri's eyes were transfixed on the ugly, overweight, man sitting in the comer with a bevy of women around him. He was at a table of six. Four women, him and a tall man with hair tied back in a pony tail. He was loud, but obviously wealthy, or just pretending to be.

"Who's that guy over there?" Uri asked their waiter.

"That's Metchnikov, the owner of the LA Weavers," replied the waiter as he put down another couple of pitchers of beer.

Uri had read about him. A Russian immigrant who was meant to have a lot of money and had bought the local basket ball team and, with the help of some local personalities, had created a media success with the ailing team. Uri had only seen the odd photo and his images did not lie. The man was gross. His napkin tucked into his shirt neck, obviously held in place by his plethora of chins, and with barbecue sauce trailing down one of them. The girls didn't seem to mind. Uri went back to concentrating on his ribs and the company he was in.

Later that night they found themselves in some seedy nightclub that wasn't really Uri's scene, but he went along with the rest. The predominantly young crowd were dancing to a heavy beat and the room was full of cigarette smoke and kids with glazed eyes. Uri had never seen so many drug-taking individuals in one place. Smoking, pill popping and snorting lines of coke and that was just in the room. God knows what was going on in the toilets. Heroin, and more, he suspected. He saw Ricky talking to the guy with the pony-tail that was in the restaurant.

"I didn't know you knew him," said Uri as he joined Ricky at the bar.

"Who?" said the young man.

"The guy with the pony-tail" replied Uri taking another sip of beer and realising that he had probably had enough by then.

"I don't, I just got some of this from him," said Ricky as he opened a sachet showing a line of cocaine nestling in the crease.

"You must be mad," said Uri angrily.

"Cool it man," Ricky was as drunk as he was going to be stoned, as he blatantly sniffed up the powder through a straw from the bar. The man with the pony-tail was doing a roaring business. 'Our fat friend obviously seemed to be involved with more than a basketball team,' thought Uri as he tried to get the guys ready to leave. They were having a good time and didn't want to go. Uri had no alternative but to stay and have another drink which was to give him a mild hangover the next day.

After qualifying, he didn't know what to do, but he would wait and see what came up. He might travel or make use of his languages, he was in no hurry. During summer vacations, Uri always worked. As a child he would wash cars or do errands. As a teenager he would be a bus boy in a restaurant. Now, as a young man, he felt that he should do something a little more serious and relevant to his education. The local newspaper's employment section was always looking for manual and clerical workers, both full and part-time. But on this occasion, there was one advertisement that caught his eye.

'WANTED, trainee/junior assistant manager to work with established import/export company. Accounts and computer skills an advantage.'

His studies involved all of that and more. He telephoned to make an appointment.

The business was small, but busy, explained

the woman who interviewed him. They imported anything that they could find a market for in California. From European wines, to artefacts. Uri's job would simply be to operate a simple stock control and present accounts for payments which the Manageress, Lisa Timothy, who would then send to their clients. The salary was OK and the hours were good. He wasn't going to make a career out of it and as long as it kept him off the streets during the summer, he, and his father, would be quite pleased and he would make some more serious decisions after he had had some fun.

Uri quite enjoyed the work. It was a small office. Apart from him and the Manageress, there was a receptionist, two lorry drivers and two warehouse/general workmen in their twenties who didn't say much and spent their time in the store areas packing and dispatching. Cases of wine would come in and go out to wholesalers. Colombian coffee, Caribbean sugar cane all was checked off, re-packed and distributed to waiting customers. Toward the end of the first week, Uri had started to reorganise the accounting system and made it more streamlined. He had checked with Lisa Timothy and she had approved the changes and congratulated him on his work.

The following week he decided he would look around the warehouse and ensure that items were being correctly logged and checked in properly. After all, his position was one of Trainee Manager. Armed with the obligatory clipboard, he started to go through the warehouse at lunchtime when everyone had gone. It would be quieter then and he could get on with it more quickly. Mexican ceramic figures, French wines, Spanish wines, Chilean wines, ground coffee, coffee beans all labelled and neatly stacked. However, there were cases that were not labelled or recorded. He would check those with old stock records, perhaps they had been there for some time. The following day he was busy at the computer when the door opened and a man went over to the receptionist. He looked up and caught his breath. He recognised him, it was the guy with the pony-tail. The girl gave him a package and he walked out again. He didn't say a word.

One day he was in the warehouse continuing his inventory checks, the unregistered boxes still intrigued him, when the two warehouse boys came in.

"What are you doing here?" said one of them.

"You should stay in your office," said the other.

"I was just checking items for stock control," replied Uri.

"Well don't," said the taller one as they both walked towards him, "keep to your computer."

Uri went back into the office slightly shaken. He was sure that they had something to hide and whatever it was, was illegal or immoral — or both.

When he came back from his lunch break, Lisa Timothy called him into her office.

"The boys in the warehouse tell me you have been sneaking around ."

"I was just checking the inventory against our stock records."

"That", she stared at him, "is my job, when I decide to do it."

"I'm sorry, I shall wait for you to ask next time." he replied.

"That's OK. Listen, I want you to take this case over to this address," she handed him a piece of paper, "someone will be there to collect it. Take a taxi."

"I have my motorbike," said Uri. But she insisted that he took a taxi. The receptionist ordered him a cab and within minutes he was on his way to the address on the piece of paper.

"How much?" asked Uri, as the cab came to a halt outside an elegant apartment building."It's on the account buddy," replied the driver, "all except the tip."

Uri reached into his pocket and gave him a dollar. The cabbie looked at him with distaste. He got out of the car and walked toward the apartment block. He passed the concierge who called out to him.

"What do you want?" he called.

"I have something for 7b" replied Uri hesitantly. The concierge told him to wait a minute, picked up a phone and, mumbled something into the mouthpiece.

"OK go on up." The lift was there waiting. He pressed seven and it started to climb. The doors opened and he stepped out onto a plush carpeted hallway with two doors at either end. 7a and 7b. He walked toward the latter and rang the door bell. The door opened and Uri stood rigid as he looked into the eyes of the man with the pony—tail. He didn't know what to do.

Before he could make any moves, the man told him to come in and held him gently, but firmly by the arm. He took him into the large lounge and then Uri's heart did a double somersault. Sitting in a huge sofa with a picture window behind with views over the city, was Igor Metchnikov.

"Come in, come in," beckoned the fat man. "Sit down. This is Benny," he said "Benny has been with me a long time, he doesn't say very much, but he listens quite a lot." The pony- tail nodded. Uri returned the nod while sitting on a chair near to Metchnikov. He took the case from beside Uri and opened it. "I expect you are wondering what this is about," said the man as he rummaged through the briefcase. "Do you know who I am?" he continued. Uri's head was still nodding affirmatively to the last question. "Well, you work for me."

"No, I work ..." his voice trailed away, as the obvious hit him.

"Ms Timothy tells me that you have taken a great interest in your work. Sometimes too great. But we will forget that. She says that you are very bright and efficient. You have a knowledge of languages, computer skills and what's more you are a fellow countryman. Where are you from originally?"

The man's voice was thick and guttural. His

accent was stronger than his father's, thought Uri as he nervously replied,

"My parents were from Chernobyl, but my father and I have been here for ten years,"

"I want to give you a bonus," said Metchnikov and handed Uri a small packet of 20 dollar bills from the case. There had to be 500 dollars thought Uri as he held it without saying anything. "It is a sort of loyalty bonus if you understand me. I'm going to keep an eye on you, because I think that you are going to go far."

"Thank you, but I don't think ..." Benny moved toward Uri.

"You were saying," said Metchnikov. There was a silence. "I am opening a new office soon on similar lines as the one you are in at the moment but slightly more specialised and I need someone who speaks Russian and English who is hard-working and loyal. The salary will be high and you will get the usual benefits. You do not have to answer me yet, but I will be seeing you again very shortly. Thank you for coming. Benny will show you out." The interview was obviously over and Uri stood up as Benny pointed the way to the door. He was going to turn around and say something, but he thought better of it.

The new offices were unobtrusive but comfortably furnished. His job was to liaise with a Dimitri Yakov in Russia regarding adoptions of poor orphan children over there looking for kind parents from the West. Most of the business would be done over the

phone, through personal contacts, but should anyone wish to meet Uri personally there would be no problem. Two girls were assigned to Uri to help and there was already a list of childless parents who could not adopt in the USA looking to fulfil their lives. The offices also acted as an administrative office for Metchnikov's other businesses. He had a car and a small expense account and had become one of Metchnikov's more legitimate employees. He was invited to basket ball games, parties and receptions. He had been given an apartment, nothing luxurious, but better than living at home with his father, who was pleased with his sons step up in life although he was not so sure of his employer. Obviously all the Russian immigrants were aware of Metchnikov and some of his activities but Uri had said that he had seen nothing untoward and that his boss was a genuine businessman who seemed to be doing very well. His father always felt that a lot of Metchnikov's business was drug related. The Mafia men, who had come from Russia with the sort of money that his fellow countryman seemed to have, was not made by being a scientist or a philanthropist. He was never sure whether his son was naive or, was ignoring what he saw, in return for a good salary and all the perks — or both!

"You speak Spanish don't you?" enquired Metchnikov as he put too many fries into his mouth. Uri cut a piece of rare steak and put it on his fork,

"Not fluently, but I studied it at school and college and of course have used it locally in LA."

"I am thinking of opening a business in Spain," said the Russian in between mouthfuls. "Time-share has been a big business in America for a long time, but our fellow Russians have now the freedom they have always wanted and they are travelling further and further abroad. They are buying property and time-share all over. And the new market is Spain. Through contacts I have made over there I have invested in a new development in Marbella which is on the South coast where the weather is good, not unlike California. I am setting up offices in Russia to send people over and I want you to go to Spain and set up what is known as a sales line, dealing specifically with Russians. Because I have invested so much money in the project I have told the Managing Director, Baz Brown, that you will be the Russian sales line manager.

You will receive a good basic salary and a very high commission. You will also be a director of the company. This is basically to avoid the problems of work permits. You will work with Brown so as he can show you the way and after that you will be responsible for looking after my investments there. Do you understand?"

"But what about the office, I thought it was doing well."

"It was. But we are moving out of that business. I need your talents elsewhere."

"But I don't know that I want to go to …"
Metchnikov cut him off, "You will leave at the beginning of the month. Everything is arranged. Now drink your wine."

When Uri arrived in Spain he could see why everyone loved it. The white buildings bright sunshine, but more importantly the air was so clean and fresh. Nothing like Los Angeles. He met Baz Brown whom he liked immediately. His apartment was elegant and comfortable, his car was small but adequate. It didn't take him long to pick up the skills needed to sell time-share and Baz even let him loose on a couple of English clients for practice. He sold to them. His young good looks and charm, with that unusual soft American accent with a very faint trace of his Russian upbringing, made him a natural salesman. Soon he had put his line together and Metchnikov had sent over some young student types from Russia who were soon in the swing of it. Permits were arranged and soon Igor Metchnikov' five investments were paying off. Largely due to Uri.

It came as a bit of a shock when the big man walked into the office at Costalite resorts one cold January morning. Over lunch with Uri he explained that he had moved to Spain especially for the winter months and was living on his boat in Puerto Banus. He had invested in other business ventures down here and if everything went well, he would probably stay longer. He was pleased with Uri and what he had achieved and invited him aboard his yacht for a cocktail party. Just like old times.

The advertisement that he had placed in the Coast's new Russian newspaper had not brought that much response, but the receptionist had set up a couple of interviews for him for that morning. She was beautiful, intelligent and warm. He had never seen a Russian girl so attractive, not that he could remember many. She was over on holiday and looking for work. Her English was quite good and she was hungry. She turned out to be Ukrainian as well and like most Ukrainians they conversed in Russian. He offered her the job. It didn't cost anything unless they sold, so even if she wasn't very good, she would be nice to have around. She did well on her first day and her smile said it all when she made her first sale.

Although all the group had had drinks together, Uri had made it a rule not to go out with any of the girls on a serious level. They had all had some fun, but nothing complicated. However, Katrina was different, but he felt that she had someone, as she had mentioned a boyfriend in Russia. He was talking to Baz about sport, business in general and, the fact that he had a meeting with Metchnikov during the day and had work to do for him, when Katrina came over to talk to him. He didn't have time to speak to her then as much as he wanted to, so took the opportunity to invite her for dinner. She accepted. His thoughts were with her as he got into the car. 'I know I shouldn't mix business and personal life,' he thought, 'but perhaps on this one occasion, I just might.'

It was always difficult to find a parking space in the centre of town at the best of times, but early evening when the bars and restaurants started to get busy, it became even more of a problem. There was a small space which he managed to squeeze into. He locked the car and walked to the entrance of Parque Marbella where Katrina shared an apartment with mad Diana. He was so surprised that the two of them had hit it off. Probably because they were opposites. He rang the intercom button. Katrina answered, "I'll come down," she called. Uri paced back and forwards for a few minutes until he heard the door open. He turned around to see Katrina, who looked exquisite. Her fair flowing hair, bright summer dress and beautiful features made his heart jump.

"You look absolutely wonderful," he said as he reached for her hand.

"Thank you," she replied coyly.

They drove along the Golden Mile until Uri made a sharp right turn into the country.

"Where are we going?" she asked.

"I am taking you to an extraordinary place owned by an extrovert English actor cum singer who has an old house that serves good food and plays good music, and it's quite romantic," he smiled.

Over dinner he could not take his eyes off her. She was witty and charming. Her eyes glistened as they talked and, he knew he had not felt like this before. They drank wine, talked about Russia and the Ukraine, he talked about America and they talked about Spain. It was nearly one 'o clock in the morning and they were the last table but one left. He called for the bill. On the drive home, she turned to him and said,

"I've had a lovely evening, probably the nicest evening I have had for a very long time. Thank you."

"So have I Katrina, very much."

He pulled up right outside the apartments. She looked at him, he turned towards her, "Would you like to come upstairs for a coffee?" she asked.

The apartment was a typical young woman's den. Warmly furnished, some fresh flowers, "I buy them," she said laughing, "Diane wouldn't think of such feminine things." She sat next to him and handed him a brandy and a coffee. Julio Iglesias played Crazy on the music centre. He leaned over and gently kissed her. Her mouth was soft and warm, she opened her lips and he kissed her deeply. Her arm went behind his head as she held him firmly close to her. His hand worked its way hesitantly up to her breast. Her young body responded to his touch. He wasn't sure that he should be doing this, perhaps it would spoil some long term relationship, because he wanted to see her again, and again. He pulled away gently, "Don't stop," she commanded him and led him into her room. He pulled her gently toward him kissing her passionately on the lips. He slipped the summer dress over her head, she un buttoned his shirt and the belt on his trousers. They slipped gently on to the bed, he deftly removed her bra and started kissing her breasts and gently sucking her nipples. She responded with her hands caressing his groin and running her hands up and down his erection. He slid his hand between her briefs and lowered them gently to her ankles and removed them with his feet. The passion was building in both of them as they discovered each other's bodies and their mouths explored new territories. She accepted him with ardour and they moved so completely together until she let out a cry of pleasure that made him orgasm in a way he could not remember ever doing before. They kissed and touched and held each other until they drifted into sleep.

CHAPTER THIRTEEN

As she awoke she moved her arm to the other side of the bed and touched his warm, still sleeping body. She hadn't meant what happened last night to happen. What would he think of her? What would happen at work? It was just that he seemed such a nice guy and he was charming, well mannered, educated and very good looking. The evening had just sort of carried her away. Nice food, good wine it had been such a lovely evening. Maybe she shouldn't have invited him in for coffee. Oh, to hell! She had done it now and there was no use crying over spilt milk. She leaned over and kissed him. His hair was ruffled and his usually clean shaved face had dark stubble. He smelt of sweet sex. The touch of her lips on his, made him stir. They kissed warmly and lovingly rather than passionately although she knew she could make love with him again.

"Good morning," she said, "would you like some tea?"

"Russian?" he enquired.

"No, I'm afraid not. I think it's English, it has strings attached."

He laughed, "Yes, OK." She went into the kitchen and poured a fruit juice from the packet in the fridge and put the kettle on. He came out carefully behind her and put his arm around her,

"Where's Diana?" he asked.

"It's her day off, so she went out with a boyfriend last night and isn't coming back until tomorrow night."

"Good, I wouldn't like her to see me here."

"Why not? Are you ashamed?" He took hold of her and pulled her toward him and kissed her gently.

"Of course not, you fool, I just don't want to compromise any of us. Anyway I want to keep this relationship private and very, very personal." She kissed him again. Drinking his tea quickly, he said he had to go and that he would see her later at work. It was already nine o'clock and he should have been there by now and she should be there by ten.

As she got into the shower, she thought about the evening and the fact that she had not mentioned anything about the baby. She felt that she didn't want to tell him anything about her past. If this relationship is going to happen, she didn't want him to be put off by the fact that she had had a child. It was different with Gregorio. They were together for some time when she had to tell him. She would tell Uri one day, if she ever got the baby back. And, if she couldn't then what he didn't know wouldn't hurt him. Poor Gregorio, what was she going to do. She was going to have to tell him what was happening. She would do it this evening. She still needed some advice about her child and she did not know what to do next.

The day passed uneventfully, she did one sale out of two tours which pleased her. Uri was as aloof as he possibly could be, but was failing miserably when it came to eye contact. They exchanged smiles.

He didn't mention anything about seeing each other that evening and she hoped that that was because he had previous arrangements. She felt it was not her position to ask, so she left it.

That night at home, she sat on her balcony and began to compose a letter to Gregorio.

'My Dear Gregorio, It seems such a long time since we last saw each other. Since I last wrote to you I have found out where my baby is. She lives in Madroñal which is near a town called San Pedro, not far from Marbella, which is where I am working. She is so happy. The family are very wealthy and can provide her with so much I am almost frightened to go further. But my heart still aches when I think of her. Andrew Burnet is a businessman and she, she is called Denyse, is a fashion designer. They spend some time here and some time in America. I have missed you and have needed your advice. I miss my sister too and I know she would be able to help. Dear Gregorio, there are so many miles between us and I have had much time to think. I love it here. The weather is good and the way of life is so wonderfully different from anything we know. I am not sure that I want to return to the Ukraine and the Soviet life. Please try and understand and give me time to sort myself out. I will keep in touch and let you know how things are. With fondest love, Katrina'

She read it through. She had said everything and nothing. He may read between the lines but there is nothing that he would do. She would leave it a while longer before telling him about Uri. And she would only do that if she wasn't going back.

She also wrote a letter to the pawnbroker who had her Grandmother's ring asking for its return. She would go and get a money order and send it off as soon as possible.

That night she went to bed confused but contented.

The next day at work Uri came up to her. "I missed you," he said, "can we go out this evening for a drink and then maybe a pasta or something?"

"That would be nice" she replied, "to save you coming up I will meet you at the Coffee Doc below the apartments at about eight thirty. Is that OK?"

"Fine," he smiled, "I look forward to it."

As the weeks went on Uri and Katrina saw each other regularly. They had managed to keep it very quiet at work and not even Diana was sure what was going on.

She knew that they had seen each other on a few occasions, but she did not know that the relationship was as far advanced as it was. She knew that Katrina had not been home on several occasions, but she thought it could be someone else. Not that she interfered, or cared, she was a good flat mate to have and, they never discussed each other's personal life.

Katrina had made a couple more trips to spy on the family and had done nothing more about it. As she was dressing to meet Uri for dinner, she knew that she had to tell him about the baby and her desire to get it back, or at least meet with the parents. The door bell rang. "I'll be down in a minute," she called over the intercom, and hurriedly checked her hair and her make-up for the last time.

He kissed her as she came out of the entrance and they got into the car to drive to El Estudio in San Pedro. A small family run Italian restaurant where the food was good and the prices reasonable. They were shown to a small table in the comer. Uri ordered some wine and they began to talk. It always amazed Katrina how they always found something to talk about. Very seldom did they talk about work, but they discussed the culture of the three countries they had been in. She, learning about America and, he learning more about the new Russia, which was different from the one he had left behind.

Their main course arrived and the young girl topped up their wine glasses.

"Uri, I have something very important to tell you." A look of panic crossed his face.

"Nothing terrible I hope."

"It depends how you take it," she looked at him.

"You're not pregnant are you?"

She laughed a poignant laugh. "No my love, I'm not. But tell me would you mind if I was?" For a moment he was lost for words.

"I don't really know. I have never thought about it. I suppose it would depend on the circumstances. If you were to make me feel that we had to commit ourselves only because of it, I might reject it. But if it was what we both wanted at the same time, who knows?"

"Well, I'm not. But your comments may be relative. When I was a young girl ..."

She began to tell him the whole story from beginning to end. She told him about the baby selling ring that was discovered in the Ukraine and how the witnesses and the doctor were all dead and how they had never found the ring leader. He sat rigidly listening to her every word. He did not interrupt her, but listened patiently.

"And now, all I want to do is see my baby and find out more about how they came to get her. But I don't know what to do next. I suppose I was hoping that you may have some ideas."

Uri picked up his wine and swilled it around his mouth. She looked at him intently. He seemed far away and she wondered whether she had distanced him, by relating it all to him.

"That's some story," he finally said. "I really can't think what you can do about it. If the Burnets have legal adoption papers, then they have the right."

"But my baby was stolen," she said emphatically, "and the documents can't be worth the paper they are written on. We must be able to do something."

"Leave it with me for a few days, I'll see what I can find out." he placed his hand on hers.

"Uri, the fact that I was pregnant and had a child doesn't upset you does it?" she was unsure what his answer would be.

"Of course not," he replied, "when we are very young we do things out of a genuine desire to find out and experiment, and often we are not ready for it. It is not always our fault if we are too naive or unprepared for reality. It happens to the best of us. If it does not scar you mentally for life, then no real harm has been done. Although you are upset and want to sort out this situation, you are still a normal, mentally healthy and intelligent young woman. Whatever the outcome you will survive."

'I think I'm falling in love with this man' thought Katrina and looked at him with love in her eyes. They left the restaurant and went back to his apartment where they made love.

It was her day off so she didn't get up until nearly midday, Uri had left for work.

When she got back to her apartment, Diana was already up and had been busy packing. Her cases were at the door. "I'm glad I caught you," she said, "I'm going back home for a couple of weeks, my mum's not too well. Anyway I'm owed some time off, so I asked Baz and he told me to go straight away. So, I'm going back to the cold and damp."

"I'm sorry about your mother," said Katrina, "I hope it is not too serious."

"No, I think she just gets depressed when we are all away from home. Anyway, I'll be back soon and just think, you will have complete freedom of the apartment," she smiled knowingly. They put their arms around each other, "Be good," said Diana as she walked toward the lifts. Katrina closed the door. She would miss Diana, but it would be nice to have Uri over without concern. She went over to the kitchen unit where Diana had left some mail for her. She recognised the postmark and the handwriting on the envelope immediately. It was from Gregorio. She opened it and read it quickly first and, then slowly, to take it all in.

'Darling Katrina,

I have missed you so much and not a day goes by when I do not think about you. I am glad you have found your child and I can understand that you do not know what to do. You must feel very lonely at times without your family or friends. I can see that you are enjoying the way of life, but it will not replace your roots. But you must do what you want to do, especially if we cannot get the child back.

I have spoken to your sister and we have both agreed what must be done. I am coming to Spain on Saturday the 20th arriving from Madrid at 6.30 pm. I look forward to seeing you. Please do not try to contact me to change my mind. All the arrangements are made and I want to be with you.

All my love, Gregorio.'

'That's today damn it' she thought. 'The fool, what does he hope to achieve. What am I going to do about Uri, oh Jesus what a

166

mess!'

She phoned Uri and asked him if he was free to meet her today as she wanted to talk. He suggested lunch time at Kings, just a few minutes from the resort, at about two.

She showered and dressed, her mind in a turmoil. She didn't know how she would feel when she saw Gregorio again. She didn't want to hurt him and yet she knew she felt something powerful for Uri. Poor Gregorio, he had travelled all these miles and she was sure that it was just to check on her. What was she going to tell Uri?

The bar was packed when she arrived so she stood at the bar and ordered a white wine and took a seat on the terrace. Uri arrived seconds later. They kissed, "have you been waiting long?" he asked.

"No, I've only just arrived." He ordered a glass of beer and some Serrano Ham.

"Well, what is so important that I am summoned to a meeting?" he grinned.

"I'm sorry," she replied, "I didn't mean to drag you away, but I had to talk to you." She took the letter from her bag and gave it to him. He read it slowly, the unfamiliar lettering, stretching his forgotten knowledge of his almost forgotten tongue. He looked at her. "What does that mean to us, will you be going back with him?"

"No, of course not my love. You mean too much to me for that, but I have to see him and sort things out. Please give me a few days. Can you let me have the time off work?"

"Of course, if that's what you want."

"And could you possibly let me have a rental car for a few days?"

"You can borrow mine and I will take one from the pool."

"Thank you darling, very much." she said genuinely.

"Are you sure you know what you are doing?" he asked.

"No, but I have to sort things out now, once and for all. The baby, Gregorio, my life and us. If you want me to be around, then I want to stay."

He held her hand across the table. "I don't want to lose you," he said, "but your happiness is the most important. I will stand by you in everything you do and, if it helps you, I love you very much and want to be with you."

She squeezed his hand.

"Thank you. That means so much to me. I will let you know what's happening. By the way, I know you haven't had much time, but have you spoken to anyone yet?"

"I have a meeting with someone tonight who may be able to help. If he can, I will contact you."

They finished their tapas and Uri apologised for having to dash back. She understood. He took his work very seriously and was a loyal employee. He gave her his car keys and they held each other tightly and, kissed firmly.

"I love you," she said. He smiled and crossed the road towards the resort. It was three o'clock, she walked over to Uri's car and drove back to the apartment to tidy up a bit. She knew that Gregorio would want to stay with her and she didn't quite know how to handle it.

The flight was on time and she didn't have to wait long before the passengers from Madrid started to come through to the arrival lounge. She saw him first and waved, then her heart stopped as she saw next to him, her sister. She couldn't believe it. She rushed towards them both and her sister ran towards Katrina. They embraced, both in tears.

"Why didn't you tell me you were coming," she sobbed.

"It was Gregorio's idea, he said that you had missed me. I spoke to Boris and he told me to come." she hugged her sister harder. Gregorio stood by until the two young women released each other and he held out his arms to hug and kiss her. A natural reaction took Katrina into his arms and allowed him to kiss her, 'though short and somewhat dispassionate on her part.

They walked to the car chattering

"How are Mama and Papa?

"They send their love"

"How is Boris and little Angelique?"

"They are both fine and send their love and hope to see you soon."

The chattering went on all the way back to Marbella. Gregorio hardly getting a word in and Katrina finding it hard at times speaking Russian again. It seemed so long ago.

They got to the apartment and they were

both very impressed with where Katrina was living. She made some tea and they sat down.

"I must find somewhere to stay," said Natasha.

"Don't be silly" replied Katrina, "you will stay here. Gregorio can sleep on the sofa and you can sleep with me." Gregorio looked disappointed,

"I couldn't do that," objected Natasha, "I will sleep on the sofa."

"Let's not argue about that now," replied Katrina, "we will sort it out later. Meanwhile let's go out to eat." It was a nice evening so they walked along to Dalli's Pasta Factory and as it was early, managed to get a table on the patio. The service was friendly and efficient and they soon had their meals in front of them. By the second bottle of wine, the small talk was coming to an end and Gregorio started to tell Katrina his plan.

"We are going to kidnap Catherine and take her back to Russia." Katrina nearly choked on her spaghetti.

"You're what?" she cried in amazement. "What the hell do you think you are playing at? This isn't some second rate movie where you just go in guns blazing and steal someone from off the street. Did you know about this?" she blurted to her sister.

"Calm down a minute," said Natasha trying to placate her.

"Calm down? You must be mad - the pair of you."

"Listen a moment," said Gregorio.

"I don't want to listen to anything," said Katrina irately.

"Katrina," her sister spoke quietly, "you cannot tell me that you had not thought about it. It's just that you couldn't do anything about it. We have talked this over and we have decided that it is perfectly possible."

Katrina put her hands over her forehead, "I can't believe I'm hearing this. What are you going to do with the child when you've got her. Just go to the airport and buy a ticket and fly her out of the country?"

"My daughter is on my passport Katrina." Natasha looked across the table at her. "She can travel with me."

Katrina thought for a moment. "It's madness, it will never work."

"What alternatives do you have?" enquired Gregorio. "If you don't do this, you will never get her back, because the law will never be on your side. The child is in Spain, probably legally, and the parents are US citizens. I can't see that the authorities in Russia, the Ukraine or America will do much about it."

Katrina sat pensively and took another mouthful of wine. The smooth velvety liquid warming her throat and, stomach, which was desperately disturbed.

"How do you think you are going to do it?" she asked almost mockingly.

"You are going to show us where they live, you have already said you know where that is," said Gregorio authoritatively, "and we will watch the house for regular activities. To see when the child is alone. Regular shopping trips, trips to the park, maybe the child goes to nursery school. Whatever, we will watch carefully so as we can tell which is the best time to take her. As soon as we have her we will take her straight back to Madrid and then home. There is no point in hanging around."

"What if she doesn't want to go with you?" Katrina asked logically.

"We have some sleeping tablets," replied Natasha.

"I would want to see her." said Katrina.

"That would not be possible," continued Natasha "we must leave straight away before the child is reported missing and get out of the country as soon as possible. You do realise, don't you Katrina, that if you want your child back, this is the only way? You would never be able to stay here with her."

Katrina did not know what to say. They paid the bill and made their way back to the apartment in relative silence. Katrina poured Gregorio and her a brandy, she needed something, Natasha settled for tea. She knew Gregorio would find this difficult, the whole thing had come as a bit of a shock, but would he mind sleeping on the sofa as she wanted to be with her sister and talk things out in only the way that two women can. He reluctantly agreed and they all retired.

Katrina and Natasha laid awake talking about the plan when Katrina told her about Uri.

"But what about Gregorio and the child?

Look what he is doing for you. He loves you very much."

"I know, I know," she started to cry, " I don't know what to do."

"Well, you had better make up your mind before we all risk our freedom for your sake," Natasha was angry.

"I will have to think things over seriously. You have brought my whole life to a crossroads and I think I thank you for all of this. I have to make some important decisions." She turned and hugged her sister and they both slept a disturbed sleep.

In the morning they talked over breakfast. Katrina told them what she had decided. "I am going to show you where they live this morning. There is someone who is trying to do something for me," her sister looked at her knowingly, "and I will have to see them today or tomorrow. I also have to go to work," she lied, "and we will talk again when you have finalised the plan Gregorio." It was the nearest thing she could say or do that was some sort of decision. They drove to San Pedro and then up the Ronda road. Both Gregorio and Natasha marvelled at the beautiful views and countryside, the sun glistening on the deep blue sea and that wonderful feeling of space. "It is wonderful," said Natasha, "I can see why you like it here."

"I know," replied Katrina, as she swung the little car into the narrow road that led to the Burnet's house. The three of them got out of the car and walked nonchalantly down the lane. Gregorio took it all in, saw a vantage point where he could hide without being seen and watch the movements of the household. They got back into the car and returned to the apartment, where Katrina and Natasha prepared some lunch. The conversation was general and Katrina was desperately wanting to talk to Gregorio and tell him about Uri. But she had to decide whether to give up Uri for her child. She had to speak to Uri, because she was now not so sure what she wanted.

The telephone rang, it was Uri. "Are you OK?" was the first thing he said.

"Yes, I'm fine, but I do have to speak to you," she said, controlling the emotion in her voice.

"I have spoken to the man," he continued, "and he says he might be able to help.

He wants to meet with you either tonight or tomorrow ,I will confirm it with you as soon as I know. I miss you."

"Me too," she said trying to avoid Gregorio's eyes, "I have to see you."

"I know, I'll speak to you later. I love you." The phone went dead but she carried on holding the receiver. She was even more confused after hearing his voice. "The man I said may be able to help, wants to see me," she said innocently.

"What does he think he can do?" enquired Gregorio.

"I don't know until I meet him, do I?" she walked out of the room into her bedroom. Gregorio left her for a short while and then knocked on her door. She was crying. He went over to the side of the bed and sat next to her and smoothed her brow.

"Is there something you want to tell me Katrina?" She turned over to look at him. He had been so strong and dependable for the last couple of years. He was understanding and wanted only her happiness. This selfless act was yet another way of him showing his love. She was so confused and unhappy, she held open her arms and they kissed. At first emotionally and then passionately. She pushed him away and sat on the edge of the bed. He sat up and said nothing, waiting for her to talk to him.

"I have met someone else," she started, "I am not sure how serious it is. Well, I thought I was sure, until I saw you again."

"I'm not stupid, you know," interjected Gregorio, "I did work that out!"

"I know you're not my love, it's just that I have been so confused and now I am even more so. I do want my baby. I know the feelings I have for you, and I have to sort out my other emotions. I am going to see this man and then I want some time on my own, please bear with me, if you can."

"You must do what is right for you Katrina, and nobody else." He kissed her and left the room.

She was disturbed by the door buzzer. She glanced at the clock, it was eight o'clock. She leapt to her feet and dashed into the lounge.

"Hello,"

"Señor Uri asked me to come and pick you up to take you to see a friend," said the voice at the other end.

"I'll be down in five minutes," she said and replaced the receiver.

"It's the man who may be able to help," she turned to her sister and Gregorio. Brushing her hair in the mirror, she added, "I told you what was happening Gregorio, please bear with me. If I'm not back tonight, here are the car and house keys." She kissed them both. "Wish me luck," she called as she opened the front door and left her sister and her old boyfriend to cope for themselves.

She didn't recognise the man who met her at the door, it certainly wasn't any of the staff that worked at the resort.

"Where is Uri?" she asked.

"He is with the man you are going to meet. They are talking. He asked me to pick you up. They drove in silence in the direction of San Pedro, but the driver turned off into Puerto Banus. He placed a card in the automatic barrier and drove through towards the tower and parked in front of a huge boat. The driver got out and opened the door for her. He walked her to the boarding ramp and she shakily made her way up, to be greeted at the top by a big man with a pony-tail. He showed her through into the salon. A big fat man sat in a chair talking in Russian on a mobile phone. He beckoned her in and indicated for her to sit. She did. When he put the phone down, he turned to her and said, "Welcome to my little toy, Katrina," he said indicating the interior of the elegant yacht, "thank you for coming."

"Where is Uri?" she asked immediately.

"He will be back shortly my dear, do not worry. Would you like some tea, or something stronger?" She nodded in the negative, "Now, our friend Uri has asked me if I can help you with your problem about your baby. Now, please tell me all the story, Uri gave me only some sketchy details."

Katrina told the fat man the story from start to finish. If Uri said he was a friend and would help, she trusted his judgment, so she told the man everything.

When she had finished there was a silence. He broke it first. "Well, my dear. My name is Igor Metchnikov. Uri works for me. He has been with me for some time. He worked for me in my businesses in America. He ran my import export side for a while until I put him in charge of setting up a new operation. He was in charge of an agency in America that deals with the adoption of children from Russia to childless couples in America."

Katrina's blood ran cold. She felt sick to the stomach. She started to shake uncontrollably. She leapt to her feet and threw herself on Metchnikov. "You bastard," she screamed, "you dirty, filthy, rotten bastard. You're lying, Uri wouldn't do that." She pummelled him with her fists, but he felt no pain. Pony-tail came over and lifted her off the man. She was kicking and screaming. He pushed her down in a chair, stuffed a hanky in her mouth and tied her arms behind her and her feet to the legs. She was hysterical, wriggling and trying to scream through her gag. Her face was getting more flushed by the second. Pony-tail slapped her. It stung and she stopped immediately.

"After that brief interlude, allow me to continue," said Metchnikov as another man brought in some tea for the Russian. "Do not be upset with your Uri, my dear, he worked for me long after your baby was adopted. I have phoned my associate in Lvov, Dimitri Yakov, and he tells me you were indeed our very first client, all that time ago. Alas, our business had to close due to the interference of outsiders and the inefficiency of some of those involved. Still we did very well over the years and must not complain. I am afraid there is nothing you can do about your child, even if I was going to let you. What's done is done. Benny, I do not want any more fun today. Perhaps you would like to entertain young Katrina, you are younger and more energetic than I am." Benny smiled and came over to Katrina who was shaking and trying to scream again. Benny smacked her once more, but this time with a clenched fist. It knocked her senseless. He undid the ropes from the chair keeping her hands and legs tied as he threw her over his shoulder and carried her down stairs to his cabin. He laid her on the bed and, after pulling off her shirt, jeans and skimpy briefs, tied her arms and legs to its four corners. She had no bra on and her lovely young breasts were firm to the touch. Benny took his clothes off and kneeled on the bed between her legs. His penis hard with expectation. She started to come round and saw the pony-tail in front of her and once again tried to scream. He started to kiss her breasts and her neck, and worked his way down to the insides of her legs. She was going to be sick she was struggling and she was choking on her gag. The more she tried to scream the worse it became. She started to cry. The tears welling up in her eyes and overflowing. She could feel his tongue inside her. She wanted so much to see Gregorio now. She wished she was anywhere but here. Where was Uri? Did Uri set her up like this? He must have known that Metchnikov was an animal. She cried harder, Uri had betrayed her. He was one of them, the fucking bastard she would never forgive him. If she got out of this she would kill all of them, Gregorio, dear Gregorio, he would kill them with her. He would never let her down. The pony-tail knelt back up and leaned over her. His member was hard and throbbing as he pushed into her body. His saliva the only reason that it did not tear her. She was crying harder now, she could hardly breathe, the tears filled her eyes and she could not see. She didn't want to, she just wanted to die. He thrust and thrust, kissing her out-stretched arms and lifting his body away from hers and then pushing down with force. After what seemed an eternity, with sweat dripping from his body on to hers, he exploded inside her. He shuddered with pleasure and continued to push every drop of his sperm into her helpless body and then collapsed on top of her. She could do nothing. She lay there feeling disgusted with herself, the animal on top of her and, with Uri, the man she had trusted with her very soul. The pony-tail got up and dressed and left the room. She laid there absolutely stunned. If they thought that she was going to do nothing about this when she got back, they were mistaken, she would contact the police, go to the authorities, tell the consul her mind stopped thinking of what she was going to do, as the realisation that they were not going to let her go, suddenly hit her. She panicked even more and tried once again to scream and shout. She had exhausted herself, she must have drifted into sleep, as the next thing she knew was that pony-tail was on her again. He pushed himself inside her again, this time with no lubrication and she hurt. The more she pushed upwards at him the more it appeared she was contributing to his pleasure. He climaxed again, leaving Katrina sore and mentally and emotionally broken. Maybe death would be better.

Pony-tail stood up and put on his shirt and jeans. He walked over to the broken woman and picked up the pillow. He placed it over her face and pushed down. Katrina saw the pillow coming and the light disappear as her breathing was restricted. She pushed and screamed again and again to no avail. Gregorio went through her mind, her parents her sister, her baby, 'oh my God, my baby'. Her head was bursting now, she couldn't breathe, there were clouds in her head, she was getting cold, she wasn't in control any more. Her last thoughts had passed.

CHAPTER FOURTEEN

Uri Karpov climbed the boarding ramp to the after end of the boat to be greeted, as usual, by Benny. Uri acknowledged the bodyguard but, as normal, got no reaction from him. Metchnikov was sitting in his chair reading some papers, he looked up. "Uri, come in my friend, how are you?"

"Fine, thanks Igor."

"Business is good I understand."

"Yes, very good."

"Now you wanted to see me about a friend of yours."

"Yes. I was out for dinner with a girl I have been seeing for some time, she actually works for us. It's something I have never done before, but I have managed to keep it away from all of the staff. I don't think even Baz knows and he and I work very closely." A small look of disapproval crossed Metchnikov's face. "Anyway, during dinner she told me a story about herself. My blood ran cold, I felt nauseous, she was telling me about how she was a young girl in the Ukraine and fell pregnant to a boy whom she never saw again. She left home and went to live with her sister and registered at the local hospital in Lvov. When she gave birth, she was told that the child had died. Some years later she saw a television report that stated children were being stolen and sold to the States. She immediately went to Lvov to see the Doctor who was no longer there. She went to hospital records to find papers of birth or death on her baby but there were none. Police arrested a woman called Petrova who was going to turn state's evidence and told them about some of the mothers involved including Katrina. She thought that the adopting parents were called Burnet and lived in California. The long and the short of it is that she traced the Burnets to Spain and is trying to get the child back."

There was a silence while Metchnikov, without expression on his face, took it all in. "I thought you told me when I was working with you that the whole thing was a legitimate exercise. I didn't know you were stealing kids. What happens if this all comes out. We'll all be arrested. What made you do it." Uri started to get irate and panicky.

"Be quiet you fool," Metchnikov shouted, "Shut up and sit down." Uri did as he was told. "Be logical about this a moment and ask yourself, if this young woman of yours left home to avoid her parents knowing that she was going to have a baby, would she not have arranged to have it adopted at birth? She would hardly have arranged to take the baby home would she? If, as she says, she was one of our patients, she would have signed adoption papers, instructing the hospital to remove the baby at birth so as not to upset the mother. It is a known fact that when women see their baby, there is an immediate bond and if they have arranged for adoption, they usually renege on the agreement. It would seem that your Katrina, or whatever her name is, has obviously felt pangs about giving away her child that she is compensating by trying to find her and getting her back. Something she could not possibly do."

"But what about this Doctor Petrova that was arrested, was she working for you?" he asked forcefully.

"She was one of the doctors with whom the company dealt," replied Metchnikov calmly.

"In that case," continued Uri confidently, "why did you close the operation down if it was legal?"

"Because people like Petrova were going into business for themselves," he lied, "and were doing things incorrectly. It seemed sensible at the time to cease trading in something that was getting a bad name and concentrate on the project in hand. Time-share. Which, let me remind you, young man, is why you are here and, have the lifestyle, income and privileges, that you do. Now, if this girlfriend of yours would like some help and advice, I would be more than happy to talk to her. I will find out from my associate, Yakov, who you will remember, if we have any information on this girl — what did you say her name was?"

"Katrina Ornst," replied Uri feeling somewhat deflated.

"Ornst," said Metchnikov as he wrote it down on a piece of paper.

"O-R-N-S-T?" he looked up. Uri nodded. "And her address?"

"Parque Marbella, 480."

"And what did you say the name of the

adopting family was?"

"Burnet."

"And their address?"

"I don't know, she didn't say."

He wrote it down, "She may not even have been one of ours. And even if she was, it was all, how you say, above board, and if your conscience is playing on you, this would appear to have happened four or five years ago and you opened the main agency office about three years ago. So, you do not have any connection with this young lady's case."

"I suppose not, but I still feel responsible." said Uri.

"Well don't," continued Metchnikov. "Just tell her that I will see her tonight or tomorrow night and we will see what we can do for her. Alright?"

"Yes, thank you Igor," he said relieved.

"I will phone you, now go and have nice day. The sun is shining, we are lucky to be alive," he said sinisterly.

As Uri Karpov descended the gangway, Metchnikov called to one of his entourage to bring him some champagne. The galley prepared some smoked salmon sandwiches for him and within minutes a chilled bottle of Perrier Jouet was opened and his glass was filled. He sat down and put a sandwich in his mouth and took a gulp of the cold champagne. What was he going to do? He thought he had left this shit behind him when he flew out of the States. Things had been going quite well for the agency until some stupid kid had rumbled what they were doing and went to the police. Yakov had called him immediately as soon as Petrova had phoned the lawyer's office to tell him that police had been snooping around. Igor had told him to suspend operations immediately and, to contact Petrova and, the others to tell them to take holidays until it calmed down. He felt it would be a passing thing. Anyway, they had all the legal papers and documents, so what could they do? Yakov had reminded the boss that the papers were acquired and, although legal 'to look at', they would not stand up in a court of law. 'And don't forget' , he had said, 'it is illegal to adopt healthy Russian babies! ' If it hadn't have been for that stupid dyke they could have got away with everything. If she had gone away until the heat had died down, it would have been different. Yakov had phoned him in the States to tell him that Petrova had been arrested and three young women had come up as witnesses and were willing to identify Petrova and press charges. Metchnikov had thought long and hard as to what to do. The only link to him and Yakov was Petrova. Since Sergie Barenkov's death, one of his top aides had come over to work for Igor. He was the one who was handy at disposing of unwanted problems. It was the first, but by no means the last, that he would use Benny. He issued instructions to arrange for an accident to happen to the female doctor. Two days later she had been found hanged in her cell.

Metchnikov still felt the time was right to

close things down. Uri Karpov was a bright young man and had done a good job in the agency, but he was naive about Igor's businesses. He had best give himself something to do. A Russian contact of his had been to Spain and had told him of the phenomena of time-share on the Coast. Metchnikov knew little of how it worked, but his contact told him that the money to be made as a developer was immense. 'Look at it logically' he had said.

You build a block of apartments and value each one, at say, forty thousand dollars and you sell fifty weeks at say four thousand dollars. That gives you one hundred and sixty thousand gross profit on development. Obviously,' he had told him, 'there were a lot of heavy costs involved, such as marketing — up to fifty-five percent — but the profit was still good. On top of that, you then have the maintenance fees which can be huge.' Igor had agreed to invest and had sent money to his man in Spain. It was doing well, but he had felt he needed someone on the operational side whom he could trust, and so sent Uri Karpov. He had done well. But things were getting hotter in Russia and Yakov had told Igor that the investigators were being very thorough and that they may call in other services in America and Europe to see if there was any connection. Metchnikov decided to sell his import export business and his drug network to another operator he knew from out of town. The incumbent was happy to take on his operation and the premises that Igor owned. Igor had asked for everything to be paid out of the US. The payment for his business interests was by way of a cash payment to a Swiss account and a luxury yacht based in Barbados, complete with crew, who were familiar in the ways of the world in which the vendor and purchaser were involved. So together with his trusted aide, Benny, they had left America for the Caribbean, and then set sail for Spain.

On arrival in Puerto Banus, he was met by his contact, who guided him through the formalities and arranged for some high profile parties on board the Wave Dancer. In fact, things had been going rather well, until Uri had related this story to him. Of course he knew who he was talking about. He remembered the name Burnet, because it was their very first transaction. Whilst they could not point to him, they could point to Yakov, which in turn could well come down on him. He was going to have to do something — and quickly. He called Benny into the salon.

"We've got a problem. Did you hear Karpov's story?" As usual, the pony-tail nodded his agreement rather than speak. "I want you to get Diego to go around to her apartment this evening, pick her up and bring her here."

That evening, the salon door opened and in walked a very attractive young woman. It was Katrina. He could see what Uri saw in her, she was indeed very pretty and had a good body. He was talking to Yakov at the time and quickly wrapped up the conversation. He beckoned for her to sit down and asked her to tell him all the details while he made some notes. He needed to know what she knew. She was obviously intelligent and had worked a lot out for herself. She had even found out where the Burnets were living, which Uri had implied. However, he did not mention the plan to snatch the child, which is what the girl was telling him now. This whole thing was going too far. When she finished he told her who he was and that her boyfriend in fact ran the agency in America, she went berserk and jumped on him, hitting his chest with her fists. He felt very little, probably because of his ample padding, but her screaming brought in Benny who restrained her. He told him to amuse himself with her until he had decided what to do. The bodyguard had to hit her to quiet her down, before untying her and taking her below decks.

The steward told Metchnikov that his dinner was ready. He sat at the dining table on his own and ate four huge king prawns covered in garlic butter and lemon, followed by a fillet steak with fries and salad. He drank a bottle of 1982 *reserva* from the Rioja. He was on his coffee and brandy when Benny re-emerged.

"We are going to have to dispose of the girl," said Metchnikov.

A look of both disappointment and pleasure went over the aide's face. "I will have to leave it with you. But make sure she is off this boat between the time I go to bed and when I get up tomorrow." He went to bed in the knowledge that one of his problems would be over by the time he got up. He had to decide what to do with Uri. He had been a good boy, but he was now into something he couldn't cope with. He had got himself emotionally involved, a dangerous occupation. He was naive and head strong and it was he, Metchnikov, whose life would be on the line if everything was to go wrong. He slept.

At eight the next morning he was sitting on the sun deck with orange juice, tea and some croissants when Benny appeared. "Everything alright?" enquired Metchnikov placing a huge lump of butter on his hot croissant. In one of the few moments that pony-tail spoke, he answered his boss in Russian. "I took her up a mountain road and dumped her over the side. She should be at the bottom of ravine never to be seen again." He smiled and walked out. 'I do like people who enjoy their work,' he thought. "Benny," he called after him. The man returned.

"We have to do something about Uri Karpov I'm afraid. He knows too much for our own good." He smiled. "I will phone him and invite him to lunch on Thursday. Tell the steward and inform the crew that I will want to go for a trip on Thursday. Meanwhile get one of the boys to keep an eye on him from a distance. And I want Diego to take one other and go to where the girl lived and keep an eye on the occupants. When the sister and her ex-boyfriend go out I want them followed. And tell Diego to keep me informed of their every move. Benny grunted in the affirmative. Metchnikov dismissed him with a polite wave. He picked up the phone and dialled. "Could I speak to Baz Brown, please. — Metchnikov. — Hello, Mister Brown, how are you? Good. Listen, I would like you to come for lunch tomorrow, would you be able to? That's good. And Mister Brown, please do not mention this to Uri, I will explain everything when I see you." Igor was setting his plan up stage by stage. He didn't really like doing this as the boy hadn't done any harm — yet, but the risks were too great. The phone rang, it was Uri. "Uri, good morning, how are you?"

"Fine," he replied, "when did you want me to bring over Katrina to see you?"

"I tried to phone you last night Uri," he lied, "but your mobile phone must have been switched off or unavailable, as I was unable to get through. I needed to speak to her last night as I have to be somewhere else this evening, so I got one of the boys to pick her up. We had a long conversation, what a charming young lady, you are very fortunate, and I told her that I would get Yakov to look back through all the files and find the relative information about her and her child to see if we can get out of the adoption and therefore legally declare the papers void, in which case it would be a simple court case to get the child back." 'What an accomplished liar you are Igor,' he thought as he waited for Uri's reply.

"What are the chances?" he asked.

"I don't know yet, but I have spoken to Yakov and he will fax me as soon as he has all the information. Meanwhile I told her to do nothing and I would contact her through you when I had some information. I suggested she went away for a few days and unwound, she was very uptight and upset. She seemed to have a lot on her mind. She said her sister and ex- boyfriend were over, she may go away with them for a while."

"Yes, she had asked me for some time off. Thank you Igor, I do hope it all works out."

"Oh I am sure it will. Come to lunch with me on Thursday I will have news for you by then."

"Shall I bring Katrina?" he asked innocently.

"No, I prefer to tell you everything first. And anyway she may not be back by then." He was getting to believe all his lies himself.

"Until Thursday then," said Uri.

"Until Thursday," replied Igor, and put the phone down.

The following day at lunchtime, the figure of Baz Brown appeared at the top of the gangway. Benny showed him in.

"Mister Brown," Metchnikov got up and went to greet him. They shook hands. "Thank you for coming it is so nice to see you."

"The pleasure is all mine I can assure you," said Baz looking around the luxury of the beautiful boat. They walked out on to the forward sun terrace where the steward offered them some champagne. He showed the friendly Irishman to a seat.

"I thought we would have lobster salad, is

that alright with you?" knowing it would be. .

"That would be fine," replied Baz, as if he ate it every day.

"I know you are a busy man," continued Igor, "so I will not waste too much of your valuable time. It is concerning Uri."

"What's wrong?" said Baz quickly. . .

"Nothing. Nothing at all. Quite the opposite. He's a good boy and as you know, he has been with me a very long time. It is just that I think he has become a little stale and I believe he has some girlfriend trouble."

"He hasn't mentioned anything to me and his work is very good" said Baz. The stewards brought two whole lobsters and a bowl of green salad which he placed in the centre of the table along with mayonnaise, Hollandaise and crusty brown bread-and butter. He topped up the two men's glasses and left as quietly as he had entered.

"Yes I am sure, but you will admit that I know him better than you. It would appear that a girl he has been seeing and, has become very fond of, has a boyfriend and, he has arrived in Spain. She is at this moment spending a few days away with him and, this is upsetting Uri, as he cannot come to terms with it. However, that is only one of the small considerations. I have a new project for him in America and I want him to leave immediately. Please do not mention anything of this, as I have not yet discussed it with him."

"How do you know all about his girlfriend, I didn't know he had anyone that serious," asked Baz

"As I said Mister Brown, I do know him better than you, and his girlfriend came to see me."

"I don't know who I am going to replace him with. He is such a good man. When do you think he will be leaving?" asked Baz.

"The day after tomorrow," Igor said as he sucked the claw of his lobster.

Baz panicked, "Thursday, well that gives me no time at all."

"I'm sure you will cope," said Igor matter-of-factly. "But I repeat, none of this to Uri, or anyone else for that matter."

"No, of course not." The two men finished their lunch and discussed the success of the resort, and no more word was mentioned about Uri, or his impending departure.

That afternoon, Diego called in again. This time he told his boss that he had been following the Russian couple and they had made two trips down to the Burnet's house, where they observed the family. An older Spanish woman had emerged with the child and the couple followed her, as did Diego, and they went to a nursery school in San Pedro. They remained outside the school until two o' clock when the woman returned to collect the child from the playground. They had done that again today.

"Stay with them. Watch them closely tomorrow as they will probably do the same again." He put the phone down.

They were obviously going to try and snatch the child at some stage. But why would they do that now that Katrina wasn't around. If they hadn't have seen her wouldn't they be wondering where she was. What were they going to do with the child when they had her if the mother wasn't around. Why did people have to interfere?

The following day around lunchtime, Uri phoned in a panic.

"What is it now?" Igor asked impatiently.

"I'm worried about Katrina," he replied. "She hasn't been at home for a couple of days. I've been around to the apartment and there is no sign of her, or her ex—boyfriend and her sister. And, my car is there which means she has no transport. Where the hell is she?"

"I have no idea Uri. Diego took her back to Marbella and she asked to be dropped by the bus station. Maybe she went somewhere."

"She wouldn't go away without letting me or her sister know. I don't know what to do."

"I suggest you leave it until tomorrow my friend. If, by the time you get here, she hasn't appeared, we can go to the police and say she is a missing person. But I am sure she is alright. She is old enough to look after herself."

Igor put down the mobile phone. 'Things are getting too close to me now' he thought. 'The sooner I can do something about all this, the better'.

The phone rang again. This time it was Diego, "The couple have snatched the child from the playschool, we are following them. What do you want to do?" There was a moments silence while Metchnikov's brain worked quickly. This situation was getting out of hand. He had to stop it now, as soon as possible. "Get rid of them. Quickly, quietly and efficiently."

"All of them?" asked the henchman.

"Yes, all of them." replied Metchnikov, and hung up.

That was it. They had to make sure there were no loose ends.

The sun was setting as Metchnikov sat on the after end of his boat having a drink when Benny came up to him. "They have dispatched the parcel and it has been left in a derelict house in an area outside of Marbella. There are no traces of its origin. They have used my tried and tested method of tying it up," he said almost as if the shopping had been done. 'He was a man of few words,' thought Igor, ' and most of them succinct and to the point.' He went to sleep that night with only one major problem left and he wasn't quite sure how he was going to handle it.

Uri was punctual as usual. He walked into the salon watched, as always, by Benny. "Hello Igor," he said extending his hand. "Good morning," replied the Russian. "Please, come out to the sun deck," and they went out to where a table was laid for two. "Champagne?" asked Igor,

"Thank you," replied the young man. The steward poured two glasses and prepared the table with two seafood cocktails. "I am very concerned about Katrina," continued Uri. "She has not been seen and has not contacted anyone. All her belongings are untouched. I am going to the police this afternoon."

"That is a good idea, I will come with you," said Igor as the vessel's motors started up and the boat began to slip away from the shore.

"Where are we going," asked Uri concernedly.

"It is such a nice day, I thought we would just take the boat for a bit of fresh air. Their starters arrived. Once at sea the Russian turned to the young man.

"What would you say if I told you, I wanted you to go back to America and open a new project for me?" he asked as he pushed prawns, mussels and lobster pieces on to his fork.

"I am very happy here, thank you," he replied, "and I have no intention of going anywhere until I have found Katrina." Igor decided it was time to tell the man that he wouldn't see her again.

"I am afraid Uri, that Katrina met with an accident. I couldn't tell you before."

A look of panic went across Uri's face. "What accident, what has happened to her?"

"I am afraid she was killed."

Uri went white. He started to visibly shake. There were tears in his eyes. "You bastard. You fucking bastard you had her killed because she was getting too close to the truth. You had to get rid of her to protect yourself."

"Settle down, I did it for you as well. We were all in it together." he protested.

"You bastard, I hate you, I'll fucking kill you," he screamed. He picked up his fork and with a blood curdling scream he plunged it through the fat man's pudgy hands. Igor let out a painful roar and the noise of both men brought Benny onto the after deck. He quickly saw what had happened. He grabbed Uri, who swung out at him, and placed a well aimed punch in his solar plexus and a right hand which connected with his cheek, which sent the young man flying into the salon. The steward ran out and seeing Igor's hand, grabbed a serviette, and rapidly pulling the fork out of his hand, wrapped it around the wound. Igor let out another yelp of pain. Benny dragged the semi-conscious Uri back onto the sun deck and put him in his chair.

"You stupid, stupid boy," shouted Igor and with his good hand, he swiped him across the face three times, drawing blood from the side of his mouth. "Get rid of him," he said in anger. Benny picked him up and dragged him into a corner. Using piano wire, he tied Uri's hands together behind his back and attached them to his ankles, bending his body backwards. The man was screaming and shouting protests. Benny hit him again.

He stopped. He then wrapped the twine several times around his victim's neck. Then he dragged over a base from a sun umbrella, filled with sand to keep it weighted down, and attached it to Uri's feet. The steward meanwhile had cleaned up Igor's wound and applied a bandage. Benny came over to his boss. Igor looked at him, then walked into the salon, closing the smoked glass door behind him. Uri was struggling. The more he moved, the more the wire cut through his wrist and throat. Tears were running down his face. He was pleading with his captors. The steward and Benny lifted the helpless body on to the edge of the boat's bow and on a hot sunny day, with no one in sight, they pushed the man into the deep blue Mediterranean. The body hit the water with a splash and the weight went plummeting down, taking the screaming body with it. In seconds, there was nothing.

CHAPTER FIFTEEEN

I awoke to hear the wind blowing and the rain lashing against the bedroom windows. It was an infrequent summer storm. It had obviously only just started as, as I looked across the marina, the roads were still dryish and people were tying down the hatches on their boats and others were running for cover. The palm trees bent and waved majestically in the warm winds that were accompanying the heavy rains. These storms were a strange phenomena as they came from nowhere and invariably disappeared just as quickly. I rolled over to find the bed empty. It seemed ages since Sandy had last stayed at her own place. She had gone out with some new found friends of hers, studio associates, and said she would stay at her place for the evening. That suited me, as I had to develop some more photographs and get some invoices prepared to send off, or deliver, to clients, tomorrow.

It did feel strange getting up without her. It also seemed silly her living elsewhere. There again, we both liked our independence and freedom and, I knew she liked having her own bolt hole. So did I, come to that. But she was the first woman who had started to mean anything to me for some time. I got up and made myself some orange juice and coffee and put the morning news on in the background. I looked out over the port from the lounge windows and could see the swaying palm trees as the wind continued unabated. The phone rang, it was Sandy. "Good morning darling," she said sleepily. "Are you up and about yet?" I smiled, as I could see her curled up in her bed hibernating.

"I have been up, showered and shaved, had breakfast, developed some photographs and written half a dozen letters," I said sarcastically.

"You liar," she retorted, "I bet you have just got up and made the coffee."

"Caught out in one!" I quipped. "What do you fancy doing, if anything, today?" I continued.

"I don't know, " she said, "I'm still in bed and haven't thought about it. What the hell is going on outside?" she enquired.

"A summer storm," I said, "it shouldn't last too long. How about we have some lunch here?"

"Mmm, that would be nice. What is there?"

"I've got some bits and pieces, but if you could pick up a leg of lamb on your way over, I could make that lamb dish I do with the peppers."

"Yes, OK. I'll get up and do my bits, and I'll come over."

"Oh, and pick up a couple of sprigs of Rosemary out of the garden by the car park, will you?"

"OK. I'll see you later."

She put the phone down. I looked in the fridge to make sure I had all the ingredients I needed, in case I had to phone her back to get something else. No, it was fine. I had everything I wanted and more. The phone rang again, it was Gerry. "Hello mate," the familiar voice rang out, how are you?"

"I'm fine," I replied. "I haven't heard much from you this last week."

"Well, no. I've been doing a bit of investigatory journalism, as they say in the trade. In fact, that was what I wanted to talk to you about. I was going to suggest a game of golf, but looking at this lot, it's a bit out of the question."

"Well," I interrupted, "I'm doing lunch for Sandy and me, why don't you come over and join us? Bring someone if you want."

"That would be great. I'll come alone though. I didn't find anyone next to me when I woke up this morning, so I think I had a boring night!" he chuckled. "I'll see you about two."

"That will be fine. See you then," and we hung up.

I had showered and dressed and was in the kitchen with a glass of cava preparing the vegetables when Sandy came in. She was wet. Her coat had kept most of the rain from her body and was soaking and the umbrella had helped keep her hair dry.

"And that's just from the car to here," she said putting the shopping and some sprigs of fresh herb down on the bar "It's still chucking it down." She came over and kissed me. Long and warm. "I missed you," she said.

"The feeling is mutual," I replied kissing her again, this time putting down the knife and potato that had been in my hand and putting my arms around her. We looked at each other for a moment, and then I broke the short silence. "Would you like a glass?" I asked indicating mine. "I'll get it," she said and went into the lounge to get herself another champagne flute. "I got a leg of lamb and some strawberries for desert," she said opening the fridge to get out the bottle.

"I invited Gerry Peters to join us, he phoned this morning to tell me he had been busy working and had some things to tell me."

"Is he bringing anyone," she asked.

"You know Gerry, he has never got one long enough to get to the 'Shall we go out to friends for lunch?' stage. He'll be on his own."

"I'll just go and make myself look a little less windblown," and she disappeared into the bathroom. I sliced the potatoes, onions, peppers and tomatoes into rings and laid them alternately in a baking tray. I scored the fat on the leg of lamb and pushed rosemary into the gaps. I sprinkled the meat with salt, ground black pepper, finely chopped garlic and olive oil. I liked this dish, because once you have prepared it and put it in the oven, you just have to put together a salad, and that's it. Sandy came back and topped up our glasses.

"Looks good," she commented as I placed it in the oven. "Let's hope it tastes as good," I replied.

We sat in the lounge listening to a Verdi CD and generally talking. It was more Sandy talking to me about her new project and I avoided any more discussion about Russians or their presence on the Costa del Sol. Just before two o'clock, the door bell rang. It was Gerry.

"Come in my friend," I said as I opened the door and led him into the lounge.

"Hi Gerry" chirped Sandy, and they kissed. "Shampoo," she asked. "As long as it's alcoholic," he jested and sat in a chair by the window. "Awful bloody weather for the time of year," he laughed, "and I always thought it fell on the plain."

"So, what's been happening?" I asked. "Any news about anything?"

"Well, since I last saw you, I don't know whether I told you, my features editor on the Sunday Times asked me to find out a bit more about our friend Metchnikov. It seemed they had heard some things about him in the UK and were anxious to see if there was a story."

"And?" I said getting up to top up our glasses, "is there?"

"Well," he continued, "there seems to be more to the man than meets the eye. His boat is Bahamian registered and is in an American company name. This company doesn't seem to be doing any declarable business as there are no records of taxes or anything with the Inland Revenue. However, an application has been received by the Bahamas maritime registry, to change the name of ownership into another company name, of which Metchnikov is a director."

"That's not a crime though is it?" I interceded

"No," he carried on, having given him time to

204

take a mouthful of bubbles, "but interestingly enough, the company was an import export operator in California, based in Los Angeles to be precise, that has recently ceased trading, having sold its assets to another company."

"So?" I asked, certain I was missing something.

"The company who took the assets over, is the same one which was the original owner of the Wave Dancer. Which would obviously imply that that was how the deal was paid for. Thus trying to avoid any taxes."

"Well, that would appear to be a normal tried and tested scam wouldn't it?" I asked somewhat innocently. .

"Yes," he carried on, "but that's just the beginning."

"In that case," I said getting up, "we had better continue this over lunch. I took the meat out of the oven and transferred it all on to a serving pan and took it to the table. Sandy had already opened a couple of bottles of red wine and had put the finishing touches to the salad and joined us at the table. I out good thick slices from the joint. It was pink and juicy' and the accompanying vegetables were full of flavour. This is delicious," they both said as we all tucked in to the first, hot , Sunday lunch we had had for a long time. The rain stopped, the wind dropped and the sun came out to throw its rays on the wet canvases of the boats and, quickly dry out the roads.

"Carry on with your story Gerry," I said

pouring out more wine for us.

"Well, I have a friend who works for Newsweek and I spoke to him about Metchnikov. The Russian went over to the States around the time that the USSR broke up. He had money. Probably made illegally in his own country. He soon got into business circles and ended up buying a small basket ball team called the LA Weavers, which did well and he made some money on the product sales. But basically it was small time. His import/export business was also pretty small. It did some wines, coffees, sugar and the like." .

"What are you getting at?" I asked cutting some more meat for us. '

"OK. Well, Metchnikov left America some six months ago and arrived here in a boat worth over five million pounds. My friend in the States says there is no way that the LA Weavers and the import company together could be worth anything like that. He reckons that he was heavily involved with drugs, mainly cocaine. That, as they say in the States, is the word on the street!"

"Sounds like a story of anyone of hundreds of American, so called business men to me, doesn't it you?"

"Yes, but they aren't moored at Puerto Banus, he is. And perhaps he is plying his trade here as well. After all, there is a market, and Morocco is only over the other side of the water, isn't it?"

"So what are you going to do?" I asked helping myself to some salad and mopping up the sauce on my plate with some crusty bread.

"I've asked my pal to keep an ear to the ground and find out what he can for me. He said the IRS would be interested to know where he is, and he is going to check if he has a criminal record or, if there is anything waiting for him if he returned." Sandy got up to bring the cheese and prepare the strawberries.

After lunch we retired to the lounge for coffee and a glass of port. Gerry said he was leaving us in peace so as we could spend the last part of the weekend alone. Our evening passed peacefully. We talked and laughed, and listened to some music, before going to bed and making love.

The next morning we were both up and out early. Sandy to the studio and me to the post office to send off some photographs and some invoices including the ones to David Lewis. On my way back from the post office, I stayed on the main road and went to the Puente Romano Hotel to see Chris Yeo and deliver the photographs.

"They're wonderful as always Philip. When we have the brochure completed I will of course let you have a copy. Oh, by the way, you remember last week you were enquiring about Metchnikov. Just a little bit of information that might be of interest. He has asked us to cancel any work we are doing trying to find him a business. He is apparently not keen on investing any further in Spain."

"Any further?" I asked puzzled, "I didn't think he had any investment here anyway."

"Ah, I didn't tell you did I? He is a major investor in a time-share project in Marbella."

"Which one," I asked."

"Costalite I believe, near the Don Pepe."

"That figures," I replied.

"Sorry?" said Chris obviously not making any connection.

"Nothing, it's just that I had a meeting down there with one of their sales managers and one of the main cores of business is the Russians. So, I suppose it stands to reason that someone like Metchnikov would get involved. Thanks any way. Any more jobs for me?"

"No, sorry, not at the moment," said Chris, habitually running his hand through his hair, "but I'll let you know if something comes up."

As I got into my car, my mobile phone rang, it was Carlos "Holá Philip. Will you be in the restaurant at lunchtime?" he asked.

"I could be, I wasn't going anywhere in particular."

"Good, about two?"

"Fine. Have you got some news?"

"I'll tell you later," he said and hung up.

Being a Monday Paul was in the office doing the books, when I arrived. Lunch had got off to a quiet start with only a few tables occupied on the terrace at the time. I popped my head around the door, "Morning," I chirped. He looked up from his computer.

"Hello there, how are you this fine day?"

"OK. thanks," I replied. "How's business?"

"Thumping good weekend," he retorted. "90 on Saturday night and over a hundred for Sunday lunch."

"Great. We'll soon be able to retire."

"We should be so lucky. Anyway, I don't know what I would do. What's happening in the world of our photographic detective then, any developments? If you'll pardon the pun."

"Funnily enough," I replied, "Carlos 'phoned me to ask me to meet him here at two. Will you be out soon?"

"I've got quite a bit more to do. Julian will call me if we get busy. I'll catch up with you later."

I left the office and went back into the restaurant, to the bar, and waited for Carlos. I ordered a glass of beer and Julian put down some nuts and olives, which I nibbled effusively, not realising until then I was quite hungry. Carlos arrived just after the top of the hour. We shook hands and I asked if he would like a drink, he took a beer too, it had turned into a very hot day, the weather having been cleared of its heaviness, by yesterday's storm.

"You won't forget the barbecue next weekend will you?" he opened the conversation.

"No, we're looking forward to it. So what is it that has happened? Any further developments?"

"The parents of the child came back yesterday and identified the little one's body. It was pretty terrible. Both the parents and the nanny were in an awful state and the mother had to go to the hospital suffering from shock. They could not identify the young couple, they had never seen them before. Neither could they think of any reason why anyone should kidnap their child. They have no enemies that they know of. They have never run into anyone down here. They are comfortable, but not very wealthy. If a ransom was asked it would have had to have been in the thousands of dollars, not in the hundreds of thousands, otherwise they could never have paid. Anyway, on that side we are no further forward."

"So what next?"

"I have this morning contacted Madrid airport. I want to know from any returning Russian/Ukrainian flights if a male or female passenger failed to get their flight."

"Would that not cause a bit of confusion, bearing in mind the number that may well stay on illegally?" I asked.

"We may have more than we need, but it is a start. Things are getting worse rather than better," he continued, " this morning we had a dead body washed up on the shore at San Pedro's beach area. Well, more parts of a body."

"Yuk," I said feeling ill. I had after all had a belly full of death this last week or so. "What do you mean by bits? Sharks?"

He smiled. "Not that sort of shark, no, but someone evil is involved. Yesterday's storm must have helped bring the body ashore, otherwise it may have stayed in the sea forever until it had completely decomposed. The victim was male, around his late twenties. Most of the skin and bone around his hands and feet was missing and his head was just hanging on by the bone. There was piano wire still attached to part of his body. His throat had been cut. Either before he entered the sea or during the storm. It would appear to be the same way as our little family met their deaths at Las Cancelas. The medical examiner is trying to put things together." .

"I think in English that would be called a little play on words."

"Pardon?" said Carlos somewhat confused by my interjection.

"Put things together," I demonstrated with objects on the bar.

"Oh, I see. My English eh?"

"I'm sorry Carlos, just a little light relief. And, there is nothing wrong with your English, just my sense of humour. I'm sorry please carry on."

"Of course this murder is very similar to the way the three were killed in Las Cancelas. But, at the moment, as we are no further forward, all this does, is give us an extra body to add to the list of unidentified murder victims. But, I am more and more convinced, that they are all inexplicably linked. It seems more like Los Angeles than Marbella here at the moment!"

"Was there any identification on the body at all?" I asked pretty sure that if this was the same murderer, the answer would be no.

"Nothing at all, except that the trousers he was wearing, although badly damaged, were from Cortefiel's here in Marbella I took them into the manager this morning and asked him if they could trace the trousers. He remembered them as a batch that they had in a pre—summer sale. He is going to collect all the code numbers, and then get there accounts department to see if they can find how many were paid by credit card and, if so, the name of the purchasers. It will take some time, and it is a long shot, but it is all I have at the moment. If he didn't pay by credit card, then we will be no further forward."

His mobile phone rang. I ordered another two beers.

"*Si, digame.*" He listened intently. "*Si — si*" he paused longer, "*Si, gracias.*"

"That was the doctor with the autopsy. Our victim was punched, there are some bruises to the face and abdomen, his throat was cut by the wire before he was thrown into the sea. He was alive when he hit the water. He must have been weighted down. The doctor thinks that is why the hands and feet were in the state they were, as the wire shaved the skin and bone during the excess movement caused by the storm. However, he would have cut his own throat further by struggling when he went under. He died principally from drowning, his lungs were full of water, but he would have bled to death anyway. He had been dead for about three or four days"

"That is sick," I said feeling myself go quite white.

"Right, I must go," he said. "I will speak to you later. Thank you for the drink." He got up and left, just as Paul came out of the office. They acknowledged each other with a wave.

"You alright?" said Paul as he went behind the bar to help himself to a beer. "You look a bit pale."

"I have just been listening to the description of a pretty horrific death," I said taking a swig of beer. "I don't know how people's minds can come up with these things."

"I think you have had more than your fair share of death and the like, for one week, don't you?"

"More like a year, " I replied and got off my stool to leave. "I'll catch you later." I went out into the midday sun. Not even dogs were in sight as the temperatures hit the mid thirties. It was hot.

I had made a few extra copies of some of the night shots of David Hill's house and decided to run them up to him. The journey from the restaurant took about ten minutes due to traffic. The affable Mister Hill was just getting out of his car as I pulled up outside the huge double doors. He acknowledged me as I got out of the car. "Hello young man," he said coming towards me with hand outstretched. "What are you doing here?"

"I printed some extra shots of the house which I thought you might like," I said handing him the envelope I had in my other hand. "That's very kind of you," he said, "have you time for a drink?"

"That would be nice," I replied, following him into his house. We went out on to the terrace that led from the lounge. "Wine, champagne, something else?" he enquired.

"Wine would be fine thank you."

He opened a fridge on his terrace, "White be alright?," he asked selecting a bottle of Monopole. I nodded. He expertly opened the bottle, put it in a cooler and brought it to the table with two glasses. He poured us both a glass and brought over some nuts and proceeded to crack them. He handed me the nutcrackers and I helped myself to a Brazil nut. He opened the envelope, "They are beautiful, "he said genuinely, "thank you. Do I owe you anything?"

"No," I said, "it's in the price of the job I did for Chris."

"I tell you what," he sipped his wine, "I think this one is fabulous. He held up a shot of the pool and gardens lit up, with the house in the background.

"Would you be able to blow that up into a full size picture? Because if you can, I would happily pay your price for a framed photograph for my new apartment, just to remind me of here."

"I couldn't, but I could get it blown up in Malaga and have it framed by a friend of mine." I said taking a mental note as to which one it was. "I'll get it done this week."

He poured some more wine. "And make sure you charge me properly, won't you?"

I smiled, "Of course." He settled back in his chair.

"So this sort of thing keeps you busy does it?"

"Well, it is a combination of this and other things that helps keep the wolf from the door. I have private clients who want photos done. I work with an advertising agency and get involved with magazine and newspaper advertisements. I contribute to Marbella Marbella and I have an interest in a restaurant in town that does very well."

"How long have you been here?"

"Ten years this month, I've just celebrated the event with a party for friends." I said remembering the other evening.

"What about you?" I asked turning the tables, "how long have you been here?"

"We've had this house for a few years. My wife and I intended to retire here. We had been coming backwards and forwards on holidays for some time. After we bought the house, I went back to arrange my retirement. We sold our house in Los Angeles and bought a condo in San Diego so as we could lock it up and make more frequent trips, backwards and forwards to Spain. That left us with the house in Boston, where my wife's family were. When Pamela died I sold the house in Boston and came over here. Really, I suppose to sell this and buy a new apartment, so as I could commute between San Diego and Marbella."

"Sandy said you were in the CIA," I said cracking another nut.

"Yes, most of my life. Put it this way I retired with them. It was fun in the old days when there was an Iron Curtain, but it got a bit tame after, which is really one of the reasons that I wanted to retire. That, and I was getting too old and Pamela too ill."

"What sort of things did you get involved in?" I asked inquisitively.

"Most of it would still come under 'State Secrets', but I was involved in keeping an eye on the Russians and their activities, defections, political prisoners and that sort of stuff."

"No James Bond stuff then?" I smiled.

"A little, but I can assure you that it is mostly footwork and paper shuffling," he laughed.

We finished our wine and I made my excuses and left, feeling a little light headed, having not eaten properly.

I headed in the direction of Marbella to call in to the supermarket for some bits and pieces for home, when my mobile rang. It was Carlos.

"The manager from Cortefiel has been on the phone, he said it was easier than he had thought and is most impressed with the organisation of the company's accounts department. They have come up with a print out of thirty six names from credit card purchases made on those batch numbers. He has instructed his office to fax it directly to my office, I am going in now. I have a theory I would like to talk to you about. I will invite you to a drink in the bar around the comer from my office in about half an hour. O.K.?"

Feeling that it was more an order than a

request, I accepted graciously. In the supermarket, I decided to have a *tapa* to soak up the earlier refreshment and — another glass of wine!

I parked virtually outside of the small bar, invariably frequented by Guardia officers and plain clothes detectives, who looked remarkably shady and, indistinguishable, from the characters that they were usually investigating.

Carlos was there talking to a colleague. As I went in the officer acknowledged me and walked out of the bar.

"Sorry," I said, "did I interrupt anything?"

"No, he was just leaving anyway. What would you like?" He was drinking sherry and nibbling at a little cheese and some olives.

"I'll stick to wine, red please, and then I can pick at that bit of cheese, I haven't eaten properly yet."

"You own a restaurant and you don't eat properly," he laughed.

The wine arrived and I took a piece of cheese, he ordered some ham and another plate of cheese which I attacked quite readily.

"What if our dead man," he started without warning, "was responsible for organising the kidnapping of the child on behalf of some bigger fish, and then decided he wanted a larger part of the action and told his boss. Or, decided to go it alone, or of course got frightened and was going to go to the police?"

I looked at him smiling, "I thought you said you had a theory, not a compilation of ideas and possibilities."

"Yes, I suppose it could be a combination of that and more." He put his hand inside his uniform jacket and took out a piece of paper. It was a photocopy of a list of names. "This is the list that Cortefiel sent me. I don't suppose you recognise any of the names, especially the English ones," he said hopefully. I glanced through it quickly thinking the chances were very remote when my eyes stopped at the name. I was stunned. Surely not.

"Karpov." I said slowly. "Uri Karpov. I know him. I have met him. Only once. But I would recognise him."

Carlos was as shocked as I was. "I'm sorry to do this to you my friend, but this time you must come to the morgue. We will go in my car."

On the way to the hospital I told him how I had met him. "In your little private investigations you have not learned anything that you think you should be telling me have you?"

"No. I'm afraid I wouldn't make a very good detective." We went downstairs to the morgue. The attendant let us in and went over to the refrigerated drawer opened it, and pulled back the cloth. "Jesus," I exclaimed, "what a mess." The deep jugular cut, the loss of blood and the water damage had all taken its toll on what was once a handsome face. "He's a helluva mess, but I'm pretty damned sure that, that, is Uri Karpov."

"At last," he sounded relieved, " we have a name and something to go on. Well done my friend." He put his arm on my shoulder and walked with me to the exit.

CHAPTER SIXTEEN

Carlos Jimenez said goodbye to his *'guiri'* friend Philip Edwards and went back to his office. Philip had left Carlos the name of Baz Brown, managing director of Costalite resorts, He would go and see him, when he had finished some paperwork. He phoned the resort to be told that Mister Brown had left for the day and would not be back until tomorrow morning.

Carlos had ordered coffee and stirred a little sugar into the thick black liquid. He spread a sheet of paper out in front of him. What did he have so far? he asked himself. Using a pencil, he wrote down all the information that he had.

Uri Karpov a young man, of Russian extract, but Philip said he spoke with a mild American accent, trussed up and taken out to sea, weighted down and drowned. The piano wire and the cut throat suggest the same murderer and a similar pattern, as the two adults and the baby found in the abandoned house at Las Cancelas. The adults were unknown. They were kidnapping the child. Why? Could it have been for a ransom. Then there was the child itself. Why would anyone have murdered an innocent young girl? She was from an American family, with no apparent connection with the others involved in the scenario. Then course, there was the blonde, who seemed to have started it all. She would appear to have come from nowhere and nobody seemed to know anything about her. How was she connected with the others? He knew that she was suffocated and raped before being dumped down the cliff. She could have been killed anywhere, before being brought to the roadside. Karpov, he was obviously tied up before he was murdered. Perhaps he was known to the murderer, otherwise wouldn't the murderer have killed him immediately. Why would he tie him up with all that cord, then take him out to sea to bury him? Why not just throw him down a hill side like the blonde. Maybe he was already at sea. Yes. They could have been at sea when Karpov was tied up. Had he been the kidnapper and then fallen foul of his boss. Perhaps threatening to go to the police? And what about the blonde? Was she linked to all of this if so, how? And why hadn't anyone missed her yet? She was found at Istan, Karpov in San Pedro, but he could have come from any direction with that storm on Sunday. The others were found near Marbella in a small urbanisation. The family lived in Madroñal and the child went to nursery in San Pedro. None of it seemed to fit. The girl was murdered on Monday, the couple and the baby on Wednesday night, Thursday morning and Karpov, Thursday or Friday.

What had the police achieved? They had sent out descriptions of all those involved to the newspapers and TV. They had notified the airports to try and find people not using their return tickets. They had issued the local hotels and hostels in the hope that the couple, or the girl, were staying in hotel accommodation. They knew who the young man was and they knew who the child was. So why did he feel like someone had just opened a box of jigsaw pieces and thrown them in the middle of the room and left him without the picture to work on.

He was tired, it was nearly eight o' clock, he would go home and change and go out for a bit of supper into the old town of Marbella. He was sure to bump into someone he knew and would have a few drinks. He knew it had only been a week but this case was getting him down and had seemed to go on forever. He tidied up his desk, picked up his cap, closed the door behind him and went down to the garage to collect his car. He drove slowly up the winding roads to his tranquil country *finca* where the plants and wildlife gave him peace of mind.

He showered the day's grime from his body and ironed a short sleeved shirt and put on slacks straight from the cleaners. He opened the fridge, took out a cold beer and went out on to the terrace to watch the dusk moving in. It was beautiful here and, when it was time for him to leave this dirty world, he would be quite happy to pass peacefully away sitting on this terrace under the vines, looking up at the mountains. The next thing he knew, he had dropped off, and it was eleven o'clock. He stretched from his chair and decided it was too late to go out. He went into the kitchen and cut off some Manchego cheese and poured himself a glass of wine. He put on an operatic CD and sat back on the terrace. Anyway, he needed time to think what he was going to do about this whole thing. He desperately needed a result. And soon.

The next day he phoned the office to say he was going directly to interview someone and would not be in until a bit later. He had a leisurely coffee and some bread and took his time getting ready. There was no need to rush to see Baz Brown, he probably wouldn't be in until nine thirty at the earliest.

It was ten o'clock when Carlos went into the offices of the Costalite resort. His appearance causing a mild stir among the staff that were there. The presence of a Guardia Civil officer normally meant a check on the number of illegal residents and workers that were prevalent in this industry. He asked for Baz Brown and the secretary went to inform Mister Brown personally. The affable Irishman came into reception and shook the policeman's hand and led him through to the office. It was apparent from the outset that he spoke very little Spanish and that Carlos' English, though not excellent, was certainly better than this man's Spanish.

"Would you like some coffee?" enquired Baz, "it is proper coffee." he further explained, thinking that the big man probably thought that most foreigners drank nothing but instant.

"Thank you," replied Carlos. "I believe a Uri

Karpov works for you?"

"He did," replied Baz, "until last week." He picked up the phone and ordered the coffee.

"Why until last week? Why did he leave?" The look on Brown's face made Carlos think that the man had no idea what had happened to Uri.

"He left to return to America. He had a job offer and was going to fly back this weekend. To my knowledge, he has already left the country I'm afraid. Is there anything I can do for you?" continued Baz innocently.

"Did you have a good working relationship?" asked Carlos.

"Yes," replied the General Manager, "we got on well and he was very good at his job, I am very sorry to lose him but his career comes first." ,

"Have you got a picture of him anywhere?

Baz pointed to a group of wall pictures featuring the sales teams at certain times of the year and at special events.

"The picture on the bottom left," he got up and went towards the wall, Carlos followed, "was taken in February at a Valentines dinner in the Club House." Carlos looked intently. It was him.

"I'm afraid Senor Brown, that Uri Karpov was found yesterday morning washed up on the beach at San Pedro."

Baz Brown went as white as the crisp cotton shirt he was wearing. He staggered back to his desk. The girl came in with the coffee. He quickly dismissed her. "How why?" he spluttered. "Was it an accident, what happened?" '

"He was murdered," said Carlos emphatically.

"I don't believe it." said Baz with genuine disbelief.

"When did you last see Uri Karpov?" asked Carlos taking a note-pad from his pocket.

"Uhmm, Wednesday evening, just before I left to go home. Uri was with some clients. I said goodbye and he just waved."

"Did he seem alright?

"Yes. Fine"

"When did he tell you he was leaving for America?"

"Well, he didn't actually."

"I'm sorry," said Carlos looking up from his notebook, "I don't understand."

"I had better explain something to you," said Baz Brown, realising that the story would sound strange to the officer. "One of the largest investors in this project is a man called Igor Metchnikov." — the name made Carlos' ears twitch. He knew that name alright — "Uri used to work for Metchnikov in America, which is how he came to work here. When Metchnikov invested, he did so on the proviso that his man, Karpov, would be employed here. My director's needed the investment and I had no objection to Uri working here. As I said, he was very good at his job, very popular with guests and staff. Anyway, last week, Metchnikov asked to see me on his yacht in Banus. He invited me to lunch and we talked about business and other things, when he told me that he was

225

sending Uri back to America, to head up a new operation there. He asked me not to mention it to Uri as he had not yet told him. He said Uri was stale and he needed a change. He also mentioned he was having girlfriend trouble and he would be better off with a change of scenery."

"Did you know his girlfriend?" interjected Carlos while making notes.

"No, I told Metchnikov that I didn't know he had a permanent one. He was friendly with all the girls that work here and whilst there were always rumours about who he may be seeing, he made it a rule never to get involved with the staff. He may well have had someone from outside, but I never saw him with anyone in particular."

"Would there be any of the girls that he might have spoken to who knew him better personally? Or even a close male colleague?"

"Not that I can think of," said Baz rubbing his forehead. "There are two who he seemed to have coffee with most days, but they are on holiday at the moment."

"When are they back?" asked Carlos.

"At the end of this week I think. As soon as they get back, I will call you."

"How did Uri get on with Metchnikov?"

"They were like father and son. They were friends, but Uri always respected him."

"Do you know of any reason that anyone would want to kill Uri?"

"No! None whatsoever."

"Was he involved with anything outside this office. Perhaps drugs, or smuggling, or anything illegal?"

"Definitely not. In my opinion anyway. He was a very clean living young man who enjoyed his work and was very industrious."

"Did you not think it was strange when he didn't come back to say goodbye or collect his belongings? I take it he left all his paperwork?" said Carlos.

"To a certain extent yes. But most paperwork is finished on a daily basis and his job did not involve much deskbound work. I must admit, I thought he might have come back, but Metchnikov works in strange ways. When he decides to do something, it gets done straight away."

"One last question *Señor* Brown, could you let me have Uri's address, both here and in America, if you have it."

"Certainly, both should be on his form." he picked up the phone and asked the person at the other end to have Uri Karpov's details available for Carlos as he left.

"Well thank you, *Señor* Brown, I'm sure I will have many more questions. I would appreciate it if you did not make too much out of this at the moment until we have finished our enquiries. But please ask around your staff to see if anyone knows anything about Uri or a girlfriend," Carlos got up and extended his hand which Baz took firmly.

"I am very saddened about this, if there is anything more I can do, please let me know."

Carlos went back into the heat from the air conditioning. He sat for a few minutes in his car, making some notes. Igor Metchnikov, here we go.

The barrier lifted as he drove into the Port, already bustling with tourists, and drove to where the guard had told him Metchnikov's yacht was moored. He parked and walked up the gangway. A man in a pony-tail greeted him in Spanish. He asked if *Señor* Metchnikov was available. The pony-tail asked him to wait a moment as he disappeared into the salon. Seconds later he re-appeared and ushered the police officer into the ship's after lounge. Metchnikov came to him and greeted him in English. 'Another one who can't speak my language' thought Carlos. "Please sit down officer," said Metchnikov. "Can I get you something?"

"No thank you," replied Carlos. "I have some questions that I trust you may be able to answer."

"I will try," said the Russian, "I hope there are no irregularities with my boat and the Port. I think everything is up to date, no?"

"It has nothing to do with the Port authority's *Señor*," said Carlos taking out his note book again.

"Do you know a Uri Karpov?"

"Yes, of course," replied Igor without hesitation. "He has worked for me for some years. A bright intelligent hard working young man. Why?"

"Do you know his whereabouts at this time?"

"Let me think. I haven't heard from him yet, but I would think he is with his father by now in California. But he will ring me soon, as he has to start work on a new project next week."

"When did you last see Uri?" enquired Carlos.

"What is this all about officer? Has he done something wrong? I'm sure all of his paperwork was up together. He was a very honest boy, which is why I have employed him for such a long time."

"It is general enquiries *Señor* and I would like to know when you last saw him?"

"I saw him on Thursday. We had lunch together."

"Where?"

"Here, on the boat."

"Did he seem alright?" asked Carlos. Was he upset about anything?

"No. On the contrary," replied Igor, "we were just discussing that I wanted him to take on a new operation in the States. I am about to open a timeshare in San Francisco with some business associates and I wanted Uri to be the General Manager. He has done well here."

"What did he say to that?"

"He was very pleased, he had not seen his father for some time, and he was looking forward to a new challenge."

"What about his girlfriend?"

"What girlfriend?" said Igor.

"I understand that he was having girlfriend trouble" said Carlos pointedly.

"He did mention to me that he would be glad to get away as he had a girl who was trying to get him to marry her or something and he wasn't into that sort of commitment. He was a very free agent."

"Who was she?" asked Carlos

"I have no idea," replied the Russian, "he never mentioned her much. As I said, I don't think it was that important, especially to him, but he was just looking forward to going",

"Did you know that he did not return to work after your meeting?"

"He did imply that he was going home to pack, but I expected him to go back to say good bye. I didn't expect him. to travel until the weekend. Really, what is this all about?"

"Uri Karpov was found washed ashore on San Pedro beach early yesterday morning."

"A swimming or water-skiing accident?" asked Metchnikov, "how awful. He was such a good athlete. I find that hard to believe."

"No," said Carlos, "he was murdered."

"That can't be. Who on earth would want to kill Uri?"

"That, *Señor* Metchnikov, is what I have to find out. Oh, one final question, did you put to sea last Thursday?"

"My dear officer, what is the point of having a luxury yacht if you do not take it out to sea. Lunch on the open sea is a wonderful experience."

Carlos got into his car. He decided he didn't like the Russian and worse than that, he thought he was lying.

He went back to his office to write up his notes and to get authorisation to search Uri's apartment in Marbella. Amongst the messages, was the press wanting to know what was happening, the same from his superiors and the mayor who was also not very happy about the lack of results, and one from Philip Edward's to tell him that the resort where Uri Karpov worked was owned by Igor Metchnikov who had a boat in Banus. 'Thank you Philip,' he thought, 'I already know that.' He said he had been told only the other day and it didn't seem important to anything until Uri was found dead and he had forgotten to mention it. 'Thank you Philip, I hope you don't have anything else hidden away that might be of use to me,' he thought again.

It was nearly two o' clock. He decided he was going to Uri's apartment to see if there was anything there that may throw some light on the whole thing. He went downstairs for a sandwich and a glass of wine. Maybe his trip to Karpov's apartment will help his otherwise dead-end enquiries.

Uri Karpov's apartment was on the eastern side of town, beach-side, in one of the newer developments springing up in the revitalised Marbella. It was a low rise building and Uri's apartment was on the top floor, the fourth, with views of the sea and the mountains behind.

His office had already contacted the administrator, to make sure he was there to meet Carlos when he arrived. He took him up in the lift, along the corridor and opened the door to 4A. He left Carlos and said he would be down in the office on the ground floor, should he want anything else. The apartment was comfortably furnished. It was a bachelor's home. Large TV and video system, hundreds of CDs and a good selection of wines and other drinks. Everything was tidy. He went into the bedroom. The master bedroom had a bathroom en suite. There was another guest room with a guest bathroom in the hall. He went back to the main bedroom. The bed was made, the wardrobe doors were closed, the dressing gown was behind the door. He opened the wardrobe doors. Rows of suits, jackets, trousers and shirts, all neatly placed on the rails.

'The apartment does not look like one that someone is moving from' thought Carlos. No suitcases out, no clothes folded, nothing. A young man like this would have planned his move meticulously —- the same way he lived. He walked back into the lounge. The American kitchen to the side where there was a dining area, was also spotless, with a cup and saucer and plate in the drainer. He opened the fridge. Salad stuffs in the bottom drawer, chilled wines, not so fresh milk and some cold meats. This boy wasn't going anywhere. He never made it back after his meeting with Metchnikov. That must put the time of his death as Thursday afternoon/ evening. And it was more than likely from the boat, when it was at sea. But he had no proof. And why would Metchnikov want to kill Uri? After all according to Brown, they were 'like father and son'. But why else would he have gone out to sea in such circumstances? No, it was definitely from that boat. But why? and how was he going to prove it? He walked over to the window and looked out at the sea. The all powerful water that held so many secrets. He turned and looked down at a side table. His heart skipped a beat. There was a framed picture of Uri and a girl. It didn't need a second look. It was the blonde that fell at Philip's feet. That must have been the girlfriend that Metchnikov had said was giving Uri a hard time. But he wouldn't have killed her for that would he? Perhaps he did. He took the photo out of the frame and put it in his pocket. He continued to look around the apartment, opening drawers and looking for anything that would tie Karpov to the murder of the girl, or his own demise. There was nothing. He would send his officers over to go through everything and list it. He would also have to contact the American Consul in nearby Fuengirola to contact Uri's father. He hated having to do that job and was glad that on this occasion he was not having to do it personally. Although, he was sure that the man's father would come over, in which case, he was going to have to explain his son's murder. He hoped he had solved it by then! He locked the door behind him and went down to see the administrator.

"Nobody must enter that room," he said, " it is the subject of a police investigation. There will be some officers arriving later on to go through the place.

"Very well, but could you please sign this

form," said the little man as he placed some paper in front of Carlos, "just to say that you have the key." Carlos signed and went back to his car.

He drove back to the Costalite resort. Baz Brown was available, he would be out in a minute. He appeared at Carlos side. "How can I help?" he asked, "are you any further forward?'

Carlos held the picture out for Baz to look at. "Do you recognise this girl?," he asked. "Good God," replied the Irishman, that's Katrina.

A wave of relief came over Carlos. He was at last getting somewhere. Before he could ask, Baz told the girl to get Katrina's details.

"I knew he had seen her a couple of times but as I explained, he never got too close to anyone. He was very much the single man. But that's Katrina alright, lovely girl. She was one of the girls that I said was on holiday, who should be back this week."

"I don't think so," said Carlos solemnly, "I am afraid this young lady was found murdered at the beginning of last week."

Baz's mouth dropped in shock. "My God," he spluttered "what the hell is going on down here?"

"That's what I intend to find out," said Carlos in a rather dramatic fashion.

Seconds later the girl gave Carlos a form with all Katrina's details.

He said his thanks and walked out to his car. He sat reading the form. Katrina Ornst, single, blonde and Ukrainian.

At last he had something to go on. But would it be enough?

CHAPTER SEVENTEEN

Glasnost was received in Russia with mixed feelings, but to David Hill and the other CIA agents it was a bitter sweet sensation. Their counterparts in the KGB would also miss the sport.- Gone would be the eavesdropping and the transfer of intelligence. Gone would be the secret rendezvous and the clandestine meetings. It was going to be boring paperwork from now on. His position at the Embassy was now not necessary. Anyone junior could assume the responsibility of 'internal security'. The more important task of Chief Surveillance Officer was now defunct. He had had a good time in Russia these last few years, although his wife and daughter would be glad to have him home in the United States, as soon as possible. He had been getting too old for this stuff now anyway. He was looking forward to a restful situation in the Los Angeles office, not far from his beach home. He would also have more time to visit family in Boston and he and Pamela could enjoy their beach house in California.

He had achieved a fair amount during his time in Moscow. He had never caused a diplomatic row with the sensitive information that he had sent home, neither had he had a run in with any of the Russian heavy mob. The agents from both sides, all with 'proper jobs' to their names, were aware of each other's employment, they even attended the same parties and invariably were watching the same people. During his time there he had almost befriended a member of the security forces and they would occasionally drink together and watch ice hockey and gymnastics. The Russians were brilliant when it came to their athletes and David admired their tenacity for training, although sometimes felt that the young ones were deprived of a normal existence. They had talked about the future as Glasnost was now a reality. He would continue in the security service although he would probably be involved in some mundane pen pushing. The same sort of existence would probably be awaiting David. Crime was rife in Russia during those last few months and, it was destined to get worse. The Russian Mafia were stronger than ever. Drugs, prostitution, stolen goods and even baby selling in Rumania, were making a lot of people wealthy. It would appear that some members of the KGB were getting involved to the extent they were encouraged to look the other way. Others were more actively involved. He would have fond memories, but he had to admit, he would be glad to get home.

Thankfully, there was no need for David to work in Washington. There were satellite offices of the CIA all around America and not least in one of the 'hotter' spots — in both senses of the word — Los Angeles.

The offices in that city were a far cry from the Embassy in Moscow and the little office from which he worked, nearby. But the sun shone and the feeling of freedom lay in the air. Not that crime was any less prevalent here. On the contrary it was probably worse. It was just that here it was out in the open, but in Russia, murders and the like, were carried on behind closed doors. His office was on the third floor and he shared a secretary with three other agents. His task was immigration linked. He liaised with immigration agents and he was to advise them of 'undesirable aliens'. They ran checks on all those people applying for visas and work permits. All nationalities tried to emigrate to America, they always had, but now was the influx from a different country. The Russians had decided that they wanted to see what the free West, that they had heard so much of, was all about. Very few ever got more than a visitor's visa. Unless they were going to invest large sums of money or had some scientific background that was helpful to the United States, none of them got in.

Because of his links with Russia, a certain understanding of the language and, his contacts, he was ideal to assist the immigration offices in this manner. Not a day would go by without him being asked to check over someone's status.

He had a good family life. He had married somewhat later in life than most people of his generation, but a lot of that was due to the type of work that he did. His daughter Susan was an attractive young woman and was following the pursuits that most college girls of her age followed. She was his pride and joy, intelligent, bright and charming. Qualities, he thought, she must have inherited from her mother. He had had her rather late in life, but was enjoying the challenge of being an older parent. His daughter had said on many occasions that he was an 'alright Dad', even if he was 'a bit old!' Pamela, herself some years younger than her husband, was a stunningly attractive woman with a zest for life. She was not as shallow as some of the women that resided among the glamour and the palm trees. Maybe its because she was from a Boston family, where life was somewhat different to the Californian dream. They both enjoyed their golf and tennis and the local country club supplied them with a fair amount of entertainment including dining out with friends, who, were very few and valued. His life had made it difficult to make friends and most acquaintances were normally short-lived.

They lived well. They had a house in Boston, inherited from family — she was the only child — and had, Since returning from Russia, bought an old house in Spain. The property in Marbella, belonged to an ex-diplomat that David had met some years previously. They had kept in touch before his move to Moscow and since his return. Once, when he was on leave, they went over to Spain to see him. He had become frail and was returning to the United States and David had asked what he was going to do about the house. He was selling. Pamela loved the house, so did David. That evening they had wandered around the grounds. How would they pay for it? She still had money on deposit from the very healthy inheritance she had had from her family. Why not? They could retire there and play golf on the Coast's numerous courses. The deal was done. They spent the last few days of their vacation sorting out the legal and financial details before returning home. On the journey back they talked about David taking early retirement. They didn't need the extra money she had told him, they had sufficient. Susan was taken care of and they could sell the house in Los Angeles or Boston, whichever. They certainly didn't need three houses, especially the huge family house.

After their vacation, their return to America filled them full of excitement. Not for their homecoming, but for the future that lay ahead. He would apply for his early retirement, they would put the house in Boston and, the beach house in Los Angeles, up for sale and find a condo on the beach near to there, San Diego or somewhere, and settle for most of the time in Spain. A country they had fallen in love with. They would leave when Susan had finished college. She could come with them if she wanted, if not, she could have the condo. The chances were, that the bright young woman would do her own thing and travel the world. They set their target date for two years from then. Meanwhile, they would take vacations in their villa in Spain.

The phone rang shrilly, piercing the calm of the balmy Californian evening. David reached out and automatically put his hand on the receiver. It was Ellen, one of Susan's friends. She had been with her that evening to dinner and a party. She was hysterical. She was crying and, in between sobs, was telling David that there had been an awful accident. Susan had collapsed and had been taken to Los Angeles Memorial Hospital. He quickly pulled himself out of bed. It was two in the morning. "What is it?" asked Pamela. "It's Susan," he replied, "there has been an accident. She is in hospital."

"What sort of an accident?" Pamela cried in panic. "She should have been home at one. What has happened?" The two of them dressed quickly and were going to the bottom of the stairs when there was a ring at the door. The police had arrived to inform the Hills of their daughter's accident. But, it was no accident, it was drug related. "My daughter doesn't take drugs," David remembered protesting, "she never has."

"To our knowledge," his wife had shouted.

They were given a lift to the hospital in the black and white. They went to reception to ask about their daughter. "Just one minute," replied the duty nurse. Minutes later, a young doctor came to greet them.

"Your daughter has been poisoned by a man made, designer, drug. It was taken in tablet form. It caused her to dehydrate, which she compensated for by drinking more water. This has induced a coma. I'm sorry, but at the moment, there is nothing we can do, except wait. And pray."

Pamela was in tears. Ellen had appeared in the door way. Her eyes red from crying. She walked shakily over to David, who opened his arms to comfort the grief stricken girl.

"I'm sorry" she cried, "I didn't see her take it. I never knew she took them." She sobbed and sobbed, while David ran a comforting hand over her head. Pamela was holding on to him, her head on his shoulder. Tears welled up into his eyes. 'God, don't take my only daughter,' he prayed to himself.

They stayed all night and through into the next morning. Ellen's parents had come to pick her up and her mother had offered to stay with Pamela, but the offer was gracefully refused. David had promised to ring as soon as there was any news. They had kept a vigil by her bedside. The plethora of tubes that ran from the machine and, the drip feeds to her body, seemed to trap her and tie her to the bed. Pictures of her playing net ball, running through the park, riding and showing off her new dress for the prom were all going through David's mind. The doctor came in and asked them to leave as he was going to examine her again. They went out into the waiting area and over to the picture window and watched Los Angles rise to the dawn. That strange eerie moment when the sun breaks through and the night lights still flicker as the light fog rolls in from the sea. "It will be alright," he had said as he ran his hands through Pamela's hair. Their tranquillity was broken as the doors to the waiting room opened and in walked the handsome young doctor, his face drained and his eyes full of grief. "Please sit down," he had asked. "I'm so sorry, but Susan is technically dead. The machines are keeping her alive. Her brain is dead and her body is lifeless. It can serve no purpose to just keep her breathing by machine. I have to ask you to let me turn it off so as she can rest in peace."

"No, no. She can't be. My little girl," sobbed Pamela, "please no." She clung to David. He bit his lip hard. So hard he drew blood. He had seen so much in his life. Death, torture and misery, but nothing could compare to this. Nothing could be worse than a parent seeing their child die before them, especially so needlessly.

He nodded his head in agreement.

"I will send in a nurse for your wife," he continued, "will you be alright?" Again David nodded affirmatively, his wife now shaking and sobbing uncontrollably. The nurse came in as David was trying, unsuccessfully, to comfort Pamela.

"I will have to take her to a ward, she is suffering from shock. Let her lie down for a while, she will come round soon." She called for a chair and Pamela was taken, crying and moaning, down to a ward. David walked back over to the window and stared as ant like figures made their way around the town, going about their daily Saturday morning business. Early morning deliveries and shoppers eager to be the first to the door as if catching some monumental bargains. Children with their parents taking dogs for walks, riding bikes, walking in the park, all the normal day to day things that families do. Always did. And those that can, will continue to do so. He placed his forehead on the cold plate window, his breath causing a patch of condensation, and he cried. At first a whimper, then uncontrollable sobbing. He was no longer an 'alright Dad'.

Pamela had been kept in hospital for observation, leaving David with the task of arranging the funeral. She had suffered from severe shock and was continually tranquillised. The results of the post mortem had plunged her into even greater depths of despair. Susan had had no record of drug taking. She had been at a party at a local disco when she was approached by a group of young men who had offered her a tablet that would increase her awareness of the music and give her energy to dance all night. The Ecstasy tablet was bad and induced a heavy thirst which when quenched produces excess water in the system which invariably culminates in a coma and subsequent death. The verdict: Accidental Death. As far as David was concerned it was: 'Death by Person or Persons Unknown'; And he was going to find out whom. But first he had to bury his little girl and get his wife better and back home again. The former had been easy to arrange but difficult to see through. The service was emotional and touchingly delivered by the local Vicar: There were no Uncles or Aunts or Grandparents, but this was adequately made up for with family friends, school friends, college friends and lecturers, local police and even the managers of the disco, who provided police with as much information as possible, impressing upon the authorities that they have a no drugs on the premises' rule.

Pamela was not permitted to attend. She was in no fit state to go anyway. She had got worse over the previous week and doctors had said it would be dangerous for her to have to cope with the situation. After the service and the cremation, David was persuaded to come for a drink with a couple of his colleagues, and their wives, from the agency,

He didn't want to, but he knew he would end up going back to the house and opening a bottle of Bourbon on his own, so best he shared his sorrows with some close friends. The drinking lasted less than an hour and David thanked everyone, but said he was tired, and wanted to go home. He returned to an empty house with the resolve that he was going to do something to help find his daughter's murderer.

It did not take him long to sort out Susan's stuff. He asked Ellen, her best friend, if she felt strong enough to help. The pretty young girl appeared punctually and between them they opened wardrobes and drawers and packed things away in boxes.

"Take whatever you want," he had told Ellen,

but she said she felt funny. "She would want you to have her things, I'm sure," he had said consolingly. Ellen took some of her CD's, her favourite stuffed toy, and while packing them separately burst into tears. David sat on the bed and pulled the distraught young girl to his side.

"I'm going to miss her," cried the girl.

"So will I," replied the grieving father. "Tell me Ellen," he continued "did you know the people who gave her the tablet?"

"No. I didn't see her being given anything."

"Did you see her talking to anyone you didn't know?"

"She was a very friendly person, she often talked and danced with strangers." Ellen had stopped crying and was now feeling as if she was offering something constructive in the way of help.

"So, that night was there anyone talking to Susan, that you did not recognise as being a friend of either of you?"

"There were two guys, I had seen them before," she wiped her red eyes, "they are always at the club."

"Did you tell the police?" David had asked.

"They never asked me that question."

"Would you recognise them again?"

"Yes, I'm sure I would."

They continued their packing. Ellen came across Susan's diary and put it into her box. She felt that she would never have wanted her dad to read it, no matter what.

After Ellen had helped carry the boxes to the garage and had said goodbye, David did a final check of the bedroom, tidied up and closed the door.

He would wait until Pamela came home before he would make a decision as to what to do with everything. 'When she comes home' he had thought. She had got no better. In fact she had got worse since the funeral.

He went in every night and just sat there talking to her. She didn't move she just stared up at the ceiling. She wouldn't eat properly and had to be fed. Doctors had said that she had lost the will to live.

It was three weeks after the funeral that she was allowed home. She had got out of the car unsteadily and David had to help her to the front door. He sat her in the chair and made some tea for her. He put on the television and left her to accustom herself to her home. When he went back she had not moved.

It was obviously going to be a long hard road to recovery. The doctor had suggested a nurse to be with her during the day while David was at work and to be on hand for the psychiatrist's visits on alternate days.

David's work was suffering due to his family situation and he had asked his boss if his application for early retirement could be brought forward so as he could look after his wife. This was granted. They paid him handsomely for his services plus a sick pension as well; And, almost to the year that they had come back from Spain and, on his 57th birthday, he shook hands with his colleagues and left the offices of the CIA for what he thought would be the last time.

He had just finished clearing away the supper things when the door bell rang. It was Ellen.

"I thought you would like this," she said, handing him Susan's diary. "There was nothing of any delicate nature in there," she said coyly, "but there is a name that comes up frequently and, in the same context, drugs are mentioned. I thought it would be more use to you than the police; Anyway, you can always give it to them after if you want."

"Thank you Ellen," he said, "would you like to come in and see Mrs Hill?"

"No, thank you, my boyfriend's waiting." She turned and went down the drive.

He walked into the lounge where Pamela was sitting. He read through the diary and started talking to his wife. "There may be some information in here that could help us catch Susan's murderers," he said casually.

"For Christ's sake," shouted Pamela, throwing the cup and saucer from the side table, "she's dead and gone can't you understand, nothing will bring her back. Not God, not the police, not you or the whole of the bloody CIA: Nobody cares. She's just another figure in the statistics." And then she burst into uncontrollable shakes and sobbing. David tried to comfort her but was pushed aside. He called the psychiatrist's mobile number. Within half an hour he was sitting at Pamela's side. "Let's get her to bed," he said lifting her up onto her feet. David came over and took her other arm and helped take her upstairs.

"Go and pour me a scotch David, I'll be down in a minute."

He had already had one by the time the Doctor appeared to take his.

"I have to tell you, that Pamela is very ill."

"But she just spoke and, very animatedly I must say," said David picking up another piece of broken china from the carpet.

"That is not as good as it would appear," continued the doctor. "This means that she is perfectly capable of speaking but chooses not to. She listens to and understands everything that is going on around her, but wishes to take no part in it. All her emotion is bottled up inside her. She has not grieved fully for her daughter. Not going to the funeral didn't help, although at the time it might have made things worse. She is aware that she is dead and that nothing will bring her back. Most women in her state wander into bedrooms picking up things that relate to their children, almost pretending that they have just 'gone away and will be back soon', but Pamela doesn't do this. She is basically suffering from acute depression and is like a time bomb waiting to go off. She neither cares whether she lives nor dies. She just doesn't care about anything. She needs lots of care David and I think she ought to be in a psychiatric hospital, or she may do herself some damage."

"I've been with her for twenty three years, all of which have been wonderful and I have no intention of letting her leave this house unless it is to do what she wants to do." He poured himself another drink and offered the bottle to the doctor.

"Thank you, no! Very well, if that's what you want, but she needs plenty of love and understanding. If you need me, just call. I'll see myself out."

"Thank you Felix" said David as he sat back in his chair and fingered the red diary on the arm. He opened it and read over some of the pages. He saw the name and how he had tried to get his daughter to try some drugs, but how she had refused. His eyes moistened as he saw his life and plans breaking into little pieces, all because of some little fucking bastard, he drew a pencil ring around the boy's name, Jimmy.

It had been six weeks since they buried Susan. One evening after he had given Pamela her dinner, she hardly touched it as usual, and cleared up, he told her was going out for an hour and drove down to the 'Highball' night club to speak to the manager. The doorman called up to say that there was someone. at the door wishing to see Mr Wild. A smartly dressed man in his early thirties extended a hand. "Hello Mr Hill, how are you?"

"You know me then?" said David.

"Of course. I was at the funeral and your pictures have been in the press somewhat over the weeks. I hear your wife is not well." They walked into the lounge, all polished and cleaned. Barmen were busy stocking up their shelves awaiting the onslaught of young people that would have the cash registers bouncing by the end of the night.

"No, she is suffering from severe depression brought on by Susan's murder."

"I thought the coroner returned a verdict of accidental death," said Wild.

"What do you think?" said David, "someone had to give them to her."

"How can I help Mister Hill? I've already told the police what I know and what my staff saw. We really do have a no drugs policy here and my doormen are very strict. Obviously they can't stop and search everyone that comes in here, but they do look for the tell tale signs and the bathrooms are constantly checked."

"Surely you must know who the pushers are," said David defiantly.

"I have told you Mister Hill, if anyone is known to have anything to do with drugs, they are kept out."

"What about a boy named Jimmy? You must know if he is a pusher."

"Mister Hill, I do not know my customers by name. This is not a private club and over 400 people a night come here to dance and drink. Some nights a few people get thrown out for taking drugs, sniffing cocaine or whatever. Sometimes they get thrown out for getting drunk. We do not ban the occasional drunk, but we do remember the druggies. We do our best, but I really can't help you any further. As much as I would like to."

"Yes, I'm sorry," said David as he made his

way to the exit. "Thank you for seeing me."

"Not at all," said Wild as he watched the distressed and disheartened man make his way to his car.

When he got home, he carried out the same routine of making Pamela a cup of tea and taking it up to her in bed.

The TV was on, but the sound was off. He told her where he had been. and what had happened, but she said absolutely nothing.

As usual.

The following day he phoned Ellen and asked her if he could talk to her. She said she was going out bowling with her boyfriend Tod. David said he would meet her there as it wouldn't take more than a few minutes for him to say what he wanted. The bowling alley was packed with youngsters enjoying themselves. Susan normally came here on Wednesday nights after her studying, just for a couple of hours. He saw Ellen and her friend sitting by the bar. He walked over and asked if he could join them. The young man introduced himself.

"I just wanted to know when you would be going back to the Highball Club again" said David.

"I haven't been there since, well since Susan"

"Yes, it's alright Ellen, I understand. But I do need to know about Jimmy. Could you find out about him? Perhaps his full name, where he lives, where he hangs out. Even a picture of him or a good description."

The girl hesitated and looked at the young man. He offered no resistance. She looked back at David Hill, her eyes looked into his and he could feel her emotion and fear. "I don't think that I can ..."

"Ellen, we have got to stop this thing happening again. To anyone. Susan's life was wasted, let's see if we can prevent someone else going the same way."

She thought for a moment longer. "OK. I'll go on Friday."

"Not without me you don't," said the young man. Tod, if I'm to talk to this guy, I can't have you near me." she was confident.

"Alright, I see what you mean, but we will go separately but I'll be there to keep an eye on you." As David left he couldn't help but admire their courage. He just hoped it would help.

Saturday lunchtime David was mowing the lawn when the portable phone rang, on the windowsill, where he had left it for convenience. Pamela never answered the phone any more so it was easier to take the portable with him whenever he went around the house. It was Ellen.

"His name is Jimmy Mutch. He's in his early twenties he's about five foot ten weighing about 140 pounds, with short dark hair and his phone number is 5585519."

"You should work for the CIA," quipped David. "Well done, very well done. Are you O.K.?"

"Yes, fine. It gave me a bit of a buzz, knowing I was chatting him up for the wrong reasons."

"Or the right ones, depending on which way

you look at it" said David

"Yes, I suppose so. The only thing is he wants a date and I don't. Neither does Tod," she laughed, "so I'll just have to keep away from the place. No problem." She hung up.

He put the phone down. At last he had something. He went back inside to see how Pamela was. She was looking thin and drawn. Her colouring was grey. She never went out. He spoke to her but she mumbled something incomprehensible. He went down to his study and phoned Frank at work. He asked him for a trace on a number. No problem he had said and within minutes David had the address of his quarry.

He drove his car down through the seedier parts of town until he came to the intersection written on the piece of paper. He turned left and drove slowly along until he found the number that Frank had given him. He parked and got out. It was 9.30 am. The night rat would still be in bed. He knocked on the door. He knocked again. A muffled, sleepy voice called out, "Yeah, Who is it?"

"Delivery for Mister Jimmy Mutch," shouted David. There was a few minutes silence, before the door opened slightly. David looked through the security chain and saw enough of the face to convince him that this was the little shit that he wanted to talk to. Instinctively, he kicked the door, busting the chain, and smashing it into the kid's face sending him reeling across the squalid room, towards the bed where a young girl sat upright, sheets covering her body, screaming. In three strides David had the punk by his hair and lifted him off the floor and pushed him against the wall. The girl was still screaming. David turned and yelled at her to shut up. She did. The kid was totally vulnerable as his nakedness proclaimed. "Where do you get your drugs?" he yelled, his face right up against the young man's own.

"I don't know what you're talking about," he replied, obviously frightened.

David grabbed his balls and squeezed. The boy let out a yell. David squeezed harder.

"OK, OK!" screamed Jimmy with tears in his eyes, "I'll tell you." David released his grip. The kid stepped back and pushed his head forward connecting with David's forehead, making him feel dizzy and nauseous. He staggered as the kid made a bolt for the door. The ex- CIA man made a lunge and dragged the boy to the floor. He slapped him around the face and. dragged him up again by the hair. This time he held him against the wall by his throat and once again grabbed Him threatening to curtail his sexual activity for some time to come.

"They'll kill me if I tell you," he squealed.

"I'll kill you if you don't," replied David tightening his grip.

"Alright, alright," cried the boy. "His name is Benny, he's not American, I don't know where he's from."

"What does he look like?" shouted David pressing his thumb on the kid's Adam's apple.

"Six foot plus with long black hair in a pony tail," choked the boy.

"Where can I find him," David was now shouting at the punk to frighten him further.

"I don't know," tears were now rolling down his cheeks. David tightened his grip with both hands. The kid's eyes were bulging and sweat was pouring off his forehead. David could feel the warm wetness on his hands as the kid's fear overcame him. "Really I don't," sobbed the snivelling rat, "I only meet him in the clubs. Honest."

David released the boy and he stood there crying. The man lunged forward, repaying the compliment. His head connected with the boy's. There was a crack, a yell of pain and, the naked body slipped down the wall, with blood pouring from his nose. 'That's for Susan,' he said under his breath. He turned toward the bed, where the girl was crying, her mouth covered with the pillow to prevent the frightened sounds from enraging the violence of the perpetrator. He wiped his urine coated hand on the sheet, shook his head at her and, walked out of the room. '

He parked his car in the underground car park of the familiar office block and took the lift to the third floor. The secretary was pleased to see him as were his colleagues. Frank came over, "Hi David, how ya' doin'?" and shook his hand firmly. "How's Pamela?"

"Still bad I'm afraid. Listen Frank, thanks for your help yesterday, but I need some more."

"Shoot," replied the affable CIA man.

"The punk that I saw this morning told me

that his dealer was a guy named Benny. A six-footer with long black hair tied in a pony tail. He deals around the clubs. Now you have a friend in narcotics don't you. Would he be able to find this guy.

"Sure, he probably knows him if he's a pusher." He picked up the phone and punched in some numbers, "His name is Fernandez, Micky Fernandez. He's Hispanic, knows the streets and, the scum in them, backwards. Fernandez, narcotics," he said into the mouthpiece.

"Micky, Frank Kent. Hi. Listen have you got a few minutes, I've got something that might interest you. Ten minutes at Dino's. Fine." He put the phone down. "Come on, I'll buy you a late breakfast." They walked downstairs and across the road to the popular Dino's Diner, the haunt of CIA men, their contacts, local police and criminals, lawyers and whores. A den of iniquity and information. Two coffees and two chicken on rye with mayonnaise later, a young long-haired, unshaven, leather jacketed, young man came in. David smiled to himself. All undercover cops looked the same these days. It was more of a uniform, than a uniform. The best way to be undercover, he reckoned, must be to wear a suit or a blazer and slacks. After the introductions and a further coffee, the sandwich was refused, David started to explain what he wanted.

"I'm sorry about your daughter," said Fernandez as he spooned four heaped sugars into his coffee mug, then lit a cigarette. "No matter how hard we try, we can't rid the streets of the problem. Mainly 'cause the kids all need their kicks and can't seem to get them from normal pastimes." He stirred his coffee intently, "We know this big guy, he has been around for some time. We've not got anything on him. He's Russian. He works for some fat cat that has legitimate business here, Metchnikov. He's in import export, that sort of thing. We have never been able to pin anything on him either"

"Well now you've got something," interrupted David.

"You know better than that Mister Hill," continued the cop, "we need proof and possession. At this moment in time. we have nothing. But I appreciate the lead. Where did you get it from?"

"A friend of my daughter's, —- indirectly," lied David. "I'm sure he's the one responsible for those kids in the club getting their drugs and for selling sub standard Ecstasy tablets."

"Leave it with me Mister Hill, I'll keep Frank informed. He got up and shook hands, leaving a full mug of sweetened coffee.

"Let's go back to the office and see what we have on Metchnikov," said David.

"Wait a minute" replied Frank, "I think we should leave this to the cops now. You're not with the Agency any more, and this is not an official investigation."

"So?" continued David, "let's have an unofficial look." He smiled, "For old times' sake." The two men got up. Frank put some money on the counter and they walked back to the office.

"Metchnikov," said Frank as the information came up on the screen, "granted a visitor's visa for three months, two years ago. Applied for a green card on the basis that he was going to set up an import export business and employ American nationals. Invested money in the First National. His application is being processed and he will probably get his residency, no mention of any partners or sidekicks." He pressed print and the information was swiftly dispatched. David picked it up and folded it. "David?" Frank looked at his old friend, "that information is not for ex—CIA agents. Please don't do anything stupid. I would hate to see you in trouble."

"Thanks Frank," he shook his old partner's hand, "I'll be a model citizen."

He went back down in the lift and got into his car. He looked at the address on the sheet of printed paper, started the engine and drove slowly out of the garage. The sunlight poured into the cool car and David put on his sunglasses. 'Just like old times,' he thought as he pulled onto the freeway.

The warehouse had a smart office frontage that belied the rest of the building. There was a young female receptionist at a desk as he went in.

"Can I speak to Igor Metchnikov? said David authoritatively.

"Who wants him?" replied the bottle blonde. '

David took out his wallet. Whilst he no longer had his shield, his I.D. had CIA on it and he thought that would be enough as the girl had probably never seen one before.

She seemed unmoved, "I'm afraid he's not here at the moment, can I take a message?"

"When will he be here?" continued David looking around.

"I've no idea," she replied.

"What if I want to write to him?" he said sarcastically.

"Then just write care of this address. He doesn't come here, someone collects his mail and messages."

"When?"

"It varies. I'm sorry I really can't help you anymore. If you wish to leave a message then please do so, otherwise you will have to leave." David smiled at the girl. 'She's confident, he thought.

"No message" he said, "but I'll be back."

He stood back on the side-walk, the Californian afternoon sun beating down on him. It was past three and he had been out of the house since nine. The nurse had called in as the psychiatrist was due to visit Pamela in the morning. She would only have been alone for a couple of hours and was probably sleeping anyway. He would sit in his car for a while and watch the warehouse, just in case he saw anything of interest. By five, nothing had happened. No sign of the Russian or the pony tail. He would go home and give Frank a ring and let him know he was being a good boy. His wife had been on her own for long enough and he had to get some food for her.

He opened his front door and went over to

the flashing answer phone. There were two messages. He pressed play.

"Mister Hill, this is Detective Micky Fernandez, we've had a complaint from a kid who reckons you harassed him in his own home. I've spoken to Frank and he has said he will speak to you. Let me tell you something, ex—CIA or not, I don't like loose cannons on my patch, interfering with my work. Keep off this. If you keep interfering with police investigations, I'll run you in so fast your ass won't catch up with your feet. Have you got that?" '

"David, it's Frank. What the hell are you doing. Fernandez has been on to me chewing me out. And another thing, Metchnikov is under FBI investigation so for Christ's sake leave it alone. Do you understand David. You're retired. Act like it."

'Well' thought David, 'that's me well and truly chewed out.' He called Pamela's name and went into the lounge. She was obviously still in bed. He went upstairs into the bedroom. She was lying on her back fast asleep. He walked over and sat on the edge of the bed. A cold sweat ran over him.

On the bedside table was an empty bottle of antidepressants and a near empty glass of what appeared to be water, but on tasting it, was neat vodka. She was cold, he felt her neck, there was no pulse. He lifted her head and pulled her to his chest. He rocked her back and forward like a child does her doll and he cried. Someone would pay for all this. "I swear someone will pay for this."

CHAPTER EIGHTEEN

There were a few messages on the answer-phone, one from Sandy saying she would be home late, one from Gerry arranging a time for golf for the next day and one from Carlos asking me to meet him at the restaurant. That would suit, as Sandy wasn't going to be back until later, I could have a bit of supper there, if they weren't too busy. I showered, more to cool down than to clean up and, poured myself a large gin and tonic and sat on the terrace for a few minutes while I dried off. Half an hour later I parked in the basement and walked up to the restaurant. The terrace was full and there were people at the bar waiting for tables outside. Even though we had air conditioning people still preferred the outside during the summer. Carlos was at the bar, this time he was out of uniform. It blends better at night, he said he didn't feel quite so conspicuous, although his big frame invariably warranted a second glance. We shook hands. I ordered a further gin and tonic as the other one had gone down so well.

"Before we start, I meant to tell you about Metchnikov but I forgot, I'm sorry."

"That's OK, I found out much of that myself. I went to the resort manager this morning and Metchnikov straight after".

"What did they have to say?" I asked.

"Not much, just that Uri was due to go to America and as far as everyone was concerned, he had left to do just that. But, I don't trust Metchnikov. Have you any further information that you think I could use, that you haven't told me yet?"

"No," I replied sheepishly. "I'm sorry. I don t know anything else. It was only that I was told about the association the other day and I didn't think of it again until Uri was found dead. How did the rest of the day go?"

"We are at last getting somewhere," he said with relief.

"We know who your blonde was, at last."

"Who?" after a week of wondering, I was as relieved as he was.

"Her name was Katrina Ornst. She was Russian/Ukrainian as we assumed. She was the girlfriend of Uri Karpov and she worked with him at the time-share resort."

"Good grief, how did you find this out?" I asked impressed.

"I went to Uri's apartment and found a picture of them together, so I naturally asked Brown if he recognised her; and he did."

"So how does it all fit together, and who did it?"

"Well, that is something I'm not sure about. I reckon that Uri killed her, although it would seem he's not really the type."

"Is there ever a type?" I asked.

"No, that's true," he said returning to his conversation, "then someone killed him and the others. Metchnikov said that Uri was leaving to go to America, but he never went to the resort to say goodbye and his apartment was immaculate and did not look as if it was being left behind. No clothes were packed, his suitcases were on top of the wardrobe. So, I reckon he did not know he was going away and he certainly did not know that he was going to get killed; And, I have a feeling that Metchnikov and his henchmen had something to do with it, but at the moment I can't prove a thing. I still cannot link the others to it all, though.

"Well I think you have done well in one day considering yesterday, you had virtually nothing."

"Yes but now I need some reasoning. Why did Uri kill his girlfriend? If indeed he did. Why did Metchnikov kill Uri? — if again he did — as they seemed to be so close. Who are the other two? Why were they kidnapping a child? And who killed them —- and why? So you see Philip, I am not really that far forward."

"Not when you put it like that, I suppose," I said taking another mouthful of gin and tonic. "Are you staying for supper? I am because Sandy is coming home late."

"I would like that," he said, "I was going out last night, but fell asleep on the terrace. Today I only had a sandwich, so I'm ready for a good meal."

We sat inside, glorying in the air-conditioning. We ordered some Serrano ham. Carlos asked for a fillet steak and I had some plain grilled lamb's kidneys and we shared a bowl of salad. We just had a bottle of house red, which we got straight on to with the ham.

"I now have to ensure that a letter goes to the

family of the dead people whom we have identified," he said, "I have contacted the American Consul in Fuengirola and she will contact Uri's father. The Spanish Embassy in Moscow will have the problem of contacting Katrina Ornst's parents in Russia."

"What are you going to do next?" I asked, fairly sure that he must have a plan of action.

"I really don't know," he replied honestly. "I have to find out who the other people were, why they kidnapped the baby, what relationship they were to Karpov, Metchnikov or Ornst. And, I have to find out more about Metchnikov himself. I don't like him and I don't trust him. I will have to contact Interpol and the agencies in Russia and America. It will take time, but then, a lot of police work is time consuming".

We finished our coffees and brandies, we had changed the conversation and had discussed the forthcoming local elections, football, his barbecue the following weekend and, most other things, without further reference to the events of the last week. We said goodbye outside the restaurant which had now quietened down. He drove off and I walked down toward the seafront to walk along the *paseo* for a short while. The warm summer evening's calm was broken by the revelry of young people, enjoying Spain's hospitality. The freedom to sit outside and eat and drink until the early hours, with music to keep them company. It was past midnight when I got home and Sandy pulled up at the same time. We smiled at each other as we got out of the cars and she came over and kissed me. "Had a nice evening?" we both said at the same time. We laughed and went up to the apartment where we sat on the balcony with a brandy and watched the lights in the Marina and listened to the distant *flamenco* music from one of the Spanish restaurants. It was two in the morning before we eventually got to sleep.

I sat bolt upright in bed. Of course. It was staring me right in the face and I hadn't even thought about it. There we were with Russians coming out of our ears and the likes of Karpov and Metchnikov from the United States and we had our own, on the ground, CIA man. He dealt with the Russian immigrant population, he would surely have some contacts that might bypass the network and paperwork involved in going through proper channels. I laid back down again. I would go and see him in the morning.

The familiar face greeted me warmly despite the unscheduled call. "This is an unexpected pleasure," said David Hill, "Come in." We walked through into his patio. There was coffee on the table and he offered me some. I accepted. He got another cup and poured out the hot black liquid.

"What I am going to ask you, will sound very strange," I said getting to the point, "and you can of course tell me to mind my own business, but a friend of mine is a senior officer with the Guardia Civil and is investigating the murders that I mentioned to you the other day. We have found out that the people involved, at this moment in time, appear to be Russian. Two of them, one dead and one very much alive, seem to have come over from America It's a long shot but, I thought you may like to help." I took a sip of coffee waiting for some reaction from the man.

"I am very much retired Philip and, whilst I would like to help you and your friend, I really feel that you should go through the proper channels. It may take a little longer, but it would be better."

"Yes, I suppose it was silly of me even to think you might be able to help. It's just that Metchnikov seems to be so insulated from authority ..."

"Damn," he cried and stood up quickly as he tried to rub the hot coffee from his slacks.

"Are you alright?" I asked, seeing full well what had happened. " .

"Yes, I'm fine," he said abruptly. Did you say Metchnikov?

Yes, he moved over here some time ago and we think he may have something to do with the murder of at least one person."

He moved towards his drinks cabinet, wiping himself down and poured two brandies and brought them over. "You may need this," he said handing me a small cut glass balloon.

Puzzled I took a small sip. "Why?" I naturally enquired. He excused himself for a minute and returned with a sheet of folded paper which he handed to me. I opened it and looked at the top of the paper.

Central Intelligence Agency. ' Application for Resident and Work Permits. Russian Immigrants. Classified Information. Metchnikov, Igor

I looked at David Hill. '

"I think I had better tell you something about my past. I have not been truthful with you. Basically because there was no need to be. My life, both good and bad, would not have been of any interest to you; And, as much as I like you and your girlfriend, I did not see that I owed you any explanation."

I listened intently as he recounted the story of his years in Russia, his family, his plans, the death of his daughter and that of his wife and his brief investigations into the men that he felt were responsible. I sat flabbergasted when he had finished. He got up, looked at my empty glass and said, "I told you, you would need it." He refilled it.

"Good Lord, that is some story. I feel that I have watched a full length movie inside of twenty minutes. No wonder you hate this guy with a vengeance. Couldn't you, with your contacts, have done anything about it?"

"As I told you, the FBI were investigating and, as a retired CIA man I was told to keep well out of the way. When I found my wife had committed suicide I lost interest in everything. It was like God was telling me to leave it alone. Although in my heart of hearts I just wanted to kill the son-of-a—bitch, I felt I should sell up and get out. I had lost my daughter and wife in less than six months, had given up my job, they wouldn't have wanted me back anyway, and, the only thing I had left, was the house here that we both loved so much. But, when I got here, there were too many memories, hence the reason for selling."

I was shell shocked. "So, can you help?" I asked helplessly, feeling out of my depth.

"Come back here this evening at about eight and I will put a call in to my friends — if I have any left."

"Can I bring a friend of mine. He's a journalist that has been trying to find things about Metchnikov. Perhaps between you, you may be able to help answer a few questions."

"Sure, why not? But he mustn't write, or say anything to anyone, yet. And don't you say anything either. OK?"

"No, of course not. And thank you."

I got back home and phoned Gerry, he wasn't in so I left a message for him to meet me at the restaurant at lunchtime before we played golf, if we did. Sandy had left soon after me. I phoned her mobile and told her I would be going to the restaurant at lunchtime if she wanted to meet. She said she had a production meeting and was unable to, but she would come with me to David Hill's in the evening. I left home and called into Chris Yeo's to pick up a cheque, before going to the restaurant. He wasn't there but an envelope was waiting for me with another client's property to photograph. There was no urgency thank God, because, I had to admit, this was absorbing all my time and energy.

I put the cheque into my account in the bank on the comer and continued on to the restaurant. Paul was in the office doing his paperwork. He also gave me a cheque. If the day carries on like this I thought, it would be very satisfactory. We talked briefly before Julian came in to tell me there was a call from Gerry. I picked up the phone.

"I know it's not lunchtime just yet," said the familiar voice, "but I've got your message and I'm not doing anything, so I'll come straight over. I just wanted to check you are there."

"Fine," I said, "I'll see you in a minute." I put the phone down. "I'm going into the bar Paul, I'll see you in a sec."

It didn't take long before Gerry appeared. We had a beer and I told him what had happened.

"You had better bring me up to speed on the whole thing then, because I haven't spoken to you or Carlos since our lunch on Sunday. And it looks as if a lot has happened since then."

I started to tell him basically what Carlos had told me, when the phone rang. "It's Carlos," I said to Gerry putting my hand over the small mouthpiece.

"We have a further positive development," he said, "the girl that shared Katrina's apartment has just returned to find police officers going through her home. She is a bit upset. Perhaps you would like to come over and maybe do a bit of interpreting.

"Sure, where is it?" He told me. "I've got

270

Gerry with me, can he come along?" I looked over and saw him nodding in anticipation.

"As long as he is aware that this investigation is still not over and he cannot write or say anything."

"I'll tell him," I said cutting off. "Come on," I continued, "we're off to Parque Marbella. And you can't write, or say, anything."

During the short drive back to the apartment block, I brought my friend up to date with the happenings as best I could. "But, I promised David Hill that I wouldn't say anything to anyone, including Carlos, until after this evening."

"Well, I hope he doesn't find out you are withholding information from him, or you certainly won't be one of his favourite foreigners."

When we arrived at the door of the apartment, it was ajar. We walked in to find a young woman sitting, with her feet tucked under her, twisting a tear filled handkerchief around her fingers. Carlos was sitting opposite her, his imposing frame bearing down on her.

The other police, apart from a female officer still in the room, had obviously left.

"This is an Englishman named Philip Edwards," he said to the girl, "this is Diana," said Carlos as his way of introduction.

"Hi," I said, "this is a friend of ours, Gerry Peters. Are you alright?"

"I just don't know what's going on," she said in a thick Liverpudlian accent. 'No wonder Carlos couldn't understand her,' I thought.

"Perhaps you would like to tell us what you know," I asked in my best bedside manner.

"I don't know anything," she sobbed.

"Look," I pleaded, "you are not in any sort of trouble, but this police officer is a very senior civil guard and he is investigating some serious incidents and he needs to know anything you can tell him about your flat mate Katrina." I looked over to Carlos and, in Spanish, asked if he had told her about Katrina and Uri. He said he hadn't. Was I able to? I asked. 'Carefully', he replied.

"I said goodbye to Katrina when I went on holiday a couple of weeks ago. She said she was taking some time off work, because her ex-boyfriend was coming over."

"Uri Karpov?" I interrupted.

"No, Uri is her present boyfriend," she said unknowingly, "her ex was coming over from the Ukraine."

Carlos was still having a little difficulty following her accent. I quickly translated. He looked at me and told me, in Spanish, to ask his name.

"I don't know, I don't think she told me. If she did, I don't remember."

"What did he look like," I continued.

"I don't know, I never saw him, I've told you."

"No pictures or anything?"

"Look," she said almost shouting at me, "the girl was going out with Uri when I left, perhaps she ran off with her ex. I don't bloody know."

I sat on a pouf near her chair. We're sorry to do this to you," I looked at Carlos and, again said in Spanish, that if we were going to get anything further from her, we would have to tell her what had happened. He nodded. I continued, "but we do need to know as much as you can remember Diana".

"You see," I took a deep breath, "Katrina has been killed. She has been murdered and we are trying to find out who did it."

She looked at me, her eyes wide opened, her head shaking backwards and forwards. "No," she cried, "that can't be. Why?" Tears rolled down her cheeks.

"That's what we are trying to find out," I said pathetically.

"Ask her boyfriend Uri," she said.

"Why?" I continued to, "do you think he could have done it?"

"I don't know. I wouldn't think so. They were both very much in love. She knew she was going to have a problem with her ex. She was going to have to let him down gently. She was happy here, and with Uri."

I briefly translated the relevant points to Carlos. "Diana, Uri has been found dead as well. From what you say, it could have been the ex—boyfriend. We must find him."

She looked at me in horror. I thought she was going to faint, or throw up — or both. The shock was too much. She just kept saying, "I don't believe all this, I don't fucking believe it."

The policewoman came and whispered something to Carlos. He repeated it to me in Spanish.

"Diana," I held her hand, she pulled it away

from me,

"I don't believe it," she continued.

"Diana, listen to me, the female officer is going through Katrina's stuff and she can't find anything that appears to be personal. You know, like letters from her family, family photos, that sort of thing. Do you know where she kept those sort of things?"

She stopped rocking and looked at me. She looked back down at the floor. She was silent. "Yes," she said quietly. "In the cupboard above my wardrobes. I've got more cupboards than her. It's in a black vanity case." I translated to Carlos, who gave the nod to the officer.

"Do you know anything about Katrina or Uri that would help us?" I asked.

"No, she didn't talk about her past very much. She said she had a mother and father whom she loved very much, but felt she had let down. She had a married sister, and, this ex— boyfriend. She was seeing Uri and had fallen in love with him and the feeling appeared to be mutual. I was sworn to secrecy by both of them, because Uri never liked to let people know if he was seeing members of the staff. It was against his principles."

The female officer returned, this time with a handful of letters with Russian postmarks and some pictures. "Look," he said to me as he showed us pictures of her with Uri and some of her in Red Square, with what must have been, her Russian boyfriend. And then one of him on his own. "Do you know who this is?" he asked in Spanish. I shook my head. "This is the male found dead in Las Cancelas, with the child". The look of disbelief on Gerry's face together with the incredulity on mine, prompted Carlos to say "things seem to be getting more involved by the day. We will have to take these letters away for translation. It will probably take some time."

"Is there anyone you would like us to call Diana?" I asked.

"No, thank you. I'll be alright, I think."

I gave her my card. "Look, if you have a problem or you remember anything that might help, call me."

"Thank you," she said tearfully. We all got up to go.

"I am sorry to had to have put you through all this," said Carlos, as he put on his cap to leave. We all left and closed the door behind us.

"She'll be alright," I said. "She seems a very plucky girl."

"Lucky?" asked Carlos surprised.

"Sorry Carlos, Plucky. It means she has spirit. 'Cojones'."

"Yes," he laughed, "she probably has."

Gerry came back with me to the house where we had a drink and waited for Sandy to return. We sat down and went through everything we knew. "Well, if the dead guy was her ex-boyfriend, that destroys my 'the jealous lover' theory. But where do the baby and the other woman come in? And, what has Metchnikov got to do with it? And, if he did kill Uri, why?"

"I don't know," I said matter-of-factly, "but, what I do know, is, that if I was Carlos, I would be thinking that the whole thing was very complex and I would be praying for a break."

Sandy was home just before 7.30. She had a quick freshen up and we got to David Hill's just after eight. He let us in through the big wooden doors. I introduced Gerry.

"A journalist, I understand?" said David.

"Off duty," replied Gerry.

"I thought you were never off duty," countered David with a smile.

"I have been told I am tonight," said Gerry returning the smile.

We walked into the lounge where David had laid out a few pickies on the table and some glasses.

"Open the wine, if you would, please Philip, while I make the call. I'll put it on the voice box so as you can all hear. Now, you must remember, I haven't spoken to this guy in some many months, so I don't know what sort of reaction I will get."

He dialled the number and waited for the connection. A female voice answered. "Can I speak to Frank please?"

"May I ask whose calling?" came the reply.

"David Hill"

"Just one moment please."

"Obviously a new girl," he said glancing over to us.

"David, you old son-of-a-bitch. How the hell are you?"

"OK thanks Frank, and you?"

"Yeah, you know, same old same old. Where are you, still in sunny Spain with all them *señoritas*?"

"That's right. Listen buddy, I need a favour."

"The last time you asked me that" he interrupted, "you got me hauled by my ass and nearly got yours thrown into jail."

"Just listen to me for a moment. You remember Metchnikov?"

"How could I forget?"

"Well, he's here in Spain." There was a silence. "Did you hear me?"

"You bet I heard you. How long as he been there?"

"About six months or so, I guess."

"Shit." Another silence. "Listen buddy, you're going to get yourself into a lot of deep shit again if you get involved. This guy is the subject of a big CIA and FBI investigation. Since you left — and I think a lot of it is your opening a can of worms when you were here — we have been investigating Mister Metchnikov quite considerably.

That warehouse you went to appeared to be the front for more than a legitimate import export business. It is likely that it was used to distribute cocaine, and other nasty stuff, from Colombia and other holes in the ground. If that wasn't all, your man Metchnikov is also wanted by the Russian and Ukrainian police, for questioning, with regard to a stolen baby ring between their countries and the good old US of A — and from our own home town of Los Angeles. He appears to have disposed of his business interests here and disappeared. There is a federal warrant out for his arrest and his associate, Benny Grokholsky."

"Ask him more about the baby ring," I said in a loud whisper.

"Whose that with you David?" asked Kent.

"Just one of my *señoritas* topping up my glass Frank," said the CIA man without missing a beat. "Tell me about this baby ring."

"Well, Metchnikov was heavily into racketeering in his home base of Lvov, wherever that is, and he was approached by some hospital doctors with the idea of selling babies to wealthy American and European, childless couples. He even set up an agency in Los Angeles. He did well until the Ukrainian police uncovered some of the people behind it and he skipped to America long before the shit hit the fan. They only contacted us a few months ago, by which time our Russian friend had flown yet again. At least we've got him now."

"Where is he David?"

"I'm sorry Frank, what did you say, I can't hear you, the line is breaking up."

"You son-of—a-bitch, you know damn well you can hear me. Tell me where he is."

David hung up. We all looked at him. "Let him do his own investigation," he quipped, "it won't take him long to find out. He knows I live in Marbella and even the CIA will work out that he has a boat in Banus. But it gives your police commander the edge if you want to tell him."

"He's sure to want to talk to you," I said taking another mouthful of wine. "You don't mind?"

"No, I guess not. Anything to see that bastard behind bars."

We left David Hill after drinking another couple of bottles of wine and made our individual ways home. Gerry promising that as we had missed golf today, we should take a rain check. I said I would phone the next day.

When Sandy and I got home, I told her the story that David had told me about his family and Metchnikov.

"Poor man," she said, "you would never think that he had had that much heartbreak in his life."

"No, he hides it well. And, it wasn't that long ago. We are only talking of some months."

"What do you think Carlos will say?" said Sandy as she slipped off her clothes and crawled into bed.

"I should think he would be quite happy to get the information, but it still doesn't tie Metchnikov to the murders. This baby smuggling ring is interesting though."

"Do you think that Metchnikov was involved in it down here?"

"I wouldn't think so. I hardly think people here will pay that sort of money for child adoption. Anyway, family ties are so strong here, the chances of a single girl giving birth without the family knowing about it, would be unlikely. That's the sort of thing

Americans do. Anyway, tomorrow I will go and see Carlos and tell him what happened and get him to meet with David."

I slipped into bed beside Sandy. She put her head on my chest. "How's work going?" I asked.

"I thought you'd never ask," she said.

"I'm sorry, it's just that with everything going on......."

"I know, she said kissing my body gently, "you've had a lot to occupy your mind. It's OK. Mainly paperwork and pre-planning to be honest. It'll be a lot more fun when it gets going."

Within minutes we were both fast asleep.

I knocked on Carlos Jimenez's office door. "*Pasa*," came the familiar voice. I walked in to see him at his desk with a pile of papers in front of him. "*Holá* Philip," he said looking up. "Paperwork, I hate it."

"We all do," I replied, "except town hall bureaucrats".

He smiled, "And police officers? Sit down my friend. *Que Pasa*?"

"I met with a guy a few days ago that happens to be an ex CIA man. He's retired and lives in the Los Naranjos park area. In conversation, it came out that he was involved in Russia and later, back in America, with Soviet immigrants and their movements inside the States. One person he knows a lot about is Metchnikov." Carlos looked at me intently, "So I thought you may like to meet him."

"Indeed. But what can we learn from a retired agent?"

"He still has friends in the Agency and it just might cut a few corners for you."

"Is he prepared to talk to me?"

"Yes, I thought we could go up at lunchtime if you were free."

"Yes, come and meet me here at two, We'll go in my car."

"OK, by the way, I suppose it's still too early, to ask if you have had the letters translated?"

"They went to our foreign department. They are looking for a Russian translator. It's taken us long enough to have English and German translators. Russian is still very new to us," he said sarcastically. "All we have at the moment is a murdered girl and her two boyfriends, two names we know and the other we are waiting to find out. A murdered woman whose identity is completely unknown and a dead child for which there appears to be no motive for her killing. Apart from that Philip, it is a lovely day."

He picked up the next sheet of paper and started to scribble. I took it as my cue to leave.

"Carlos Jimenez, this is David Hill." The two men shook hands.

"I'm afraid I speak no Spanish at all *Señor* Jimenez," said David apologetically.

"That is no problem" replied Carlos in his best English. "I speak a little, understand more, and if we have a problem, I'm sure our friend Mister Edwards will be able to help us." We sat down and as usual David offered us a drink. Carlos refused graciously and I therefore felt I should do the same.

"Philip tells me you may have some information regarding certain persons that may assist us in finding those responsible for some particularly horrible murders that have happened recently." Carlos got out his notebook. David Hill repeated the story that he had told me about his past and family, then related, virtually verbatim, the conversation that he had had With Frank Kent. I had to intersperse occasionally to assist in some of the more difficult words, but apart from that, Carlos' understanding of the situation was obvious.

"Thank you Mister Hill, you have been most helpful," said Carlos as he lifted his ample frame from the chair. They shook hands. I shook hands with David and we left.

"So," I asked as we got in the car, "what do you think?"

"There is more to our friend Igor Metchnikov than we thought. It is obvious from what your friend has said that the rest of the world is after him as well, in which case we had better get to him here first — in Spain."

Carlos dropped me at my car around the comer from his office and I made my way to the restaurant. I promised Paul that I would discuss the promotion of a supper theatre evening that we were holding the following Monday night. We spent the afternoon having a light lunch and discussing the promotion, not just for the evening, but for the rest of the year, up until Christmas. It was after six before I left to go home. I was back before Sandy. I went into the kitchen, opened a bottle of wine, poured myself a glass and started to prepare a salad supper. It was definitely going to be a night in.

The phone rang at 8.00 am. It was Carlos. "I have the translations," he started straight away, "our male friend was called Gregorio. The woman was Katrina's Sister and, it looks as if the murdered girl was Katrina's daughter."

"And good morning to you," I quipped, "that's what I call a good start to the day." .

"The letters are from Katrina's sister saying how happy she is that Katrina has found her baby girl and asks what she intends to do now. There are also letters from Gregorio saying how much he misses her and how he is looking forward to seeing her again and also how pleased he is that she has found her baby girl after her long search. She obviously never told him about Uri. I have a feeling that the other murdered woman is her sister. Gregorio has said what time he arrived in Malaga from Madrid, so I will get a passenger list. I have got to go and see the Burnets to see if this child was indeed Katrina's and that they adopted her through Metchnikov's ring."

"Do you want your friendly interpreter?" I asked hopefully.

"I suppose so. I'll pick you up in half an hour."

"What's happened?" said Sandy as she came

out to get her juice and coffee. I told her the latest developments and that we were nearing the end of the line. "I am pleased for Carlos," I said, "he has been upset that this sort of thing has happened in Marbella. You know what the people who live here are like. They don't like bad publicity, it's not good for business."

I showered and dressed quickly and, went downstairs, just in time to see Carlos' Citroen Xantia drive up. The journey to the Burnet's took less than twenty minutes. We talked on the way. He had phoned to say he was coming, but not the reason why. Just that he had some questions. The big gate to the drive was open and we drove straight in. Andrew Burnet came to the door. He greeted Carlos and, I was introduced. We walked into the beautiful rustic lounge, full of pastel shades and huge sofas and antique pieces that were attractive and functional. Wealth, I thought, without ostentation. "You will forgive my wife if she doesn't join us," said the educated American, "but she is still in a very distressed state."

"We quite understand," said Carlos sympathetically, "and what I have to say would maybe distress her even more.

Was your daughter adopted *Señor* Burnet?" A look of surprise passed over the man's face.

"Yes," he replied, "how did you know?"

"That doesn't matter at the moment. Was your daughter adopted in Russia?"

"Have we done anything wrong officer?"

"That is not for me to say *Señor* Burnet. I am

investigating a murder in Spain, not the legalities of an American resident. Please answer the question."

"Yes, actually from the Ukraine" said the distraught parent emphatically.

"Was this arrangement made with a man called Metchnikov?"

"No," replied Burnet equally emphatically, "the man we dealt with was a lawyer named Dimitri Yakov."

Carlos looked at me slightly confused. This was a new name in the game. Even David Hill's man in America had not mentioned him. He was obviously a front for the business.

"You have never heard of Metchnikov?" continued Carlos.

"No."

"Does the name Katrina Ornst mean anything to you?"

"No, should it?"

"Did you meet the mother of your child?"

"No, we were told that she had died at childbirth. Catherine was only a few weeks old when we picked her up. What is this leading to officer?"

"*Señor* Burnet," Carlos prepared himself for a long statement in English. "Your adopted daughter appears to be the baby of a Ukrainian girl named Katrina Ornst, who was found dead last Monday week, less than three days after, your child, the young woman's ex-boyfriend and, her sister were found murdered on the outskirts of the town. They would appear to be the ones who kidnapped your daughter from the nursery school. They in turn were murdered by persons unknown — at the moment — but we feel that this man Metchnikov may have been behind it. Does the name Uri Karpov mean anything to you?"

"No, it doesn't. But why would anyone want to kidnap our child?"

"Metchnikov was behind a baby stealing operation. They would convince young mothers with little hope and, usually no money, that their child had died at birth, or soon after, and then, sell them to childless couples like you, from America or Europe. Young Katrina would appear not to have been so easily taken in and set off from the Ukraine to find her child. She managed to trace you here, and seems to have fallen foul of our Senor Metchnikov and confronted him with it, probably threatening to denounce him. He then had her, her sister and her ex-boyfriend, as well as the child, murdered."

Burnet sat in a state of shock. "That is horrible and disgusting. What would make a man do such a thing?"

"That, *Señor* Burnet, is something we will never know, but I promise you I will do everything I can to make sure he and, his associates, Will never be able to cause such grief to anyone ever again. If you have any paperwork on the adoption, I would appreciate it, if you would give it to me."

The man got up to stretch his long legs. "Everything I have is in our house in America. I will ask my housekeeper there to fax it to me and I will bring it to your office as soon as I receive them."

"I would appreciate that *Senor*, once again my deepest sympathy to you and your wife and thank you for your time."

We walked to the car in silence. As we drove away from the house I said, "Phew that was pretty heavy Carlos. No wonder you said it would be better if his wife was not present. So that's what you think has happened?"

"Yes, but where does Uri Karpov fit in? Unless Karpov was actually in love with Katrina and she told him about the baby. He in turn was aware of Metchnikov's involvement in the baby ring and confronted him about it and he too was murdered. This is all too much for a provincial little policeman in semi-retirement in the fishing village of Marbella," he looked at me smiling. I got the feeling that now he was closing in, like the Matador with the bull, he was going to enjoy the kill, "but I think we've got the bastard."

CHAPTER NINETEEN

David Hill closed the door behind his guests and went back into the lounge and poured himself another glass of wine. So Metchnikov and the pony tail were in Spain and his old friend Frank had brought him up to date with the charges levied against him. It looked as if he had been a busy man all of his life. Drugs, prostitution, stolen babies and murder. Just the sort of people Agents, and the law, love busting. If they can get them in a corner first, arrest and imprisonment becomes attractive compared to what an angry law enforcement official can meter out. And here was this evil bastard and, his long-haired gofer, within minutes of his own home. He had never been so near to the men responsible for Susan's and, his wife's, death. The hidden anger and bitterness was rekindled. How he would love to walk up to the man and place the barrel of his gun in his mouth and watch him piss himself just like the little punk in LA. He could do that he thought, without any compunction. He went out on to the terrace. The night was balmy. He loved the smell of the *Dama del Noche* and, the gentle breeze stroking the palm trees. How Pamela loved this house and Marbella. They used to sit out here and she would claim she could hear the palm trees whispering. A tear came to his eye. He missed her. He would miss the house, but there were too many memories here. Anyway the house was too big for one. He had no desire to be with another woman, so he would be better in a smaller place. His mind went back to Metchnikov and Benny. But it had been the name of Parkov that Philip had mentioned earlier in the day that had intrigued him. He knew that name. He was pretty sure that Alexi Parkov was the physicist that he had helped out of the East all those years ago. He had had a son who would have been in his twenties now. So, what was the connection between Parkov and Metchnikov? He went over to his desk and took out his telephone directory and looked for the number of Steffi Alan, the American Consul. He knew her from years ago when she was an under consul in the American Embassy in Moscow with his old friend Tony Friers, from whom he had bought this house. He had met her several times since, both in the States and, here at Thanksgiving dinners and Fourth of July parties. She only worked in her office in the mornings, so he would have to contact her at home.

"Steffi Alan, how can I help you?" came the refined American voice.

"Steffi, it's David Hill. How are you?"

"Hi David. Fine thanks, and you?"

"Good thanks, good. Listen, do you remember Alexi Karpov, the guy I got out of the East?"

"You must be psychic, I had to phone him the other day."

"To tell him his son was dead?" interrupted David.

"Yes," she said, pausing, "how the hell did

you know?"

"Let's just say a little bird told me. I need to speak to him, do you have his phone number?"

"I do," replied the consul, "but he will be arriving in Malaga from Madrid tomorrow morning, so he will be en route now."

"If you are meeting him, do you mind if I come along?"

"No, but what's it all about?" she asked.

"I'll tell you tomorrow. I'll meet you in the arrivals lounge."

He cleared up the glasses and put them in the washer and tidied the lounge. He was feeling an adrenaline rush now, just like the old days. If he could get to Metchnikov first, that would sort out a few old debts. But he needed to know why Karpov's boy had been killed and what he was doing with Metchnikov.

The following morning he arrived a few minutes before Steffi. She walked into the arrivals lounge and gave him a hug.

"Long time no see," she said with a broad, welcoming smile. "You guys that live in the posh end of town, don't mix too often with the likes of us."

"You know me Steffi, I keep a pretty low profile and am just happy in my home. Until I sell it that is."

"Yes, how are you keeping," she said knowingly, holding his hand.

"I'm bearing up. I tend to block it all from my mind. Look," he said glancing at the arrivals board, "we've got a few minutes, let me get you a coffee and I can tell you what this is all about." They went over to the cafeteria and he ordered two coffees. They sat down and David explained briefly what had happened and his reasons for wanting to speak to Alexi.

"You won't get him involved in any of your weird and wonderful CIA antics will you David?"

"Ex CIA, if you don't mind," he smiled. "No, I just want to know what young Uri was doing with Metchnikov. You can be with me when I talk to him if you want," he said.

"I'm sure that won't be necessary. Do we need a sign with his name on?" she asked, "or will you recognise him?"

"Let's find out, shall we? I'm sure the years haven't altered us both that much." said David, as they moved back into the lounge to greet the arriving passengers from Madrid. After a few minutes he saw a man in his late fifties, with hair greyer than he expected and, who appeared to be stooping with sadness. The man looked up and saw the face of the CIA agent. At first there was a look of puzzlement, then the realisation that he knew him. A smile crossed his wizened face as his step quickened and he dropped his small travel bag at David's feet and opened his arms in welcome. David responded with a hug. The two old comrades stood for moments as Alexi said in his deep guttural voice, "David my old friend, how are you?" Tears were running down his cheeks.

"I'm fine," replied David, himself finding the

reunion a little emotional. The news of his son had obviously taken its toll on the old party member. He pulled himself away and they looked at each other for a few minutes.

David broke the silence, "This is Steffi Alan, she is the American Consul who spoke to you on the phone."

"Hello Mister Karpov, please accept my condolences for your terrible loss." she said in perfect ambassadorial jargon.

"Thank you," said Alexi, "but what are you doing here?," he said returning to his conversation with David.

"It's a long story Alexi and one that can be better discussed over a good Vodka?"

"Do they have such a thing in this country?" he asked laughing.

"I am sure two old soldiers like ourselves will be able to find some."

"I'm going to leave you to it. Please don't get into any trouble, I don't want to be called out to get you two out of jail," she commented, "and I mean, be careful David," she reiterated as she kissed him on the cheek. "Goodbye Mister Karpov."

He waved to her, as the two men walked toward the car park.

The two large blue label Smirnoff went down without touching the sides. "It's a long time since I did that," said the Russian. "It's not bad, but not as good as the real thing," he laughed as he pointed to the barman to refill the glasses. "We have come a long way since that night in East Berlin, my friend. And maybe if we had waited a little longer, all that cloak and dagger stuff would have been unnecessary, I could have just caught a plane," he laughed a poignant laugh.

"Ah, but the US government needed you then," said David.

"Yes, yes, I suppose so. I read about your daughter and your wife, and about you retiring from the CIA, I'm so very sorry." David acknowledged with a smile. "So tell me David, what are you doing in Spain and why are you at the airport? Does it have something to do with Uri's death?"

"I'm afraid so Alexi," said David as he put his finger on to his glass to indicate to the barman that that measure was sufficient. "Let me explain. When I retired from the CIA I came over here. After my wife died I really didn't think I could stay on there. And now, being here, I feel I have to sell my house and buy something smaller. So, I put the house with an agent, who sent around a photographer, a very nice man in his early forties, who I have got to know. He is friends with a senior police officer who has been investigating the death of your son and some other people, under mysterious circumstances."

"What mysterious circumstances?" interrupted Alexi, "I was told that he was killed in a boating accident."

"Well, yes that is true," said David, "but they think he was killed deliberately."

The man took another swig of vodka and looked sadly into David's eyes waiting for him to continue.

"Was your son working for Igor Metchnikov? Asked David pointedly.

The Russians eyes glazed over and he smashed the small tumbler on to the table. The noise of breaking glass caused those nearby to turn inquisitively, hearing it above the background music and chatter. Blood came from the tensely gripped hand. David offered him some paper serviettes.

"Are you alright?" he asked trying to look at the wound. It was only a small cut, that Alexi could obviously not feel and certainly wasn't worried about.

"Metchnikov," he said slowly, "I cannot say the word without feeling sick to my stomach. So it was him that killed my son."

"Why do you say that Alexi," David asked.

"Some years ago my son started to work for Metchnikov. At the time the man had a high profile, you are probably aware of that, and was almost respectable on the surface. But I knew he was into drugs and other illegal activities. Men like that who come from Russia could only have made their money in that fashion. Uri was a bright young man with a great future, but he chose to work in Metchnikov's office during summer vacations. Uri started to work in the evil man's import export business. I think Uri was impressed by the money and the people. He was offered a job within Metchnikov's operation which paid him good money and gave him an apartment in town away from his papa," a tear came to the man's eyes as he remembered, "I begged him not to take the job, but like all young men, — just like us hey David? — he was impressionable and loved the excitement. I kept telling him to be careful and when he told me he was coming to Spain I told him not too. He took no notice of me, but he must have said something to Metchnikov because a few days before Uri left for Spain, I had a visit from two of Metchnikov's goons, telling me that if I so much as squeaked to anyone about anything that I knew or thought I knew, Uri would disappear, without trace."

"What sort of things would that have been Alexi," interrupted David.

"I was never too sure. Metchnikov was a sly bastard and could buy his way out of everything, but Uri used to tell me he was in charge of an agency. A service agency that supplied goods between Russia and America. It was only after he left and the news hit the media about a stolen baby adoption ring, that I put two and two together. No one ever came to my door about Uri though, so I assumed that he was in the clear and that maybe his life here would mean a clean slate, even if he was dealing with Metchnikov."

David started to tell the man everything that he knew, which was not that much but it was sufficient to know that Metchnikov was responsible for the deaths of both men's only family. They would have to make a plan of action.

"You will stay with me," said David and I will drop you off at the police station so as you can talk to the man who is handling the enquiry. Shall we do that first and get it over with?"

"Yes, as much as I have no desire to see my son's dead body, I have to formally identify it so as the Consul can arrange to fly him back home."

"Don't let the police know that you have met with me. I think they would probably not like it if they thought I was involved."

David dropped Alexi off in front of the Guardia Civil offices and, having given him his number, told him to phone when he had finished and he would come and collect him. They waved and he drove off to his home to have a coffee and something to eat. He was not used to drinking vodka before breakfast and it had had the undesired effect. Come to think of it he had not had a vodka since the old days. Alexi Karpov, who ever would have believed that some ten years on, they would meet again? In Spain of all places. David had been responsible for getting Alexi out of Russia. The American government had wanted him. He was a physicist of some note in his home country and he'd been working with nuclear reactors. He had managed to contact David through the embassy and had told of his desire to leave the oppression of communism. He had lost his wife and wanted to take his son to the West where he felt sure a better life would await him. David had spoken to his boss, who had arranged the political asylum, all David had to do was get him out of the East and into the West.

It had been done before and successfully.

This time there was a young boy involved, but no matter, they would give him a mild sedative that would make him sleep through the precarious trip over the border and the inevitable flight to freedom. It was tragic that a man like Alexi, who had achieved so much in his professional life, should have lost so much in his personal life.

Not only had life dealt him a severe blow with the death of his wife, he had lost his home and now his only son. That Metchnikov certainly did have something to answer for.

The toast and coffee, whilst welcoming and sustaining, did not negate the effect of the vodka and he was in a fairly deep sleep when the phone rang. He stood up and went over to the desk and picked up the receiver, it was Alexi. "I am finished with the police David and, am in the bar opposite the office."

"I'll be there in ten minutes and we will go for some lunch."

The two men sat on the terraces outside restaurant Antonio's, in Puerto Banus, eating Paella. David pointed out the ship that Philip had mentioned to him.

"That huge ship is Metchnikov's?" asked Alexi.

"Yes," replied the ex CIA man, "and we've got to figure a way to get on it and surprise our Russian friend."

Alexi looked at him perplexed. "What on earth do you think you can do?"

"I'm not sure yet, but give me time."

The two men made their way back to David's villa. His mind was trying to work out a plan to get on the boat and, more than that, a way of getting to Metchnikov. He pressed the automatic gate entry button in the car, and the two big wooden gates opened. Alexi looked at the beautiful house as they drove into the drive. "The CIA paid well," he said.

"More our family money," said David as the car pulled to a halt outside the front door. "I'm afraid the CIA paid their agents about as well as the Russians paid their physicists."

"*Touché*," said the scientist.

"Make yourself at home," said David as he opened the door to the guest room. Alexi went toward the window and looked out over the gardens and the surrounding countryside.

"A far cry from Los Angeles, hey David?"

David smiled and went back into the lounge. He opened the terrace windows and looked out over his gardens. 'What am I going to do?' he asked himself.

Over coffee the two men sat and discussed what, if anything, they could do. They talked until the sun started to go down and they had got no further. Alexi was tired from his journey and so they stopped the discussion and opened a bottle of wine and sat and talked about old times. The two old comrades talked about their lost partners and their lost children. Two different worlds, brought together by two different governments to suffer similar fates by a character that neither of them knew or had ever met. Life played strange tricks.

Relaxed from the wine and tired from

thought and travel the two men made their way to bed and slept soundly.

David was up first and went into the kitchen to put on some coffee. He went back toward the guest bedroom and knocked on the door. "Come in," said the sleepy voice.

"Good morning," said David, as he went over and opened the window to let in the early morning sunshine. "Did you sleep well?"

"Yes thank you," said Alexi, "especially with the help of the wine and a long journey."

"I'm making coffee," continued David, "would you like some?"

"That would be very nice," said Alexi, " I will come into the lounge, but first I must have a quick shower, if I may."

"Of course," said his host, "the towels are in the bathroom.

David checked the coffee and went into the shower himself. The two men met in the lounge as David opened the patio doors that led out on to the terrace.

They sat taking in the tranquillity of the early summer morning, drinking their coffee, when the door bell rang. David looked at his watch as he went over to the intercom. "Yes," he spoke into the voice box.

"*Un paquete para Señor Hill.*" came the reply.

"Just a moment," said David and pressed the entry button, allowing the inner door to the large entrance gates to open. He walked toward the front entrance of the house and opened the heavy wooden door. He had no sooner pulled the door from its frame than it slammed into him with a violence that sent him stumbling back, until he tripped over himself, winding himself as he landed prostrate. He looked up to see the barrel of an automatic pointed at his throat. "What the fuck ..." he was caught short as the man with the gun stood on his groin and put his finger to his lips.

Alexi called from the lounge, "Are you alright David?" His voice curtailed as the other man grabbed him by the neck and pulled him out into the hallway. The man holding David down, lent forward and pulled him to his feet. "Someone wants to talk to you," he said, and pushed him toward the front door. They went out on to the quiet tree lined street and the two helpless men were bundled into the back of a car. The driver pulled away and it was only a matter of minutes before it was obvious that they were heading towards Puerto Banus. Despite David's insistence, the men gave no indication as to the reason for their abduction. They said nothing as they drove through the barrier to the Port and pulled up alongside, the recognizable shape, of the Wave Dancer.

The doors opened and the two men were bundled gently up the gangway, to the after deck, to be greeted by Benny, the pony tail. They were pushed into the salon and saw Metchnikov sitting in the comfortable sofas. The men frisked the two visitors.

"Welcome gentlemen," said the Russian gangster as he indicated to Benny, to make them sit. "I'm sorry your invitation was somewhat unorthodox and perhaps a little rough, but I'm sure if I had sent you one through the post, you would not have responded so readily."

"What do you want with us?" asked David as innocently as possible.

"Please do not treat me like an idiot, Mister Hill. You and, our mutual friend, Mister Karpov are well aware as to why you are here. I'm sure you have been thinking of a way of getting on to the ship to see me, this has just saved a bit of time."

"Why are you doing this Metchnikov? What purpose will this serve?" asked David.

"I have been made aware, by a mutual friend, that you and your misguided friends here in Spain, are going to make a futile attempt to arrest me, for some trumped up crimes, that people seem to think I, and my associates, have committed. I just thought it would be good if we can clear the air. You Mister Karpov think I led your son astray and am responsible for his death. Let me tell you, Uri was perfectly aware of what he was getting himself into, and enjoyed every minute of his work, and, I may add, was well paid for it. It was his stupidity that landed him into trouble. Stupidity that you and, your friend, Mister Hill, obviously share. And you," he looked at David, "should know better. You are an ex CIA agent who had been told to stay away, but were too stupid to listen. You have been trying to blame me for your daughter's and, your wife's, deaths. Your daughter took drugs and it was her stupidity that led to her death. Your wife, just gave up and died." David went to lunge towards the fat man, but was pulled back by one of Metchnikov's men. "Please don't do anything careless, Mister Hill, I would hate to have to shoot you here, the blood makes an awful mess of the carpet. Put them below Benny."

"What do you think you are going to do with us?" shouted David.

"Fear not Mister Hill, you will be well taken care of," said Metchnikov as he turned his back on his guests and went out onto the forward deck. The two men were pushed down below and ushered into a cabin where they were pushed to the floor and put back to back. One of the thugs took some rope from a cupboard and tied the two of them together. David tightened his muscles and tensed himself, so as to allow some movement in the ropes after the thugs had left the room. The door closed behind them and they heard the engines start up. Minutes later, they could feel the movement as the ship made its way out of the harbour.

"We are going on a sea cruise," said Alexi flippantly.

"I'm sorry I got you into this Alexi," said David.

"That is alright my friend, I have never been to sea before, I'm quite looking forward to it," he answered sarcastically. "Anyway, you did not exactly invite them to your home, did you? And, put it this way, you were thinking of a way to get on board, and they saved you the trouble."

The two men started to laugh. Part from fear

and part from frustration, as to the position they found themselves in. David started to check on the tightness of the rope wrapped around his torso. "I want you to relax as much as possible Alexi, while I try and wriggle out of these ropes."

"Ah, once a CIA man, eh?" said Alexi as he did his best to relax allowing David to wriggle his arms from behind his back, unsuccessfully. After a while he stopped. "I'll try again in a minute," he said.

The vessel had gained speed in the last few minutes. They had been at sea about an hour when David could hear the sound of a helicopter and then the rat-tat of machinegun fire. He tried once again to release his hands from the rope. The door opened and one of the men came in and pulled David and Alexi up from the floor. David instinctively lifted his head up and under the chin of the armed man. There was a sickening crunch and the man let out a yelp of pain as he staggered backwards momentarily disorientated. That was sufficient time for David to release his hands, burnt and bleeding from the rope, as the man raised his gun to shoot, David lifted his foot in a well aimed kick to the hand that caused him to release the grip on the gun. David, with the added weight of Alexi still attached to him, stepped forward and with one punch, caught his assailant on the already tender chin, causing him to buckle backwards. David pulled the rope from him and Alexi.

"Use this to tie him up," said David as he picked up the automatic. He opened the door of the cabin and looked carefully around him. The boat was travelling faster now as the sound of gunfire continued. He climbed the metal stairs from the crew quarters where they had been incarcerated, to the upper decks, when there was a terrific explosion and at the same time the boat took wild evading action causing David to be thrown off balance and plummet down the stairs, ricocheting from side to side. He landed in a crumpled heap at the bottom of the stairs.

CHAPTER TWENTY

Gerry and I were in Carlos' office when a messenger arrived from the courts with the warrant for Metchnikov's arrest. Him, the pony tail and anyone else on the boat, that could be brought in for questioning. Carlos then phoned the Port police to inform them that he was coming down to Banus and to meet him at the entrance to the Port. He put on his bullet proof vest, along with all those accompanying him, his jacket and cap, checked that he had his gun and looked at us. "OK. you two. Because I promised you the story you can come along, but under no circumstances get involved and, do not do anything, that will put you, or anyone else, in danger. Is that understood?" We adjusted our vests, put both our feet together and mockingly saluted. "Sir!" we cried. A smile went across his face. "I'm being serious, these people are evil and cold hearted and I want to be able to have dinner with you when this is all over. Let's go." Outside the entrance to the police station were a group of officers. Two of them with machine guns. There were two Nissan Patrols and a Citroen staff car. The driver opened the front passenger door for Carlos and we climbed in the back. The others got in their respective vehicles and the small convoy headed out toward the Golden Mile. I looked at Gerry a mixture of excitement and nerves was apparent in both of us. The lights on the vehicles were flashing although no sirens were on. We pulled off the *careterra* into the entrance of the Port. The gates were opened immediately and there were two police officers waiting for us to arrive. Carlos opened his Window and the two young officers went over to his Window and saluted. Carlos acknowledged by touching his peak. "I am going aboard the Wave Dancer to arrest the Russian owner," said Carlos, stopping mid sentence as the two men looked at each other with horror on their face. One turned to Carlos and told him that the boat had indeed left about an hour earlier. "Shit," said Carlos exasperated.

We drove up to the place where the boat should have been. He spoke into his radio, explaining the situation to the dispatcher and asked that helicopters were sent up to trace the yacht and that the Coastguard should be notified. "And send me a boat too, I want to follow the bastard myself." We got out of the car and he called on one of the two officers with a machine gun to join him. Several minutes passed and you could see that Carlos was getting impatient. One of the Port officers came over to him to tell him that they had tried making radio contact with the boat, but they had obviously turned off their receiver or were ignoring the call. The police launch pulled up alongside and Carlos, his officer, Gerry and myself joined the two officers already on board. The launch pulled out into the marina and headed for the open sea. "Which direction do you think they have gone? " I asked.

"They will either have gone to Morocco because its quicker, or they may even be hoping to cross the Atlantic, where, if they make enough headway, it will be safer."

"In which case they will be going through the Straits."

"Yes and they have had an hour's start on us and, as he probably knows we are after him, he will be going at his top speed," Carlos' voice was drowned out by the propeller noise of the low flying helicopter as it made itself known and the pilot's voice crackled over the radio.

"Which way do you think he has gone sir?" asked the pilot.

"He may attempt to get to Morocco in which case he won't be far from there by now, or he could have gone towards the Straits."

"OK," replied the pilot and sent his chopper nosing off toward the right. The police launch was now at full speed and crashing through the waves. If anyone wanted to be sea sick, this was now their opportunity. I had already started to take some pictures. A good one of the helicopter, some of the launch before we got on board and one of Carlos on the radio.

Gerry was furiously scribbling and we looked across at each other with a sense of satisfaction. The story we all wanted and the winding up of the dreadful events of the last couple of weeks was coming to a close. The radio crackled into life. It was the helicopter pilot, he had spotted the craft going toward the Straits of Gibraltar. He had called out to the occupants but they had ignored his requests to heave to. What was he to do next?

"Just keep him in sight until we get there," said Carlos. "Doesn't this thing go any faster?" he snarled at the helmsman. The officer edged the throttle forward to its maximum and we seemed to gain a little speed. Carlos asked to be patched through to the Coastguard at La Linea, the border town with the Rock of Gibraltar. Their main task in life these days was to prevent illegal immigrants from Morocco and cigarette smuggling from the Rock to Spain. When they answered he asked to speak to the commanding officer. They chatted for a few seconds, then Carlos explained the situation. The officer in charge said he would dispatch two vessels immediately. The radio crackled again. It was the helicopter pilot again, saying that he was being fired upon from the vessel and was pulling away from them. There was an audible sound of machine gun fire hitting the metal of the helicopter and a cry of panic from the pilot shouting, "I'm hit. They've hit the props, I'm going down." there were no further shouts from the pilot as the radio went dead. A billowing of black smoke could be seen rising from the sea.

Our launch was now making good speed and keeping up, not far away from us, was the Marbella Coastguard. The radio burst into life again. It was the Coastguard from La Linea telling Carlos that they had sighted Wave Dancer.

"Be careful," ordered Carlos. "They have

already used fire power to destroy one of our helicopters." The officers of the La Linea Coastguard said that they would just circle them and slow them down until Carlos got there. The hot summer sun was beating down on us and the sea spray was having a cooling effect as the boat ploughed through the waves tossing the foam to the sides.

"There it is", cried the officer at last, pointing to the craft that had slowed because of the two Coastguard vessels that had started to circle around their quarry.

Carlos turned to me, "Philip I would like you to speak to them over the loudspeakers. I do not want there to be any confusion over my demands, because of my English."

"Sure," I replied "what do you want me to say?" He briefed me quickly and we approached the huge yacht.

"This is a police vessel, this is a police vessel. On board is the Deputy Commander of the Guardia Civil Marbella. He has a warrant for the arrest and questioning of all persons on board the vessel Wave Dancer. You are requested to heave to and allow our officers to board and then escort your vessel back to the Port of Banus. There is no escape. Please all come to the after end of the boat where we can see you and keep your hands on your heads. I repeat, come to the after end of the vessel keeping your hands on your heads. You have two minutes to comply with this order." The yachts motors were still running and the ship had hardly decreased speed. After a couple of minutes, the boat started to slow. We in turn did the same. One of the officers went out on to the front of the boat to go alongside. Carlos went to the cabin door while the other officer steered the boat. Gerry was sitting on the floor, writing furiously and I was now taking pictures. Three people came on to the after deck of the luxury yacht with their hands on their heads. I framed the three in my lens and then I heard the sound of machine gun fire. I instinctively threw myself on the floor, almost knocking Gerry sprawling. The windows on the cabin shattered as splinters of wood and fibre showered down on top of us. There were cries of pain from the man at the helm as he slumped to the floor. Carlos shouted as the impact from a stream of bullets passed over the front of the cockpit, hitting him and throwing backwards on the bulkhead, his face full of fear and pain, as blood flowed from his face and shoulder. He collapsed in a heap on the floor. I heard the engines on the yacht increase in sound and speed as the vessel accelerated forward. I crawled along the deck to the door and looked out carefully. The yacht had ploughed through the two other vessels that had grouped around the yacht waiting to board. The impact had caused one to be holed, the other seemed to have damaged its mechanism. The yacht was escaping. "What the fuck was that," cried Gerry "Jesus, is everybody dead? Look at Carlos." The man on the forward deck was slumped across the bow. I took the wheel and accelerated after the yacht. "What are you doing? called Gerry. "You want a story?" I said over the noise of the engines. "We can't let them get away now, for our sakes, for the ones that were murdered, and for him." I pointed at our lifeless policeman friend sprawled on the deck in a pool of blood."

"Jesus, Philip we'll both be killed," shouted Gerry as I pushed the throttle forward. The people on the after end had gone back inside, presumably secure in the thought that they had disposed of two vessels and killed the occupants of the third. We'll go alongside," I said somewhat confidently, "and I'll try and get on board."

"What? cried Gerry incredulously, "who the hell do you think you are, James fucking Bond?"

"I'll be OK you just keep that machine gun aimed at the deck on the back of the boat. When I get on to the after ladder, I'll tie the rope to it so as you don't get lost."

"You must be off your chump," he said quaintly. "And I've never used one of these," he said lifting the weapon up.

"Don't point it in my direction then," I shouted.

There was still no sign of activity from the after end of the yacht. I was now doing the same speed as the Wave Dancer. I manoeuvered our launch slightly to the side of our quarry, because of the wake that the yacht was creating. I told Gerry to take the wheel while I attempted to jump on to the after ladder. But it was no good, I could see, I couldn't make it. We kept pace with the yacht. Just then we heard the sound of another helicopter approaching and the on board radio once again crackled into life. They asked to speak to Carlos. I picked up the hand set and pressed the two way button. "Carlos Jimenez and the officer on board appear to be dead, the two other craft appear to be in difficulty. We are trying to board the ship now."

"Stay where you are!" came the reply. And the helicopter flew over us and started to fire warning shots over the yacht. We could not see from where we were, but it seemed that retaliatory gun fire was coming from that direction. "I'm going to make an attempt," I said, "with this." I picked up a rope with a grappling hook at the end. I took the hand gun from the dead officer and checked it was loaded. Gerry took the wheel and watched aghast, as I balanced on the side of the moving launch and hurled the hook over the starboard side of the yacht, the sound of gunfire echoing in my ears. On the third attempt the hook gripped itself to the inner bulkhead of the open deck. I tugged firmly, attached it to a capstan, and, with my heart beating in my shoes I launched myself from the police boat toward the side of the yacht, like a mountain climber abseiling between two points. One major difference, these two points were moving. I had my legs out-stretched waiting to make contact with the side of the yacht.. Years of the sports club were now proving their worth as I pulled myself up on the rope. My hands were burning and my arm muscles strained as I climbed slowly but surely up the side of the craft fighting against the movement of both vessels and the wind. I reached the top and threw myself over the side on to the deck. I made sure the grappling hook was well secured. Intermittent gun fire was still audible as the helicopter was darting backwards and forwards at least keeping Metchnikov's gunmen happy. I went around to the after deck and peered carefully into the salon. I could see the Russian throwing papers into a suitcase.

Out through the other side I could see pony tail and one other, hidden behind the lowered lifeboat, exchanging haphazard fire with the helicopter. I pulled the gun from my belt and summoning up all the courage I could muster in my best Rambo style, I walked through the doors. Metchnikov looked up in panic. "Who the hell are you?" he asked. As he turned to call for help I felt fear creeping up the back of my neck.

"Just stay exactly where you are and put your hands on the top of your head."

"Piss off."

I pulled back on the automatic, loading the chamber. His arrogance slowly fading as he realised I may well use it. "I recognise you now. You are that photographer who took those pictures for the magazine. Look, I'll give you a hundred thousand dollars if you just jump off the boat!"

"What's wrong, I said, "don't you want to kill me like you did the others?"

Beads of sweat were appearing on his bald head now, even more than was running down my forehead.

"I didn't kill anyone he said, "Benny did. That's what he is paid for. And he will enjoying doing it to you. You will never get off this boat alive."

"We'll see about that," I said, "but for now, let's go onto the bridge together and stop this boat."

He lead the way up top as I kept my gun firmly placed in the small of his back, praying to God that he wouldn't do anything stupid as I had no idea whether I would have the guts to pull the trigger. Real life bodies were slightly different than targets at the gun club. As we approached the helmsman he turned and, with panic on his face, pulled out a gun.

"Don't you fool," yelled Metchnikov, "he's got a gun in my back."

I pushed Metchnikov down on a seat. "Keep your hands exactly where they are. You," I pointed the gun at the other man, "bring this vessel to a standstill." There was a pause as he looked at the Russian. "Now!" I shouted, menacing him with the automatic.

"Do as he says," said Metchnikov. The man pulled back the throttle. The boat slowed and the helicopter circled as the sound of gunfire disappeared. I pushed the man toward the stairs and told Metchnikov to follow him. When we got to the salon, pony-tail and the other one were just coming through the forward doors. In a rare moment of conversation, pony- tail said, "What the fuck is going on. Who is this guy?"

"Don't go any further," I said, "or I'll kill him."

"He's got a gun in my back," shouted Metchnikov.

"Who gives a fuck," shouted Benny and let off a round above our heads in the salon. The other guy made a lunge towards us. I took the gun from behind Metchnikov and raised it instinctively upward and outward and pulled the trigger. The tiny jolt to my hand making my wrist flick. The man caught the full blast before I even heard the crack of the bullet leaving the barrel. As if he had been hit by a cannonball, his face caved in and blood spurted from the front and back of his head. His nose and eye had taken the full blast of the shot. All this seemed to take place in slow motion.

As he hit the deck, there was further sounds of gunfire from Benny's machine gun and I felt Metchnikov's body quiver. The bastard had shot his boss and the other man. I pushed the fat man forward and fired a shot in Benny's general direction and rushed back upstairs to the cockpit. I locked the door behind me, but the rattle of gunfire soon splintered the wooden door into shreds. I dashed out onto the open deck. Benny appeared at the doorway to the cockpit I pulled the trigger hitting the window by his side. He fired showering the deck with bullets. I jumped down from the top deck to the one below. Turned quickly to align my sights and as I did so, I slipped and my gun went skimming across the polished surfaces. As I ran toward it, there was a ripple of machine gun fire and the noise of the helicopter's loudspeaker instructing my assailant to put down his gun. His response was to lift the gun and fire a hail of bullets at the helicopter's screen and jump for cover behind some covered deck equipment. The chopper pulled back. I ran for the gun again, this time his aim was perfect and he pushed the gun right along the deck out of reach. I turned to look at him looking down at me from about 15 feet away. There was nothing I could do. There were two rapid shots. Benny's smug look turned quickly to fear as he dropped his hands leaving the weapon attached to his fingers like a damaged mechanical appendage. He fell to his knees and then crumbled to the floor. A wave of relief and nausea washed over me and then I saw Carlos standing there with his pistol in his right hand. Blood thick and congealed to his face and on his uniform. He sat down on the nearest object. I started to laugh and didn't know whether to cry. I went over to him and put my hand on his good shoulder. "Thank you my friend," I said.

"No — thank you," he put his hand on my arm to help lift himself up. As we stood up, I saw one of Metchnikov's men out of the corner of my eye. He lifted a gun in our direction but before he could aim there was a burst of machine gun fire and, twisting and turning to the impact of the bullets he writhed to the floor. Standing behind him was David Hill.

"What the hell? " I spluttered, "It's the US cavalry."

"Carlos turned and looked at David. "What are you doing here Mister Hill? I should have you arrested for interfering in police business." He smiled, "but thank you."

"We had better check down in the crew quarters," said David, "if you are angry with me now, you'll be even more angry when you see who I brought with me. I hope he is alright." A man was lying on the floor with blood trickling from the back of his head. David pulled him over. He groggily came around.

"Who the hell's that?" I asked.

"This," replied Carlos, "is Alexi Karpov, Uri's father, who should not have been here either. What on earth is going on? You have a bit of explaining to do Mister Hill."

Leaving David to help Alexi up, we went back up the stairs to the salon to see Gerry with his machine gun pointing towards Metchnikov, who was bleeding from his legs.

"He's not going anywhere," said the journalist.

"Did you get your story?" I asked.

"I should say, and I've got a few pictures of you doing your Man from Milk Tray bit. They might not be as good as you could have taken, but there was nobody else to do it as you were playing heroes at the time. You must be stark staring bonkers."

"Yes, I must be."

"Now you can really show your abilities," said Carlos, handing me a bottle of Perrier Jouet and a tray of glasses.

"I was just checking things out and this looked as if it had been prepared for a victory party, and I guess the best team won."

I opened the bottle and poured out five glasses while Carlos went to the radio and called for assistance. We toasted the relative success of the operation and the arrest of the man we all wanted.

Within half an hour a police and an ambulance launch were coming alongside the yacht. Two paramedics, accompanied by two police officers, came aboard and saluted Carlos. He made little effort to respond and just sat there drinking his champagne. One medic went over to Metchnikov and the other attended to the burly policeman and David and Alexi.

The two policemen handled the gruesome task of straightening the dead bodies and covering them with sheets.

"The bullet went right through your shoulder and missed the bone," said the young paramedic to Carlos, "and one skimmed past your cheek and took the bottom off your ear lobe. You were very lucky. You'll live."

"This one needs treatment for his legs. He has virtually lost one of his knee caps." Metchnikov kept drifting in and out of consciousness. They brought in a stretcher and between us we hoisted him down on to the launch. Carlos was between Gerry and I as we helped him down on to the police launch and one of the officers took command of the other boat.

"I'll bring the yacht back in shall I?" I asked hopefully.

"Yes, if you can stand the passengers" replied Carlos turning to look at me, "and make sure you do bring it back," he laughed.

The motors on the three boats burst into life and they made their way towards Marbella. I went up top and started the engines of the super cruiser. I edged the boat around in the general direction of Marbella and Puerto Banus. The smell of death hung in the air, despite the fresh wind that was coming up.

The hot afternoon sun had started its westerly descent casting ripples of bright light on the water. I stood pensively, as I controlled the power of the vessel, thinking of the events of the last week or so. If anyone had told me ten years ago that I would be involved with baby snatching, drugs, murder, a chase at sea, being shot at and playing desperados, I would never have believed them. But this was the Costa del Sol — and anything can happen here.

EPILOGUE

Sandy and I drove up to the *finca* in the blazing afternoon sun. The land outside the house was already filling up with cars as we pulled the BMW alongside Gerry's Sierra. He was standing at the gate waiting for us. He kissed Sandy and gripped my hand tightly. "Been doing any more stunts lately?" he asked.

"I'm joining the SAS next month," I said jokingly, "they've heard of me!"

As we walked onto the back terraces by the pool, there was a spontaneous round of applause. Carlos walked over, one arm in a sling and the other extended in greeting "Hello my friend," he gripped my hand, " you seem to have overcome your ordeal well. He was a very brave man," he turned to Sandy, "very stupid, but still very brave." The wine flowed, the prawns sizzled on the barbecue, the women clapped and sang their *Sevillanas*, the guitarists played their *flamenco* and the Spanish sun shone mercilessly on the gathered crowds. Some sheltered under the vine covered terraces, others, especially the young, swam in the pool. We sat with Gerry, David Hill and Alexi Karpov. Their heads bandaged like war wounded. We carried out the inevitable post-mortem into the events of the last two weeks. Carlos came over with a plate of king prawns and some bread. One of his colleagues arrived with another jug of wine.

"*Salut,*" he said raising his glass. "I think we

may have to make you two honorary Guardia Civil officers," he took a swig. "Metchnikov will appear in court on Monday and be charged. He will then be held until a court date is set. All the paperwork on the boat is being gone through by our special task force. It is proving most informative."

"What I don't quite understand," I said, "is how and why Metchnikov had his men pick you up, David. How did he even know where you lived? You weren't aware that he was here until I told you, so, how could he know where you were?"

"You remember I phoned Frank Kent in the States?" he said, I nodded, "well, it appears now that he was in the pay of Metchnikov. After I left, and they had told me to keep out of their investigations, Frank got involved. And, as can happen, the lure of easy money, overcame Frank's loyalty. Retirement for him was not far away, and as I have said, an Agent's life is not a wealthy one. He's been arrested now and faces a long time in jail."

"Yes," said Carlos, " and thanks to David and his conversation with his old boss in Los Angeles, a man from the CIA is arriving tomorrow and, between our two governments, we will be talking to a senior police officer from Russia. It would appear that Metchnikov was indeed the ringleader of a huge baby selling racket and a senior man in the Russian Mafia network. A nasty piece of work I believe is the expression."

Jane Mendez came over. We all stood and she greeted each of us in turn. "So these are the three musketeers," she smiled. "I suppose you will be writing the article for me Gerry and will want to be paid substantial amounts of money?"

"I will — on both counts — and it will be slightly different than the one the Sunday Times is running. So will the money, I'm sure." We all laughed. "And you," she said looking at me, "you should write a book."

"I'm a photographer not a writer," I replied.

"You should," said Sandy, "we all said it would make a great story. You did as well."

"Who knows," I said, "one day I just might."

GLOSSARY

Autovia	Ring road/motorway
Ayuntamiento	Town hall administration
Bragas	Knickers
Calamaritos	Baby squids
Churros	A doughnut type mix, deep fried and served with sugar or dipped into hot chocolate
Corrida	Bull Run
Cojones	Literally, balls. Spirit, daring.
Carlos Primero	Good Quality Spanish brandy
Cava	Spain's 'Champagne'
Carretera	Main highway
Diario Sur	Local newspaper also printed in English every Friday
"Diga Me"	Literally "speak to me" used frequently to answer the phone
Ducados	Black tobacco in un tipped cigarette
ETA	Terrorist group in the North of Spain fighting for Catalan independence
Expresso	Small intense black coffee
Finca	A parcel of rural land, more commonly used

	to describe the house that is on the land. Usually associated with old, rustic properties
Guiri	Slang word used by the Spanish to describe foreigners
"Hasta Mañana"	Literally "Until tomorrow"
"Pasa"	"Come in." When used as
"¿Que Pasa?"	it means "What's wrong - What's happening?
Pacharan	A liqueur drink with an aniseed type flavour
Paseo Maritimo	Sea front walkway
Residencias	Legal requirement to reside in Spain
"Tengo una cita.."	"I have an appointment with ..."
Venta	Country inn, restaurant

Printed in Great Britain
by Amazon